Once Upon a Wager

Julie LeMense

Crimson Romance
New York London Toronto Sydney New Delhi

CRIMSON
ROMANCE

Crimson Romance
An Imprint of Simon & Schuster, Inc.
1230 Avenue of the Americas
New York, NY 10020

For information about special discounts for bulk purchases, please contact Simon & Schuster Special Sales at 1-866-506-1949 or business@ simonandschuster.com.

The Simon & Schuster Speakers Bureau can bring authors to your live event. For more information or to book an event contact the Simon & Schuster Speakers Bureau at 1-866-248-3049 or visit our website at www. simonspeakers.com.

ISBN: 978-1-4405-8158-8
ISBN: 978-1-4405-8159-5 (ebook)

For my wonderful husband, Darren, and my three boys, Jack, Max, and Ben. They endured countless discussions about Regency era romance during the writing of this book, a threat to testosterone levels if ever there was one.

Acknowledgments

My thanks to everyone who read this as a manuscript, offering their time and advice, especially my sisters, Dani, Jean, and Kathleen; my sisters-in-law, Catherine and Mae; my friends Chrisanna, Constance, Donnamarie, Kari, Meg, Renee, and Tricia, not to mention Catherine's book club. Thank you, also, to Julie Sturgeon, my editor, who made my final draft so much better than my first. And lastly, thanks to my mom and dad. Even now, I can hear Dad saying, "What are you reading, Julie? Not another romance book!"

Part 1

Chapter 1

July 1808
St. James Street, London

Alec Carstairs, heir to the eighth Earl of Dorset, looked down at the letter on his desk, torn between feelings of frustration and something else he refused to acknowledge. Her handwriting was as awful as ever—undisciplined, like the young woman herself— but he knew better than to blame any long-suffering governess. Annabelle Layton did as she pleased. She always had, regardless of the consequences.

> Alec,
>
> I am sorry, as you well know. Two years is past time to forgive me, don't you think? The whole episode is best forgotten. You needn't miss Gareth's party again. I do not, I believe, have a sickness that is catching.
>
> Please say you will come.
>
> Your erstwhile friend,
>
> Annabelle Layton

A ragged sigh escaped him, the force of it sending the missive skittering across his desk, a Tudor-era monstrosity sent over from his family's London town home. Of course he'd forgiven her, if that was even the right word. She'd been so young then—just sixteen—uninhibited and free, with little thought for propriety or decorum. Forgetting the incident, however, was another matter entirely. It had irrevocably changed the way he saw her … to his everlasting shame.

"My sister insisted I hand deliver it," Gareth said, dropping himself into a tufted armchair across from the desk, startling Alec from his thoughts. He'd all but forgotten Layton's presence in the room, an unintended slight that had thankfully gone unnoticed. Alec's distraction would only have piqued Gareth's curiosity. After all, Gareth, like Annabelle, wasn't easily ignored. Both were golden haired and blue-eyed—a gift from the stunning Lady Layton. They'd been the boon companions of his otherwise lonely childhood. But none of them was a child anymore.

"Say yes, Carstairs. If you are any kind of friend, you'll not make me go back to Astley Castle by myself. God knows I'd rather stay in London."

So would Alec, but he undoubtedly had different reasons for that sentiment. "My schedule is very full, Gareth. My father has secured a new seat for me in the House of Commons, and I must memorize the current legislation. It sounds like another excuse, but it is not." And it wasn't. Not really. Alec felt the press of his new position closing in all around him: the impressive bachelor lodgings, the tailored wardrobe from Weston, the stacks of leather-bound folios packed with Parliamentary proposals. The eighth earl insisted that his son's surroundings reflect his recently elevated status.

"Have I ever told you your father frightens me? I swear his face would split down the center if he attempted a smile."

"He is stern," Alec admitted, "but only because he takes his responsibilities so seriously." As a child, he'd been frightened of his father, as well.

"Well, he is a spoilsport all the same. You're only twenty-five. Why must you bother with the Commons?"

"I'd rather talk about the party, Gareth. I should think you'd be eager to attend. It will celebrate *your* birthday, after all."

"Yes, but who knows what they've planned? Last year, the order of precedence going into dinner was decided not by titles, mind you, but by the high scores from an archery contest Annabelle organized out on the lawn."

Alec refused to smile, despite the temptation. "Surely she didn't lead the way into dinner? She hasn't even made her debut." To do so would have been highly improper. But not atypical.

"How did you know Annabelle won?"

"Of course she did. You're forgetting we taught her the finer points of the game." Just as they'd taught her to shoot pistols, bet on cards, and ride bareback. He'd had a hand, he supposed, in making her into the hoyden she'd become.

"Annabelle will always play to her interests," Gareth admitted. "Which means that this year, there will be lots of dancing at the party. She's mad for it, all of that spinning and skipping about. I ask you, who wants a Scottish reel back home when I can dance with the high-flyers in Covent Garden? Now there's a dance I don't mind doing."

An inappropriate image of Annabelle came to mind, but Alec forced it aside, turning his focus on her brother. "You look as colorful as any bird-of-paradise in the Garden, Gareth. That satin waistcoat is nearly blinding in the afternoon light. My eyesight may not recover."

"Just because Brummell dresses like an undertaker doesn't mean that I have to be similarly sepulchral. Especially when there is a party I must attend. Say you will come. I don't know the reason behind your estrangement with Annabelle—and do not deny there is one—but I'm certain that she's to blame. She can be a maddening creature. Still, she misses your friendship. She said … let me think … that it 'had more value than you have lately accorded it.' I had to promise to say exactly those words."

Ah, their friendship. Old and inviolable once. Annabelle's barbs, like her arrows, were always well aimed.

With a deep breath, and before he could stop himself, Alec took a sheet of parchment and scribbled a few words upon it. He then folded it upon itself. He extracted a stick of sealing wax from a side drawer, heating it briefly above the beeswax oil lamp on his desk. He dripped a small puddle of wax where the folds met, and pressed it with his signet ring. Satisfied the seal would hold fast against Gareth's attempts to loosen it, Alec handed him the note. "I will be there," he said. "But I have little doubt I will regret it."

Gareth merely chuckled. "If you're going to regret something, make the pain of it worthwhile. Come join me at The Anchor on Park Street. I plan on getting well and truly drunk before I meet up with Digby to play cards. It will lessen the sting of my certain defeat."

"Damien Digby is an ass. He makes you risk too much."

"I can only stand one respectable friend, Alec. And that would be you," Gareth added, "in case you're wondering."

"You say 'respectable' instead of 'boring' to spare my feelings, I know. Go on without me. If I'm to travel to Nuneaton for your birthday, there are things I must do." Like memorizing names, organizing arguments, and—above all else—practicing a brotherly smile.

After Gareth departed, Alec pushed away from his desk, and walked over to the study's large bay window, which looked out upon St. James Street below. Bracing his hands against the sun-warmed panes, he watched carriages and pedestrians move down the cobble-stoned thoroughfare, regretting his impulsiveness. Undoubtedly, his decision was a poor one. What would Annabelle read into his reply?

Annabelle,

I've missed our friendship, too. I will see you at Gareth's party. But you must promise to keep your clothes on.

Sincerely,

Alec Carstairs

As he waited for his father to join him in the library at Dorset House, Alec took a brief glance at its worn leather tomes, all lined up in an orderly fashion along dozens of age-darkened wood shelves. This was Henry Carstairs's domain, the inner sanctum where he built his political coalitions, and entertained allies with brandy after dinner. On the rare occasions Alec had been in London as a child, it had also been the room where Father meted out his punishments. Perhaps that was why Edmunds, their butler, had seated him here, rather than in the family drawing room. The earl's note had hinted at his strong displeasure, though Alec was long past the age of birch rods and bloodied hands.

As if summoned by his thoughts, the earl strode into the room, a sheaf of papers tucked under his arm, his reading spectacles perched on the edge of his nose, making his eyes seem owlish. Trim and fighting-fit, Father would make for a very intimidating owl indeed, though Alec now bested him in height by two inches. He was no longer the small, sickly boy who had so often been ignored, along with his mother. He'd finally earned his father's attention, even his respect, despite their high price. Standing quickly, he offered a quick bow. "Good morning, Father. You wished to see me."

"Take your seat," the earl said, settling into the large baronial chair behind his desk. "I was not happy to learn that you are going to Nuneaton for the Layton boy's fete, when you should be here preparing for the Commons."

"Even allowing for travel there and back, I will only be gone three days. I'll be bringing along the summaries prepared for me, and I've memorized the names of all the members, as well as their political positions."

His father shifted in the chair, displeasure obvious in the tight set of his jaw. "I expected you to join us for dinner tomorrow. Lord Fitzsimmons and his daughter, Jane, will be in attendance.

He's proven a useful ally in Parliament, and the girl is a reliable and sober sort. She'd make a good wife for you."

Of late, Father had mentioned marriage repeatedly, and Miss Fitzsimmons in particular. "I'm sorry I was not informed of your plans," Alec replied. "I cannot attend. I've already accepted the invitation to Astley Castle."

"To travel there for a such a short trip, when our Arbury Hall will have be readied. I think it an imposition."

The Hall, which bordered the Layton estate, was kept in a constant state of readiness, because Father expected nothing less. It wouldn't be wise, though, to point that out. "I won't be staying at the Hall. I'll stop by to have the carriage checked and to greet the servants, but I will sleep at the castle. They'll have a number of overnight guests."

"Those guests won't be from the best families, I can assure you. And the Layton boy is drinking and gambling himself into the grave. I don't like that you associate with him."

"I don't share his vices, Father."

"No, but never underestimate the allure of recklessness. The boy is shockingly irresponsible, and the girl is at an age now when your childhood friendship might be mistaken for something more."

"I am well aware of that."

"Annabelle Layton is the sort that invites scandal. The whole family is, which is something we can't afford, not if all my plans for you are to be realized."

"They are good people who mean no harm."

"They are remarkably odd. Lady Charlotte is weak-minded, and Sir Frederick … I've rarely met a more compulsive man. Nervous and awkward, but mention some sort of flying insect, and he'll prattle on for hours. Lepidopterology is all the rage, but I can't abide butterflies."

When Alec was a child, quiet in a lonely household, the Laytons had seemed exuberant, exotic even. They'd lived and loved with abandon, while he and his own mother had been starved of affection. Alec couldn't fight back a flash of anger at the memory. But those days were past. With hard work and dedication, he'd found a way to earn his father's love. And not just for himself.

But it was true that Gareth was increasingly a victim of his weaknesses. Just yesterday, he'd tried to talk Alec into a large wager. Lord Chetwiggin's grays were racing against Lord Sherford's blacks in a torchlit sprint on Hampstead Heath. Alec and Gareth would leave for Nuneaton beforehand, but Digby was placing a bet in Gareth's stead. Undoubtedly, it would be made for far more than he could afford.

"I'll not return with a passion for lepidopterology, Father. I can withstand a brief exposure to their family." And to Annabelle.

Those owlish eyes were fixed upon him, their expression severe.

"You mean to disagree with me on this?"

"Shall I break my word, then? That is not the man you've raised me to be. This will be a party in the country with old friends, and nothing more."

The room was ominously quiet.

"If you must go, then go," his father said at last. "But remember who you are, and what I expect. Don't do anything that will have unfortunate repercussions. And stay away from Annabelle Layton."

• • •

Annabelle was thrilled to see the familiar handwriting on the back of her note, but she was less thrilled reading it. In fact, only the most rigid self-control kept her from stomping one of her darling green half boots on the stone floor of the terrace. Could he not be done with it? Did he not remember the heat of that morning? The very air had simmered, like a pot set to boil. She'd been unable to sleep. Astley Castle's fountain, hidden from view in the formal gardens, had beckoned like the wellspring of salvation.

She'd known full well that her behavior was scandalous. Ladies did not swim in fountains after all, but the water had felt so wonderful. And she *had* been wearing clothes: a linen shift, even though the water made it rather revealing. Certainly, she'd not expected Alec to be out wandering the castle grounds at dawn, a witness to her shameless display. He had gone utterly still at the sight of her, like a pillar of salt caught between Sodom and Gomorrah.

Even now, she could remember his eyes. Something had burned in them, and she'd hoped, despite her embarrassment, that he'd finally understood she was no longer a child. That she could be more to him than a friend. But the past two years had laid waste to those notions. The only thing burning that day had been his indignation.

Later—after she'd been trussed back up in a suffocating corset and a long-sleeved gown—he'd warned her about the dangers a young woman could face, sounding just like Parson Withersby at a Sunday service. Not that the parson had ever been so breathtakingly handsome.

Since then, however, Alec had come up with an astonishing array of excuses to avoid her. The amusing letters they'd once exchanged with great regularity were now limited, on his part, to polite inquiries about her well being. He was too busy in London being molded into the man his father thought he should be. A man who was hidebound and self-important.

Startled from her pique by the sound of laughter, Annabelle leaned over the terrace balustrade, looking out onto the back lawn. Her parents were chasing butterflies—her mother's hair unbound and floating behind her, her father's shirttails flying like flags in the breeze, both of them swinging their nets with wild abandon. Their plan was to catch dozens of the colorful insects, so they could be released in the Great Hall during Gareth's party. However, she'd have to speak with Mother about that. Those plans had to be changed. Annabelle wanted this party to be remembered for its decorum. If only to shock Alec.

• • •

"Gareth, that is the largest trunk I've ever seen," she said the next morning as her brother burst into the hall in blur of color. "I hope it means you will be staying for a while. It would do both you and your purse some good."

"I can't be poorly dressed at my own birthday party," Gareth said, wrapping her in a quick hug after instructing the footmen to take his belongings to his room. He was wearing a bright green jacket over a puce-striped vest and fawn trousers—obviously a statement of high, if unfortunate, style. "Besides, there's nothing wrong with my purse. I've had a rush of luck at the tables lately, and I'm expecting to hear the news of my biggest win yet once Digby arrives."

"Who is this Digby? You've not mentioned him before."

"Damien Digby. I met him a few months back. He has got a gift for picking winners. I think you'll like him."

She doubted it. She didn't like anyone who indulged her brother's gambling habit. He regularly exceeded his allowance. Whenever he came home from London, he and Father closeted themselves in the study, arguing about money in angry whispers.

Of course, he invariably returned to the city with an additional bank draft. Her parents liked to joke that Gareth could charm the stripes off the famous zebra at Astley's Amphitheater. With a ready smile, he was so undeniably good-looking that most of her friends were madly in love with him. He got whatever he wanted. They both did.

Which is what made the matter of Alec Carstairs so infuriating.

"You shouldn't be spending so much of Father's money, Gareth. Have you forgotten that I'll be going to London for the Little Season in September?"

"How could I? You prattle on about it in every letter. I've warned all of my friends. We're going to decamp en masse to Brighton."

"I will ignore your insults," she said, fighting back a grin. "Tell me, what does Alec think about this Mr. Digby?"

"You can guess the answer to that, Annabelle. Honestly, Carstairs has forgotten how to have fun. Any day now, I expect to find he's gone old and arthritic."

Even so, he was still the most handsome man she'd ever seen. And tonight, she would not be ignored. Mrs. Markum from the village had made up the most beautiful dress for her. It was the palest of cream silks, shot through with silver thread, and delicately embroidered with tiny flowers. Her hair would be pulled back with the clips Father had given to Mother on their wedding day. They were shaped like butterflies, the wings sparkling with dozens of small diamonds.

Tonight, she would dare him to find a trace of the girl he pretended her to be.

• • •

Just as evening fell, Alec walked up the crushed stone drive to Astley Castle. Despite its rather grandiose name, it was more accurately a fortified manor house, although it did have a moat. Briefly the home of Lady Jane Grey, England's unfortunate Nine Days Queen, it had also served as a garrison for Cromwell's forces during the Civil War before passing into the Layton family. Tonight, however, the house gave no hint of its troubled history. Japanese lanterns were strung, not only in the trees leading up the drive, but also in those surrounding the house, and the effect was magical. In the early dusk, a gentle light bathed the grounds, softening the lines of the old home, coloring it with pale pinks and darker purples. Alec heard strains of music and conversation. In fact, it appeared to be a remarkably conventional party, which was something of a surprise. Surely, circus animals were lurking somewhere.

The oversized front door was open to the evening air, and dozens of people were assembled in the Great Hall, which was brightly lit with wall lanterns. Chandeliers decked with wax candles flickered high above as Gareth's parents received their guests. Sir Frederick, who often panicked in crowds, was hiding his misgivings well, and Lady Layton was radiant beside him. Gareth stood next to her, dressed in a colorful approximation of evening attire, but he seemed distracted. His eyes were darting the crowd and looking for someone. A footman with the champagne tray, no doubt. Alec did not see Annabelle.

But then familiar, melodious laughter washed over him, and he turned. A willowy, honey-tressed blonde stood at the center of a crowd of adoring men. Her face was hidden from view, but her gown—the color of moonlight—caressed her curves like a lover. Alec braced himself, every nerve taut. As if sensing his presence, she looked over her shoulder and smiled.

God in Heaven, he should never have come here tonight.

Annabelle had been only four years old the first time he saw her. He'd joined his mother on a neighborly visit to Astley Castle, and the little girl had utterly charmed him, struggling to sit still while Lady Layton served tea to her guests. Delicate, soft, and pink, like a rosy-cheeked doll, she'd roused all his protective instincts before kicking him in the shins to gain his attention.

If only he could see the girl she'd once been in the woman standing before him. Even two years ago, there had been hints of her, hiding in the body of a goddess. But there was nothing childlike about Annabelle now. She was spectacularly lovely, with arched brows, high cheekbones, and cornflower blue eyes that took his breath away.

Excusing herself from her admirers, she walked toward him with a slow smile. Then again, walking was not the right word. Swaying was the better choice, and all he could do was stand there, heart slamming in his chest as she approached, the gossamer silk gown caressing her curves. Were it dampened—as was the fashion with London's faster set—it would be almost transparent. Just like that morning when she had gone swimming in the fountain, casting a spell over him like a sorceress.

"Alec, how nice you could join us this evening. I worried that in the end, something pressing would keep you in London. So often in these past two years, that has been the case." Once, she'd have embraced him impulsively, laughing all the while. Now, she gave a surprisingly ladylike curtsey, extending one gloved hand. He leaned down to press a kiss upon it, and if his lips lingered a moment too long, he was rather proud of his self-control. It had been just enough to breathe in the scent of her—a familiar mix of honeysuckle soap and the lemon drops she loved. But there was also something new. Something dangerous.

"I wrote that I would be here, Annabelle. I am man who honors my obligations."

She tilted her head, angling it up toward him, her eyes bewitching beneath half-lowered lashes. "Is that what I am now? An obligation?"

She would scramble his wits if he wasn't careful.

"Of course not. We're old friends, despite the distance between us."

He'd been referring to the distance between London and Nuneaton, but he was certain she had leaned closer. His body all but screamed it.

"Perhaps we can ease that distance tonight."

God above. Did she have any idea how that might be interpreted? He managed a self-conscious pat on her shoulder before stepping back, hoping he appeared collected and calm, instead of dizzy with the nearness of her.

"You are looking very well," he said after a long pause. "How … big you have become."

And with that asinine statement, he turned on his heels, vanishing into the crowd.

• • •

Why must Alec be indifferent to her, when so many other men were eager to gain her attention? There was Horace Briarly, the squire's son from the village. He'd vowed his eternal love these past three years or more. Lord Percival Spencer, the rather rakish heir to a viscountcy in Warwickshire, made every excuse to visit her father with lepidopterological concerns—though it was obvious he had no interest in the hobby. And then there was the widower, Sir Boniface, an amateur artist. He'd already presented her with a number of lovely paintings, although it was embarrassing to have six portraits of oneself. Wherever Annabelle went, men seemed to sprout up like spring flowers.

But none of them was as endlessly *fascinating* as Alec Carstairs. So noble and decent. So restrained and responsible. The one reliable constant of her childhood, he'd become the man against whom she measured all others.

Not to mention the beauty of him. Wide shoulders, narrow hips, and long legs, all encased in immaculately tailored clothing. Dark brown hair, still wavy but shorter now than she remembered. Beautiful lips, wide and generous. Prominent cheekbones and a straight nose that flared slightly. Those toffee-colored eyes that always reminded her of Cook's caramels, still warm from the stove.

Gaining his attention this evening required a new strategy. But she couldn't plot effectively if she was caught up in a conversation with Horace, who was heading her way like a hound on a scent. She quickly blessed the wall of potted palms beside the door. With a quick movement, she slipped behind them, escaping out onto the drive.

As escapes went, it was poorly planned. It was a party, after all. Guests were getting out of their carriages and walking up the meandering stone pathway to the castle entrance. Distracted by thoughts of Alec, she walked directly into a small group of men who were newly arrived. One of them caught her with his arms, steadying her before she could knock both of them down. Glancing up at the blunt-featured man, she offered a hasty apology and spun away. He called after her, but she was in no mood to speak with strangers. She headed into the castle's elaborate gardens and the swiftly descending darkness.

Passing clipped boxwoods and yews set in a pattern dating to Elizabethan times, she followed a gravel path into the heart of the gardens where a Roman folly stood, reflected in a semicircular ornamental pond, her fountain at its center. The pond was filled with gold and silver fish, and as a child, she'd loved watching sunlight shimmer on their scales through the water. Several bubbled to the surface at her approach, hopeful and expectant, but tonight, she had nothing to offer but a half smile.

There was a bench hidden behind the folly, and she took a seat there. Her collision had wreaked havoc with the elaborate coiffure her maid, Mary, had created. Annabelle fumbled with an errant clip, but that sent another wave of heavy hair tumbling over her shoulders. It wouldn't do to be seen in this state. She could only imagine what Alec would think. At least, the new Alec. The one who was so stuffy. Thankfully, though, she was alone.

Until quite suddenly, she was not.

"I was sure my eyes had deceived me, but they did not. You are exquisite."

The voice belonged to a strange man, his approach almost silent in the soft grass. Annabelle merely edged further into the shadows. "Sir, I don't wish to be rude, but I would prefer to be alone."

"But your beauty holds me spellbound," he said easily, as if he'd practiced the line.

She looked up. It was the blunt-featured man. He had light brown hair and pale gray eyes, and while she could not guess at his age, he was far older than she. "This is hardly the time for false flattery. And the party is that way." She pointed needlessly toward the house.

He moved slowly toward her. "What is your name?"

"As you well know, it would hardly be proper for me to say. We've not been introduced." Nor should she be alone with him here in the dark.

"Such becoming modesty." He smiled, flashing uneven teeth. "But I insist on knowing who you are." He took another step closer as he slowly withdrew the glove covering his left hand. "Tell me, my dear, if I trailed my fingers down your cheek, would your skin be as soft as it appears?"

So he was that sort of man. "You should know that I always carry a small pistol on my person," she said, her voice impressively calm. "Just in case an unfortunate situation like this one should arise."

"Really?" His eyes gleamed in the darkness. "Why don't I feel my hands along your body, and see if I can discover the place where you've hidden it?"

"Touch her," another voice ground out, "and I will break both of your arms."

Alec. He'd followed her, after all. He was suddenly towering over the stranger.

"Carstairs, what an unpleasant surprise. The lady and I are having a private discussion."

Ignoring him, Alec turned to face her. "Are you all right?" Taking in her disheveled appearance, he added tersely, "Has he hurt you in any way?"

"No, I am fine," Annabelle replied, masking her relief. "I merely needed some fresh air."

"I meant no harm," the man said, raising his hands in mock surrender. "I was merely engaging in an innocent flirtation with a desirable woman."

"She's little more than a child," Alec bit out. And as offended as she was by his comment, this didn't seem like a time to argue.

"She is hardly a child, Carstairs," the man drawled. "If she were, I doubt you'd be treating me to such a manly display."

She could sense the tension in Alec. He was keeping his temper in check, but just barely.

"Who are you?" Annabelle asked. "Why are you here in my home?"

"Your home?" His eyes widened with surprise. "You must be Miss Layton, Gareth's sister. He and I are very close friends."

"Of late," she said, "he has been less particular in his friendships."

The stranger darkened at that. "As it turns out, we are business partners of a sort. I am Damien Digby, at your service."

Gareth had been wrong. She could not like Mr. Digby.

"How utterly perfect you are, Miss Layton. When your brother spoke of your beauty, I thought he exaggerated. I can see now he was being coy. I will look forward to seeing you inside."

With a cold look at Alec, he turned and strode purposefully toward the house.

• • •

"Don't you know enough not to run off without a proper escort, Annabelle?" Alec demanded, anger sharpening his voice.

At his tone, her own temper flared. "I was more than fine, Alec. I've grown … what was the word you used? Oh yes, big. I'm big now, like a sturdy tree out in the lawn. Perhaps if you think on it, you can come up with an even more unflattering term. In the meantime, I will take care of myself."

"Don't be foolish. You don't know what a man like that is capable of."

"You heard him say he meant no harm." Even as she spoke the words, she knew they were false. She'd seen the look in Digby's eyes.

"He is a cad, the very worst sort." Alec put a hand to the edge of his cravat, as if it were suddenly too tight. "And much as it pains me to say so, you are at an age when such men will seek you out."

"I cannot help the fact that I've grown up, Alec. I'm sorry the end result of it has been so unfortunate."

He met that statement with a long moment of silence, merely watching her in the moonlight, a muscle twitching in his jaw. "I don't think that is the right word."

She didn't want to find out which word he would choose instead. Her confidence had been battered enough for one evening. "I have to return to the party." She started to move away, but he put his hands on her shoulders to still her.

"Have you really taken to carrying around pistols, Annabelle?"

"Of course not. I was bluffing. I would never ruin the line of this lovely dress."

His eyes sparked briefly with amusement, and perhaps admiration. "Lovely as your dress is, you can't return to the party looking as you do. Let me help you."

He reached down to loosen one of the diamond clips tangled in her hair, and slowly worked it free, standing so close she had to remind herself to breathe. He smelled of sandalwood and crisp, clean linen. "This one will also have to be reset," he said, moving to the other clip, his amusement fading. In moments, the rest of her hair tumbled down to her waist, and he ran his fingers through its long length in an effort to smooth it. Then he cleared his throat, dropping his hands to his sides.

"I'm not much of a lady's maid." He tucked the clips into her gloved hands and stepped back.

"People will wonder what we've been doing out here in the dark," she said, daring him to think of her that way. But his face was inscrutable, and she fought back a stab of frustration. "Of course, no one would suspect you of misbehaving. You are far too honorable. You're practically my brother."

"I am not your brother, Annabelle. And I'm not as honorable as you think." Abruptly, he turned toward the castle. "Follow me to the servants' entrance, and go up to your room from there." She hurried to keep up with his long strides. "Go straight to your maid," he called over his shoulder. "Dinner will be served soon. Your absence will be noticed if you don't hurry."

He was dismissing her, because she was a foolish girl he neither wanted nor needed. It was evident in every terse, clipped word.

When they reached the house, she passed quietly through the doorway leading into the kitchen. In the confusion, as the staff prepared trays of food to be brought up for dinner, she was able to slip by unnoticed. In moments, she was up the stairs.

• • •

Only when she'd vanished from sight did Alec allow his careful control to slip. The ghosts of his past were all around him. He and Gareth and Annabelle, rolling down the hillside over there on that warm spring day, laughing aloud as governesses and tutors ran after them, bemoaning grass stains and inappropriate behavior. That long ago summer night, sitting with Annabelle on the bench behind the folly, her hand in his, because while she loved to look up at the stars, she was frightened of the dark. That afternoon when he'd come down from Oxford for a visit, and she leapt into his arms. His only searing thought had been, "how beautiful you've become." That morning two years ago, when everything changed.

He hadn't been able to sleep. It had been intensely hot, even at that early hour of the morning, so he'd gone for a walk, hoping for a breeze. Hearing her laughter, he'd been drawn to it, never expecting to find Annabelle dancing in the fountain, a pagan goddess of the dawn, water coursing over every nearly naked curve. The pink tips of her breasts had been visible through her wet shift, and he'd felt like the worst sort of lecher for wanting her. Even now, he hardened at the memory, his mouth dry as dust.

Annabelle was free in a way he'd never been, full of life and laughter. She was warm, vital, and sparkling, like flames in the night. But never had someone been more unsuited to the path that he must follow. His happiness was not his own. It did not matter that he wanted her, that he could no longer deny his desire. How shocked she'd be to know that while he had been untangling her hair, he'd been imagining it wound around him, her body naked beneath his own.

Chapter 2

Annabelle returned to the party just as the first course was served, hopefully with no one the wiser. No one besides Alec, at least. She sensed him watching her at every opportunity, but whether to keep her safe or avoid her path, she didn't know. Course after course was served to the throng of seated guests. There were soups, sweetmeats, and baked fowl; meats, terrines, and savory tarts; sugar-glazed fruits and desserts—all presented by white-gloved servers moving with almost orchestral precision.

Even without the butterflies they'd planned on, it was perfect. If only Alec would ask her to dance, the evening's earlier trials could be overlooked, but he hadn't asked. She despaired that he ever would.

Gareth's friends from school, however, were gratifyingly kind, paying her ridiculous compliments. Handsome Benjamin Alden, the Viscount Marworth, recited such effusive poetry she'd laughed out loud in response. Gareth's new friends from London, however, were less appealing, their regard inappropriate. As she escaped two of them with the excuse she was needed elsewhere, a voice rang out. "Belle!"

She turned to see her brother weaving his way toward her, the lecherous Mr. Digby close behind. Surely there were more appealing friends to be had in London? Of late, though, Gareth was more impressed by flash than substance, and Digby was the perfect characterization of that.

Drawing up beside her, Gareth planted a sloppy kiss on her cheek, a sure sign of advancing inebriation. "Annabelle, you must meet Damien Digby, one of my very oldest and dearest friends."

She knew full well he was neither.

Digby's eyes fixed on her décolletage as he made his bow. "Miss Layton, I've been anxious to make your acquaintance. Will you stand up with me for the next dance?"

She'd rather have all of her teeth pulled out. However, as one of the hostesses for this evening, it would be rude to decline. Not that Digby was willing to wait for an answer. He'd reached his arm out to clasp her elbow, his gloved hand clammy with sweat. She shuddered as he strengthened his hold, pulling her toward the dancers near the orchestra.

He was a scoundrel, and richly deserved a kick with some force behind it. Thankfully, though, her evening slippers were spared the bother when a voice behind them said, "I believe the dance is mine."

So Alec would dance with her, but only when she needed rescuing. With a triumphant smile at Digby, who'd suddenly dropped his hand, she turned to face Alec. "Thank you, Lord Carstairs. You've saved me from making a scene." She took his extended arm, and together they moved past the disgruntled Digby toward the center of the room.

A Scottish reel was starting up. As they bowed and withdrew, hands held high to spin in a circle around the dancers to their left and right, there was no place in the world she'd rather be. Long ago, Alec had taught her the steps to this very reel. He had a natural, effortless grace, and as they followed the intricate pattern of the dance, he smiled at her, the tension between them forgotten. When a lock of his hair fell forward over his brow—the merest hint of disorder and vulnerability—she felt her breath catch. The evening was suddenly sparkling and full of promise. But then the dance was over, as quickly and as unexpectedly as it had begun.

"Annabelle, will you walk with me?"

She'd walk with him all the way to France if he asked. "Of course, Alec." She rested her hand in the crook of his arm as he led her toward the double doors open at the edge of the room, their curtains fluttering in the breezy evening air. With a quick movement, they were outside on the patio, and when the first strains of music for a quadrille began, the other couples out in the moonlight rushed in to take part, leaving them—at least for a few moments—alone. "I saw him approach you," Alec said once they'd reached the edge of the patio, away from the noise and light of the doorways. "You must be careful around Digby."

"He only asked for a dance. There can be little harm in that." Why were they discussing the odious man when she was alone with Alec at last?

"Digby wants more than a dance. You must trust me on it."

"At least he wants *something* to do with me," she said, her voice sharp with frustration. "I've wanted to ask about your trip here, and what you thought of the dinner. How things are with your father. How long you will stay in Nuneaton. But you no longer tell me anything, not even in a letter, and tonight, you've avoided me at nearly every opportunity."

Guilt flashed across his handsome face. "You've been hounded by men all evening, Annabelle. I didn't wish to expose you to further gossip."

He was not telling the truth. "So I'm being gossiped about?" she said flippantly, to hide her hurt. "I rather like the idea of that."

"You are the talk of the party, Annabelle. Although perhaps that's not a surprise."

"Other than that incident in the garden, I've been on my best behavior," she insisted. "I've been remarkably restrained."

"Yes, you have," he said with the ghost of a smile. "Maybe that's why people are talking."

"Well, if you've heard them, what are they saying? Don't keep me in suspense."

"I suppose it depends on whether you are speaking with the ladies or the gentlemen."

"Has Mrs. Balleymood been spreading lies again? I did not trip Thomas at last month's races on the town green. He fell when I sped past."

"I don't doubt it," he replied, sounding in that moment like the old Alec, his voice warm with affection. "But no. The ladies merely want to know the name of your modiste. That dress has caused quite a stir."

"It is pretty, isn't it?" she said, twirling in a circle to show off every aspect, only to find that when she faced him again, his gaze had darkened. "Do the men like it, too?" she asked, trying to fill the sudden silence.

"That is rather a leading question, Annabelle. But just this once, I will humor your vanity. Yes, they think that both you and the dress are beautiful."

She was used to such compliments, of course, but not from him. Of late, he was far better at masking his thoughts than at sharing them. "What about you, Alec?" she asked. "Do you think I'm beautiful?"

"I think we are old friends, so the kind of notice that the others are paying you would be inappropriate."

She took a deep breath, knowing full well that she'd regret her next words. "What if I wanted to attract your notice?"

"Annabelle, you shouldn't say such things," he said, all traces of humor gone. "A man will get the wrong impression of your motives."

"I'm not looking for a lecture on propriety," she said. "You know I always say more than I should. I was just wondering ... what you think of me."

He looked down at her in the moonlight, his mouth a grim line. In the ballroom, the next set of music was nearing its end, while her question hung in the air. As the moments stretched on, she wished she had the courage to walk away, rather than wait here, desperate for his answer. But then finally, he spoke. "I think you are impossibly beautiful."

The smile burst forth before she could stop it, or attempt some degree of maidenly modesty. "Horace Briarly said the same thing when he tried to kiss me."

"That boy from Hinckley? He should be horsewhipped."

"He is no longer a boy. He's quite handsome, in fact, but of course, I'm saving my kisses." She tilted her face toward his, certain that he would see the invitation there. Her breath quickened with anticipation.

"That's as it should be, Annabelle," he said, his voice low and serious. "Save them for someone you can make a future with."

Could he possibly have misunderstood? Impulsively, she reached up and pressed her lips to his. Alec reared back in surprise, but she clasped her arms around his neck, pulling him toward her, unwilling to let go. His lips were warm. He smelled of sandalwood still, and something spicy—shock, no doubt—but the feel of him was glorious. His heartbeat was pounding against her chest, his hair silky beneath her fingers. Even as he held his arms at his sides, refusing to touch her, she pressed closer, trying to erase the distance between them.

But he was completely still, like a pillar of salt again. His mouth was unyielding, and she suddenly knew that he didn't share her feelings. He felt none of her longing. He was holding his breath, waiting for her to be done.

Embarrassed, she slowly withdrew, easing her hands away, and then her lips.

Only to have his arms clamp like manacles around her, pulling her flush against him, trapping her there. She could feel the tension in his body, everything about him tight and hard. He angled his head down, capturing her mouth, a rush of wine-scented breath mingling with her own, making her feel lightheaded and needy.

With a low moan, he sucked at her lower lip until she opened her mouth, his tongue slipping in, slick and insistent. Annabelle shuddered with the intimacy of it, desperate to feel more of this new sensation as he gathered her closer. He swept his hands along her waist, over the curve of her hips, and down the swell of her backside, cupping her against something heavy and hot. All the while, he explored her with his mouth, as if she was something sweet and he craved the taste of her. Caught up in her desire, she knew only that she'd never felt this way. She would give him all of herself for the taking, if only he would ask.

But then inexplicably, he stopped. With a muffled curse, he dropped his arms and took several steps back. He crossed his hands behind him, as if to keep them occupied, and watched her, his eyes hooded, his breathing uneven.

How could he control himself so quickly? She still felt dizzy, as if she'd been drugged with laudanum.

"God above, I knew better," he said. "I should have stayed as far away as possible."

That cured her dizziness. Had she given him such a disgust of her, then?

"That should never have happened, Annabelle. It was wrong. Please, you need to go back inside."

"I am sorry." She could barely speak the words. "I suppose I've confirmed all of your worst assumptions."

"I'm angry at myself, Annabelle, not at you. I took advantage."

"If anything," she said, watching him beneath her lashes, "I was the one who took advantage."

"Do you hear yourself?" His voice was sharp now, even pained. "Can you understand why I have stayed away? You can't tempt a man like that. I warned you I'm not so honorable."

"Is it such a bad thing to kiss me? I've wanted to kiss you as long as I can remember."

For several moments, he simply gazed at her, his face inscrutable. "Well, then," he said quietly. "We have kissed. You have indulged your curiosity with no thought for the consequences. I don't have that luxury."

He turned, vanishing into the darkness as she touched a hand to her lips, where she could still feel his kiss.

• • •

They didn't speak for the remainder of the party. Indeed, Alec studiously avoided Annabelle, dancing with any number of unknown girls because he didn't trust himself to be near her. He felt certain he would violate all the rules of propriety, making an even bigger ass of himself than he already had.

Not that it stopped him from watching her. Every time someone asked her to dance. Every time she smiled at another man, conquering another heart. When she retired from the party, putting a safe distance between them at last, he was torn between regret and relief. She had kissed him, but he'd committed the unpardonable sin of kissing her back. God knows where he'd found the strength to stop before he completely lost his head. He'd underestimated his own reckless longing.

Recklessness seemed to abound this evening. Gareth was drunk and unsteady on his feet. He'd spilled wine on several guests—including Dr. Chessher, an esteemed surgeon from the neighboring village of Hinckley—and seeing to his drunken friend was a good excuse to leave the party early. It would put both of them out of their misery. But when Alec suggested as much, Gareth's reaction was immediate.

"Can't. Meeting Digby after midnight in the study," he said haltingly. "Working the wager out."

Alec had forgotten about the Sherford-Chetwiggin race. "How much did you lose?"

Gareth's face leached of color, and he looked away, his eyes darting about the room. "Won't tell you that … too shameful. Good old Digby, though. Fronted me all the money." Then he shifted uncomfortably. "'Course, I haven't got it."

"I'd rather pay your debt than have you beholden to that snake," Alec said. It of course wouldn't solve anything, but old loyalties were difficult to ignore.

"Don't like sh—nakes," Gareth mumbled. "Won't mess you up in this, though. Digby'll make it right." He took a sip from his wine glass, only to find it empty. "He's found a thing or two worth the money." Gareth leaned in, as if sharing a secret. "Giving me a fair shot, too. We're to race for it in the morning, just like Fitz … Ford."

"What do you mean race? You're in no condition to race."

Gareth, though, had already wandered off in search of the footman with the wine tray. More worrisome was the fact that Gareth was terrible with horses, his hands like rocks with the reins. And Digby damn well knew it.

• • •

As the clock on her mantel chimed, Annabelle punched her pillow in frustration. She couldn't sleep. Whenever she closed her eyes, she was back on the patio with Alec. Back in his arms.

He'd said it was wrong, that she shouldn't have done it, but she couldn't agree. Even as a little girl, she'd loved the feel of him, constantly finding excuses to touch him, if only to reassure herself. Alec had always looked out for her. He'd made her feel safe in a family that thrived on chaos.

And now—well, she better understood the fluttery sensation that came over her whenever he was near. The first time she'd felt it, she was watching Alec and Gareth swim in their favorite lake near Arbury Court. It was the summer her body began to change and curve, growing in very specific places, becoming long and lean in others. She'd wanted to swim alongside them, but not when wet linen underthings revealed those frightening changes, so she'd sat at the water's edge, fully clothed in a sweltering riding habit. When Alec walked out of the lake, pants clinging to his long, muscular legs, his bare chest dripping with water that caught the sunlight, she'd been breathless. Mesmerized by the way his muscles flexed as he leaned down to pick up a cloth, the way his flat stomach tensed as he wiped the water from his body. She was breathless now just thinking of it. She'd never looked at him in the same way again.

The clock on the mantel chimed again, interrupting her thoughts. Somewhere downstairs, people were arguing. In this old, stonewalled house, sound tended to reverberate, amplifying even whispered conversations. A benefit or a curse, depending on your perspective.

She tried to ignore the noise, but it was hard not to wonder who was arguing and why. She was quite thirsty, come to think of it. No wonder she was having such a difficult time falling asleep. Perhaps she could sneak downstairs, and get something from the kitchen. If she heard anything along the way, no one could accuse her of eavesdropping. Absolutely not.

She crept out of bed and went to her corner armoire to retrieve a matching wrap. Belting it tightly over her nightgown, she stepped gingerly into a pair of boiled wool slippers, took the candle from her bedside table, and sneaked out into the hall. She turned down the back stairs. Without windows, it was darker than the night. The muffled voices were louder now, angry in tone, and coming from the study, which shared easy access to the servants' stairs. She continued on, trying to quiet her steps as she neared the room. Not that its occupants would ever know she was nearby, given the volume of their voices. The door was slightly ajar.

"You can't mean to participate in this, Gareth."

It was Alec. Temptation at its worst.

"He has no choice, Dorset," someone said derisively. The damnable Digby. "A gentleman of honor pays his debts. I'm giving him a chance to win everything back, after all."

"There is no honor in this, you whoreson." It was so unlike Alec to speak in vulgar terms that Annabelle was desperate to hear more. Really, though, she must pass by. It wouldn't do to be found here in the dark in her nightclothes, in the company of three men no less, even if one of them was her drunken brother. She wasn't lost to all propriety. But then a fight broke out. She could hear something—perhaps a small table——being tossed aside, and the sound of shattering glass. There was a struggle, and then a wheezing noise, the sort one associated with a crushing case of influenza, or a constricted air pipe. Or worse.

She rushed into the room. Gareth was standing by the fireplace in wide-eyed disarray, his cravat undone, a half-empty glass of claret spilling out of his hand. Shards of crystal were scattered at his feet, the remnants of a decanter he must have dropped. It was Digby, though, who drew her attention. He'd been threatening earlier, but he was hardly threatening now. He was gasping for breath, the starched linen of his cravat twisted into a stranglehold by Alec, who stood above him, furious and deadly, like an avenging angel.

It took the span of several heartbeats for anyone to react to her presence. Gareth turned toward her, flushed and clumsy. Alec, after a moment's hesitation, dropped Digby, shuddering with the effort to contain his temper. When he took in the state of her undress, he looked away quickly. "Annabelle, you must get out of here," he said, his face grim in profile. Digby, sucking in great gusts of air, turned to watch her, his face still mottled.

It took a moment to find her voice. She was shocked by what she'd seen. "Why are you fighting?" She turned to Gareth. "Why didn't you stop them?"

He looked heartsick. "Don't … be angry with me, Belle," he pleaded. "Didn't mean for thith … this to happen."

Obviously, the late hour had done little to sober him. "Oh, Gareth," she said, suddenly wary. "What have you done?"

"Don't worry," he slurred. "I'll win. Promise."

At that, Alec bit back another curse. Setting aside her candle, he grabbed a blanket on the armchair by the fire, and draped it over her nightclothes. "Please, Annabelle," he said. "Don't ask questions now. You must return to your room." Before she could answer, he took her by the arm, leading her out of the study and back up the stairs. In the glow of the candle he carried, his beautiful features were cast in stark relief, his face implacable.

"Alec?" Her voice was barely above a whisper, as if speaking softly would blunt the violence of what she'd just seen. "What is Gareth trying to win?"

At first, it seemed he would not reply. When he did, she could still hear the anger in his voice. "A drunken wager."

"But why were you fighting?"

"I'm sorry you saw that." Reaching her door, he stopped and turned. "I shouldn't have lost control of my temper." He was struggling with it still, though. His jaw looked like it was carved from stone.

"Were you really trying to hurt Mr. Digby?"

He watched her in the candlelight. "Absolutely."

"I don't understand," she said, shaking her head, trying to dispel the fear gathering within her. Gareth was in trouble, and she'd never seen Alec like this.

"I know, Annabelle." His voice was softer now. "But the fighting is done. You must try to sleep." He opened the door to her room, and she crossed over the threshold before turning back toward him. How easily he fell back into the role of her protector. Evidently, it was the only one he wanted.

"Will you please help Gareth?" She hated the desperation in her voice.

"I will try." The hall was so quiet and still she could hear their mingled breathing. He handed her the candle, burned low now and flickering. "Good night." Then he drew back into the darkness, pulling the door shut behind him.

• • •

Digby was seated in the armchair by the fire. Gareth had barely moved, as if his mind were still trying to process all that had gone on before. Alec startled both of them as he reentered the study. "If this damnable race must go on, I'm going to be a part of it."

Gareth's face lit with relief, but Digby merely snorted in disdain. "So much for your protestations, Carstairs," he rasped, a hand moving protectively to his neck, which was lashed with bruises. "This settles a debt between Gareth and myself. You have nothing I want."

"I hardly care if you want me there or not," Alec said. "And I doubt a man like you can resist a wager of 10,000 pounds."

Digby's eyes bulged. Even Gareth was shocked. It was a fortune, an astounding amount to wager on a horse race. Ridiculous, but he could think of no other way.

"Why would you risk so much money, Carstairs?" Digby smirked, though he'd barely regained his composure. As if Alec would confide his motivations to the cheating bastard.

"If you win, you are 10,000 pounds richer, more than enough to cover Gareth's debts to you. I should think that's all you need to know."

"How noble you are … to rely on your father's money and prestige to rescue a friend," Digby taunted. "What happens if either of you wins the race?"

"You leave the Layton family the hell alone," Alec replied. "And I personally see to it that you're forced from the shores of England." Preferably in a boat destined for the bottom of the Channel.

Both men were watching him carefully, trying to decide whether he was serious. Alec was deadly serious. "Very well," Digby replied. "The three of us will race our own traveling carriages, since that is what we have at our disposal. Each of us will have a groom or a friend to judge the finish. We'll race along the King's Highway until it intersects with Two Boulders Road. The first carriage to turn and pass safely between the boulders to the finish line is the winner." It was a treacherous route, with two enormous rocks perched on either side of a narrow, rutted path. There was only enough room for one carriage to pass at a time.

Digby looked briefly at the clock on the fireplace mantel. It was just past two in the morning. "We will race before breakfast, so as not to disturb the others. We hardly want a crowd bearing witness.

"Besides," he said, turning toward Alec, his eyes malevolent. "I race best on an empty stomach. It makes me hungry for the win."

"Then I should expect that you will remain hungry."

Chapter 3

Someone was scratching incessantly at Annabelle's door, whispering in a halfhearted attempt at stealth. In her fatigue, she barely understood what was being said. Squinting an eye open, she saw a room still cloaked in darkness. It was barely dawn.

"Damn it, Annabelle, this is important!" said the whisper, louder than before. Last night came flooding back—the angry words and the vicious fight—and she slipped from her bed toward the door. She opened it as quietly as she could.

"Oh, Gareth, you look awful," she said, pulling him into her chamber. "Father has warned you about the pitfalls of intoxication." Haggard and hollow-eyed, he was dressed in a coarse jacket and stained trousers, a satchel over one shoulder.

Given his reputation as a dandy, that alone made her heart pound with concern.

"I know, Annabelle. And he was right. I am the worst of brothers. I am so sorry." She noticed that his movements were unsteady. He was as forlorn as she'd ever seen him.

"Why are you sorry? What is going on?"

He looked everywhere in the room but directly at her. "I'm going to fix it. Alec is helping me. Please don't worry."

"You can't keep relying on him to solve your problems, Gareth."

"I know. I can't explain it, Annabelle, but I seem to have forgotten how to cope with any sort of responsibility. I am so ashamed of myself."

"Shame solves nothing. What is this wager you've made?"

He tensed. "It is nothing … just a carriage race."

She was doubly worried now. Gareth had never been good with horses. "Can you not reconsider?"

"Everything will be fine," he insisted. "But I don't want you anywhere near the course. I won't have you climbing into the back of my carriage when I'm not looking."

"We both know I'm the better driver," she added unnecessarily. "But you and I are too old to race together. I promise to be good."

"I wish I could believe that," he said. "I am taking you off to Arbury Hall this morning. I've sent a note ahead asking the housekeeper to expect you."

"That hardly seems necessary. I'll stay in my room until the race is done."

"And miss all of the excitement? Come now, a lock and key couldn't keep you away, and well you know it." Reaching for the satchel, he continued, "I've brought you a quick change of clothes, an old set of mine. You can't be seen gallivanting about at this hour of the morning."

"Have you told Alec about this?"

"There wasn't any time. Meet me downstairs in the kitchen in five minutes."

There was so much he wasn't telling her. Whatever he claimed, there was no good reason for her to be sneaking from Astley Castle before daylight. But if Gareth was in trouble, she would not fail him. "Give me a moment."

He crept from the room, closing the door behind him, and she dressed quickly, impatiently donning an ill-fitting jacket and pants and boots three sizes too large. A low-slung hat successfully covered her hair. Mother would be appalled were she to see her now. She hurried downstairs to meet Gareth, and together they rushed out into the early dawn.

• • •

It would be a pretty day. As the sun peaked over the horizon, it etched slashes of gold on the thick summer grass. The leaves high above in the trees rustled in a gentle wind. Despite the cool air, it was comfortable and caressing. But none of that was significant now. They ran to the stables; she still didn't know why they must hurry. And it was ominous, of course, that she didn't know. She was wearing boys' clothing and sprinting across the back lawn before even the sun had risen in the sky, like a thief stealing away from a crime.

She could hear men talking in the distance. Gareth suddenly came to an abrupt halt, breathing heavily, eyes wary. He listened for a moment and then swore. Turning to her, he said in a tense undertone, "Run to the back of the stables. Go through the side door. Climb into the back of Father's carriage, and for God's sake, stay out of sight."

Annabelle ran as fast as she could, her feet sliding in the oversized boots as she sprinted through a thicket of trees along the edge of the lawn. When she reached the stables, she slipped through the side entrance, but she could barely see the carriage. It was too dark.

With a combination of sight and feel, she found it. She unlatched the narrow door and clambered through, pulling it shut behind her. She reached for the blanket stored beneath the rear passenger bench, but someone had moved it. She felt about for it on the floor. The carriage boards were unexpectedly smooth, and the smell inside was different—more linseed oil, less horse.

She'd made a mistake. Gareth had been given a new carriage for his birthday, and there was little doubt she'd climbed into it. She could hear the creak of the stable doors as they swung on their hinges, and the sound of approaching voices. Panicking, she hid beneath the forward-facing bench seat.

"Such a surprise to see you out and about so early, Gareth." It was Digby. "Are you making an escape?"

"I have as much a chance of winning this race as you do, Damian." Annabelle could hear the anxiety in her brother's voice. "I'm merely eager to start."

"Indeed," Digby replied. "I've been seeing to the horses. They're fed and ready to go. The only thing left for me to do is win. Then we will discuss the stakes."

They were beside the carriage now, close enough for her to hear Gareth's quick intake of breath. "We agreed on Alec's stakes last night."

"What if I prefer your original proposal?"

"About that, I don't know what I could have been thinking."

"You were thinking like someone who owes a debt of 8,000 pounds and has very few options for repaying it."

In the carriage, Annabelle was mute with shock. Eight thousand pounds! It was an exorbitant amount. It would take years for even her father to cover the debt.

"You're right, of course." Gareth laughed nervously. "But the stakes have changed."

There was a long silence. "I think your conscience is a bit late to the festivities," Digby said with little pretense at civility. "What will your lovely sister say when she learns you've practically beggared an estate you don't even own?"

Dear God, what had he done?

"You're not the gentleman I thought you were!"

"I'm a gentleman when I need to be," Digby replied matter-of-factly, as if they were discussing the weather. "This morning, I'd find it far too limiting."

She could not hide any more. She had to confront them. But as she edged from beneath the bench seat, she heard another person approach. "I thought I heard voices out here. Gareth, is everything all right?" She would know him anywhere. Dear Lord, what would Alec say if he saw her, dressed as she was? She remained hidden.

"Ah, it's Carstairs to the rescue again," Digby mocked. "But there's no need, is there, Gareth? We're simply readying everything for our race on Two Boulders Road." Her brother did not reply. "Since we're all here, I say we get under way, even though we planned on a later start. You there! You boys!" he called out. The stable hands must have just arrived for work. "You will be our judges. My own man is outside, tending to my horses, and I've already seen to the others. We've merely to hitch them to the carriages to set things in motion. I see no reason to delay, do you, Carstairs?"

"The sooner this is done," Alec replied, "the sooner the Laytons are safe from you."

After a long pause, Gareth quietly agreed. Annabelle could hear horses backing up to the carriage, and straps being tightened and tied. Someone hopped up onto the driver's perch. It had to be Gareth. She could feel the carriage pull forward, its wheels creaking as they rolled out of the stables. "Gareth!" she whispered. Either he didn't hear her or he wouldn't reply.

She was frightened now, her heart racing. He obviously didn't want her presence to be known, but how could she exit the carriage without being seen? They were moving slowly along a route to somewhere. The start of the race, she realized suddenly. Then they stopped, and she was filled with a terrible sense of foreboding. The horses were pulling against their harnesses and pawing at the ground, ready to run. Something horrible would come of this. She could feel it.

A starting gun fired a single shot in the distance. With the crack of a whip, they were off.

• • •

Adrenaline was raging through Alec. The three carriages were racing side by side, each trying to gain a foothold and shuddering with the strain of their speed. He briefly turned toward the others to access their positions. Gareth was closest to him, his eyes straight ahead, his face pale and nervous. Digby raced beside Gareth, urging his horses onward with the blistering lash of his whip, utterly focused and intent. Alec turned his own eyes back to the road. He had to win. More than anything, he wanted the satisfaction of humiliating a man who sought to harm those he cared for. Gareth was a lifelong friend, whether his father thought him suitable company or not. And Annabelle had been so worried for her brother last night, tense in the candlelight and utterly luminous.

He couldn't think of it now. His horses were stirring up a maelstrom of dust on the King's Highway, and he needed to win every advantage. He sped on, urging his horses faster. They were purebred Yorkshires—a marriage of hot-blooded Arabian stallions and English Cleveland Bays. The carriage itself was beautifully sprung, an example of exquisite craftsmanship. His father demanded the best, and for that, at least now, Alec was thankful.

Within minutes, he opened up a slight lead, just as Gareth's inexperience was beginning to show. He was holding his reins too tightly, the bits tearing at his horses' mouths as they tossed their heads in confusion. God, Gareth needed to loosen his hold, or they would rebel. Digby, for his part, was unleashing a furious attack on his team to urge them forward. Their mouths were foaming, their eyes terrified by the cruel mistreatment, and Alec swore loudly in disgust.

He redoubled his efforts as Two Boulders Road loomed ahead. Responding to a deft slap of the reins, his horses surged forward with a burst of speed, and he pulled into a defiant lead. He couldn't risk a look behind to see who followed next. From the sounds of the horses, Alec was a few lengths ahead of the others. God willing, Gareth was holding his own. As he threaded his carriage through the pass marked by the boulders, he saw the Layton grooms up ahead, preparing to judge the finish line. It was within his grasp.

Then something went catastrophically wrong. The back of his carriage gave a groan, and there was a deafening snap. He spun his head around to see what had happened, and less than a moment later, the world lurched wildly. His back left wheel had sprung free, but somehow the horses and the carriage cleared the road before tumbling over violently. He fell from the driver's box, landing with a bone-jarring crack on the roadside. For several long moments, he was disoriented, his vision blurry. Shaking his head to clear it, he felt a stab of excruciating pain. Jaw clenched, he had to squint to focus his eyes.

Suddenly, though, he saw everything with hideous clarity.

His back wheel had spun into the air, and then landed hard, bouncing directly into the path of Gareth's carriage. Digby was far behind. His horses must have rebelled at his mistreatment, taking him out of the path of danger, but Alec watched helplessly as Gareth panicked and overcompensated to avoid the wheel, jerking his reins hard right toward one of the road's namesake rocks. His horses, already spooked, were sprinting at full speed, and only at the last minute did they take note of their direction. Trying to avoid a collision, they veered wildly and sent the carriage careening out of control. Gareth was flung from his seat, and there was an earsplitting crash as the horses fell, and shards and spikes of lacquered wood spun up into the sky.

Alec sprinted through his pain to the scene of the destruction. The horses were screaming. One was already back up, and rearing in terror, but the other had broken a leg and would have to be put down. Shocked by the scene, he didn't immediately see Gareth. But then his heart stilled, and bile rose in his throat. His friend lay in the grass, blood trickling from his lips, his head bent at such an unnatural angle that Alec knew, without a doubt, he was dead.

He heard a soft moan. He wondered, at first, if it had come from him—the first spilling of grief—but then it sounded again, coming from the wreckage itself. He turned to find little that might resemble a carriage. It was nothing but a pile of cracked boards at odd angles and broken wheels. He flung himself at the remains, fueled by panic, and tossed aside splintered wood, a crushed copper lantern, a section of the carriage roof, a small door split in half. Had he imagined the sound? In the bright morning light, though, something shimmered. He tore away another layer of the wreckage. And felt a pain so stunning that surely his gut had been ripped in two.

Because there, newly revealed and utterly still, was the ghostly pale face of Annabelle Layton, eyes open, her honey blond hair matted with blood.

He tore at the last of the debris that covered her, until Annabelle was free of it, her body lying awkwardly against the remnants of an upholstered bench seat. Hands shaking, Alec tore off his gloves and felt for her pulse at the base of her neck. It was weak but alarmingly rapid. Her breathing was shallow, her skin cool and clammy.

Someone drew in a sharp breath behind him. "Is she … is she dead, too?" Digby gasped, his face drained of color.

"No, but she's in shock." He could hear the fear in his voice. "Take one of your horses, and get to the castle as fast as you can for help." Alec turned to the groom who was running toward them. "Ride to Hinckley, and beg Dr. Chessher to come right away. Meet us here. I'm too worried to move her." The other groom was looking down at Gareth's broken body, silent and still. He'd just cut free the one unharmed horse. Alec called out to him. "We will need clean linens for bandages and a board to hold Miss Layton. You'll need to pad it as best you can. And send two carts, one for her, and the other one … we'll need it for Gareth. Hurry!"

His heart was pounding, as if he'd sprinted for miles. Trying to keep his hands steady, he gently examined Annabelle's head to assess the extent of the injury there. She had a gash the length of his thumb on the left side of her head, above her ear. He could feel bone beneath his fingers. He felt along her shoulders, tracking her blood with his hands along the jacket she wore—a man's jacket, inexplicably. When he carefully pulled it open, and pressed along her left side, she flinched, though she was still unconscious. She had two, perhaps three broken ribs. He continued probing with his hands over the curve of her hips, clad in an old pair of boy's riding breeches. His hands stilled. There was more blood. Lots of it. The breeches on the left side were soaked through. The scent of it hung in the air.

He leapt to his feet and sprinted back toward his carriage. He would need the knife in his coachman's travel box. There was also a blanket he could cut into strips. In the distance, he could hear the cries of the injured horse, softer now.

His own horses were unscathed. One of the Layton grooms must have unhitched the team from his carriage, which lay on its side in the grass. After grabbing the items he needed, he ran back to Annabelle. Kneeling down beside her, he took a deep breath, and gingerly sliced open the breeches with his knife.

What he saw nearly turned his stomach. Her leg had been snapped in two, her thigh bone stabbing through the skin, blood oozing from the wound. Alec ripped the linen cravat from his neck and tied it tightly around her thigh above the break to fashion a tourniquet. *God, please let it work!* Moving quickly, he shredded his carriage blanket, draping strips of it over the wound. They were immediately soaked, but as he pulled them away and applied new ones, over and over again, the bleeding seemed to slow. He was desperate to believe it.

He took more of the strips and pressed them as gently as he could against the gash above her ear. Head wounds bled profusely, but how could Annabelle lose so much blood and live? His hands were covered with it, faintly chilled and sticky. And she was so terribly still, her eyes yet open, as blue as the spring sky above him, the pupils dilated and round as the full moon.

Alec heard the heavy thunder of approaching horses. They were coming in from every side. He could see Digby with Sir Layton and several men. One of the grooms and an accompanying footman were speeding toward him, riding in carts that were piled with supplies. From the other direction came Dr. Chessher, racing in at a full gallop, his horse laden with medical bags. He could also see Mrs. Chessher close behind, a formidable woman who helped her husband in emergencies.

Alec could hardly take in the unreality of it all. It was a beautiful morning, bright and still cool, yet here at the junction of the King's Highway and Two Boulders Road, the world as he knew it was flying apart, splintering in different directions like shattered glass. His oldest friend lay no more than a dozen feet away, dead in the grass. And there was every chance that Annabelle would not survive.

People were swarming about him. Dr. Chessher moved with efficiency and purpose, but he was obviously alarmed. He barked out orders for supplies from the cart: ice; water; fresh bandages; straight, clean boards; threaded silk; the smallest of needles; scalpels; clamps; an ample dose of laudanum. Annabelle was finally stirring, moaning faintly, but Alec knew that a few more minutes of unconsciousness would have been preferable. It would be desperately painful when Dr. Chessher reset her leg. If it could be reset.

Mrs. Chessher rushed over with the laudanum, as well as the doctor's bag, which the surgeon tore open, hurriedly setting out tools on a fresh linen cloth. Alec could feel her hand on his shoulders as she gently drew him away from Annabelle. He could see Digby aimlessly walking along the road, picking up pieces of the wreckage. The grooms were padding a flat board; it would be used to ease Annabelle's move to the horse cart that would bear her home. The men who had come with Digby were standing around Gareth's body, ready to carry it to the litter that would transport him back to the castle. Sir Layton was standing beside the body of his only son, his chest heaving, tears rolling down his face and onto his jacket.

A woman's scream split the air, and they all turned. Annabelle was writhing in anguish as Mrs. Chessher held her down, aided by the footman who'd brought the cart. The doctor stood above her, struggling to pull her leg straight so that he could align the bones. He swore at Alec to stand back when he came running forward, hoping to somehow assist them. So instead, Alec watched, helpless as Annabelle suffered. She was staring straight at him, covered with her own blood, her eyes wild with fear. During the war, he had seen soldiers like this, terrified men torn apart, caught between the last few moments of life and death, but dear God, this was Annabelle. His beautiful, irrepressible girl. He would give anything, promise anything to save her.

She fainted then, and he whispered a prayer of thanks. With the break set at last, Dr. Chessher tied a splint crafted with boards and cotton batting to her leg. He then threaded his needles and sewed shut the skin about her thigh wound and head. Mrs. Chessher, her face glistening with perspiration, declared that every wound needed a good drink—-an old superstition, it seemed—as she swabbed the sutured flesh with alcohol from a bottle, and then took a restorative swig herself. Alec hardly cared, so long as it had a chance of working.

The footman and Dr. Chessher lifted Annabelle onto the padded board, and then into the cart that would take her home. The one bearing Gareth's body soon followed behind, and then Sir Frederick, and Alec, and the rest fell in line to follow.

Once at a carnival as a small child, Alec had been fascinated by an artist who'd rendered dozens of palm-sized drawings, each of them minutely different. They'd been gathered in book form, and as the artist flicked through them, his thumb quickly separating every page, the drawings had come alive. The subject had been a little dog who'd sprinted across a precisely rendered street, narrowly avoiding an out-of-control carriage, a meaty bone the prize for a journey fraught with danger.

If only Alec could play the pages of this day in reverse, so time moved backward, and accidents were undone, and foolish words were unspoken.

If only shattered bodies could be made whole again.

Chapter 4

As he draped another cold, wet cloth across Annabelle's brow, Alec was certain he could see steam rising. She was burning up. "Mary, I think we must call the doctor back," he said in a low, harried voice. "There must be a way to bring her fever down."

The young maid, face tense with worry, shook her head gently. Little older than Annabelle, she had served the Laytons for most of her life. "Dr. Chessher said to expect this, my lord. Cold cloths and water, he said, and laudanum. The fever has to burn itself out."

Of course, Mary was right, but Alec wasn't accustomed to this desperate sense of helplessness and regret. He'd lost all track of time. Had he eaten today? It didn't matter. He had no appetite. Not when she lay there, looking impossibly young and fragile, her head wrapped in linen cloths, her leg bruised and swollen so badly he feared it would break through the splint Dr. Chessher had fashioned. A double incline plane, he'd called it. Rather than a single flat board keeping her leg stiff, it was made from two boards, allowing her knee to be elevated and bent slightly. Supposedly, it was better suited to her type of injury and would help her retain mobility. If the leg could be saved. If Annabelle lived.

The biggest threat was infection, and little could be done to prevent it. Willing to try anything, Alec and Mary were following Mrs. Chessher's superstitious habit. They'd applied so much alcohol to Annabelle's wounds, the room smelled like a distillery. Whether he was dizzy from the fumes or exhaustion, he could not say. Since the accident, he'd stayed by her side, returning to Arbury Hall only to bathe and change. It was flagrantly improper. Father, above all else, would be furious, but Annabelle's parents were beside themselves and unable to care for their daughter.

They'd crumbled in the face of disaster, a telling sign, his father would say, of instability.

Sir Layton was overwhelmed by Annabelle's severe injuries. He'd come several times to her chamber, face ashen, eyes tormented, hardly noticing Alec in the room. If only Annabelle were one of the butterflies in his collection, he kept murmuring, he could make her better. He had the glues and the supplies to keep her preserved under plate glass. His confusion was alarming.

As for Lady Layton, she hadn't been in to see Annabelle. Not once. She hadn't even met them at the doors of the castle that terrible morning. Upon hearing of the accident that had claimed her son, she'd taken to her bed, immobilized by her loss. According to Mary, she barely spoke a word to anyone. It was not healthy. As if the fear and grief he felt were healthy. Or the anger.

What had possessed her? When she was young, Annabelle had made a habit of sneaking into the carts he and Gareth raced through the countryside, but she should have been past such foolishness by now. Yet she'd dressed in boys' clothing to disguise herself. Doubtless, Gareth hadn't even known she was there, or he'd never have allowed the race to get under way. Again, Annabelle had done as she pleased, but never had the consequences been more tragic. The proof lay there, broken and bleeding, on the bed.

He dropped his head into his hands with a long, shuddering breath. If only he'd controlled his temper. Or stopped the race. The thought that she might not recover was more than he could bear.

• • •

It was almost midnight. Annabelle was sleeping peacefully, her lips slightly parted, her breathing soft and steady. Her cheek, so smooth beneath his hand, was cooler to the touch, and Alec was dizzy with relief. Her fever had broken.

He stood slowly, every muscle protesting the movement, and stepped away from her bedside chair. Mrs. Fritchens, the Laytons' formidable housekeeper, had insisted that he and Mary get some rest. She would look after Annabelle tonight. Yet Alec found it difficult to give up his watch. He needed to somehow show he cared—that he always had. Even in ways he should not.

He slipped from the room, walking through the darkened halls, one hand on the Tudor-era wainscoting to help guide him through the old home. It was almost empty now. Following the accident, the houseguests had departed in a panic, nearly tripping over each other's belongings in their haste. Digby, of course, had fled before Gareth's body was cold. Many of their friends from university, though, had taken rooms in town for the funeral. The doors and windows of the castle were hung with black crepe, the mirrors covered. Alec felt a fresh rush of grief. It seemed impossible that Gareth was dead.

As he crept down the main stairs, he heard someone singing softly, which made no sense. Not in a house shrouded in black. The sounds were coming from the small chapel, located off the Great Hall, where Gareth's body rested in repose on a block of ice. Astley Castle was said to be haunted, and in the dark of this night, he could well believe it.

As he edged closer, the singing grew louder. A woman's voice filled the chapel, plaintive and ghostly. He looked past the doorway into the heart of the room lit by candelabra, and the hairs rose on the back of his neck. Beside his friend's catafalque sat Lady Layton, clad in a wrinkled dressing gown, hair tangled about her head, her face tortured with grief. She was singing an old nursery song, the same one she'd sung when Gareth and Annabelle were small and crying over scraped knees. The one they had always relied on to make their pain go away and set everything right.

Alec's heart was in his throat. There was no way to set things right.

As he turned back toward the hall, the singing suddenly stopped. He could hear the quick approach of her bare feet on the stone floor, and he turned to face her. "Lady Layton, I am so very sorry ..." The words died in his throat. Her eyes were wild with loathing.

"You did this. You killed my son!" She advanced on him, her breath coming in quick pants.

"Lady Layton, I assure you ..."

Holding a letter in her hands, she thrust it toward his face, moving so close he could feel her anger like a palpable thing.

"This arrived earlier," she hissed. "Read it!"

Numb with shock, he took the note. He could just make out its words in the dim light.

Lady Layton,

You have my sincerest condolences on the death of your son, my dear friend Gareth. The loss of a child at any time is heartbreaking, and it must be all the more so, considering the circumstances.

If only Lord Dorset had taken the time to ensure that his carriage was in good working order! His burden must be painful indeed, to know that his carelessness caused such a tragedy.

I will continue to pray for the full recovery of your lovely daughter, Miss Annabelle. May I beg you to keep me apprised of her condition?

With my deepest sympathies,

Damien Digby, Esq.

Like a blow from a hammer, his heart slammed in his chest, air rushing from him in a single breath.

He *hadn't* inspected his carriage on the morning of the race. Surely he'd have noticed a weakness in the wheel if he had. He'd been so caught up in his anger that he'd been unforgivably careless. He could've prevented the debacle to begin with. He'd practically forced the race with his outrageous bet. He could see that now. He'd had a direct role in Gareth's death, in Annabelle's suffering.

"I am so sorry," he whispered. He was burning up in the cold room, sweat trickling over his brow.

"Don't you dare apologize. It does no good. It will not bring my son back." Lady Layton's hands were in her hair, fingers entwined with clumps of it, pulling so viciously that the skin on her face was distorted.

"I do not know what to say." Guilt pounded through him.

"I carried him in my womb, and gave birth to him in a wash of blood. I raised him, coddled him, kissed him. Look at him now." With a shaking hand, she pointed at Gareth's pale, gray body in the candlelight.

"It was a terrible accident," he said. Yet his had been the defining role in the whole tragedy, setting events in motion until they crescendoed in destruction.

"I know what you are about upstairs. You sit like a specter, haunting my daughter's bedside, waiting and watching."

"I am only trying to help Annabelle."

"I won't allow you to ease the burden of your guilt." Her voice was rising now, gaining power. "You'll not take my last child from me. I want you gone from this house. Vow that you'll never return."

He stilled. "But Annabelle …"

She slapped his cheek in a burst of fury, snapping his head to one side. "As long as I live, if you dare approach my daughter, I will kill you myself."

"Lady Layton … please."

"You'll never see my daughter again. You'll never speak to her, or write to her. Swear it!"

He didn't think he could. He couldn't leave Annabelle like this. She needed him. God in Heaven, Lady Layton was in no condition to care for her.

"She'll despise you when she learns what you've done," she said. "If you have a shred of honor, you'll leave and never return."

He took a deep breath, trying to force back air into his lungs, and fight off a mounting sense of anguish. He'd caused Annabelle so much pain. In such a real and tangible way, he was responsible for the whole of it. Hadn't his father spoken of recklessness and repercussions? Could it be that honor was all he had left?

Perhaps it was.

"I swear it then," he said softly. He turned and made his way toward the door, his footsteps ringing like a death knell in the empty hall, their sound following him into the dark night.

• • •

He watched from a distance as the cortège accompanying his friend's body made its way to the Layton's burial plot at St. Mary the Virgin church. Alec could see Paul, the young Earl of Linley, and Benjamin, Lord Marworth. He walked with an arm around Gareth's visibly shaken father, and Alec was grateful that the baron had Marworth's steadying presence beside him. Sir Layton walked with his head down, his shoulders stooped, and with a grief so profound that Alec could feel it radiate to where he stood with his horse, hidden a hundred feet away. A woman shrouded in unrelieved black walked beside them. Though her face was covered with a heavy veil, Alec knew it must be Lady Layton.

Another wave of intense guilt rushed through him. Annabelle was not there. Even the consolation of mourning her brother properly had been taken from her. According to Mary, who had crept over to Arbury Hall with the news, Dr. Chessher was encouraged by Annabelle's improvement. She was confused, though, during her fleeting moments of consciousness. Mary had promised she'd send additional updates when she knew more. Would Annabelle's leg ever heal, or be of any use? It was devastating to think that her spirit and vibrancy might be confined to a chair. And that he was to blame.

He had written a last letter to Annabelle. Despite Lady Layton, he could not leave without saying goodbye. She had to know that he was horrified by his actions and by what they had cost her. She had to know that if she ever needed him, she had only to write and he would be there, honor be damned. He'd bribed a footman to see that Annabelle got it. By the time she was well enough to read it, he'd be gone. He only hoped his departure would bring her family, and most especially Annabelle, some measure of peace.

He turned from the distant scene, spurring his mount toward Arbury Hall. Given his plans, he had much to prepare for, even as this horrible afternoon slipped into evening.

• • •

"I warned you, Alec, did I not? I knew that going to the Layton boy's party would bring no good result."

His father was pacing the library at Dorset House, caught up in the scandal that Alec had brought back from Nuneaton. For the past hour, the earl had lectured him on the ramifications of irresponsible behavior, while Alec stood ramrod straight, hands clasped behind his back—a habit from his childhood. But Alec could not keep his focus. Not when the moss-green Aubusson carpet on the floor recalled Gareth dead in the grass. Not when the red Chesterfield sofa reminded him of the blood covering Annabelle. Or when the massive fireplace beside him looked like a portal to hell, with flames licking up at him.

That had always been one of Father's tricks, to have him stand next to the fire. As a child, Alec had never known if he was sweating because of its heat, or because he was frightened by the punishment to come.

This time, no punishment would be harsh enough.

"The only consolation," his father continued, "is that it happened far from London, and that gives us time to mitigate your part. Everyone knows Layton was headed for a bad end."

"And what of Annabelle?" Alec asked quietly.

"At least she had not yet made her debut. It would be harder if she had. As it stands, she is nameless, faceless to almost everyone here. We will agree that it was a tragedy, and offer all the proper commiserations. But that part of it will pass quickly."

In that moment, fists clenching, Alec hated his father.

"It will not pass quickly for me."

The earl stopped pacing, and looked at Alec, focused and intent. "You have tried to hide your attraction to the girl, but I know you better than you know yourself. In the end, her role in this only proves that I was right to push for the distance between you."

No matter her role, there was every chance she would spend the rest of her life paying for his mistakes. "Annabelle did not deserve any of this."

"Whether she did or not is a moot point. We must redouble our efforts to introduce you to the proper circles in Parliament. The members will forgive this youthful indiscretion if you show them what you are made of, the intelligence that you have."

Ironically, Alec's reputed intelligence had been the very thing that had recalled his father's attention to his only son. He had taken first honors at Oxford in *literae humaniores* and in mathematics. When his father had asked for a sampling of his supposed knowledge, Alec had recited Cicero's famous speech before the Roman Senate in 63 AD, castigating the counsel, Catiline, for his abuse of power. Of course, he had recited it in Latin, all 317 lines of it.

How long, O Catiline … will that madness of yours mock us? To what end will your unbridled audacity hurl itself?

His father had watched him quietly that afternoon, his surprise evident in the first genuine smile he'd ever offered. When Alec had finished, he'd said, "I had no idea you might be worth something." Not the warmest compliment to be sure, but even so, the words had felt like a benediction. Because after that, Alec and his mother were no longer forgotten, packed away like an ill-fitting suit of clothes. All of his life, Alec had been desperate for his father's approval. And now, he would throw it away.

"Father, I cannot take up the seat in the House of Commons. I cannot stay in London."

The earl halted in mid-stride, turning toward Alec, his expression disbelieving. "Don't be absurd. It is more important than ever that you take your place here, and prove that you're not the worthless fribble that Layton was."

"I am going to serve with the army on the Peninsula. I have used the money that Grandmother left me to purchase a commission. And this has nothing to do with Mother. She should not be blamed for my actions."

The heat coming off the fire was nothing compared to the fury of his father. With a curse, he turned on his heel and walked toward his desk, yanking the stopper from a bandy-filled decanter set upon it. He sloshed a long pour into a waiting glass, and flung back the contents in a single gulp. After a deep breath, he turned back to face him. The disdain in the earl's face made Alec feel stupid and unworthy, all his gains lost in a single moment. But in this, he would not back down. He could not.

"So you will fight in Spain," his father spat. "Or Portugal, or wherever they send you, and for what?"

"For penance. To make some good out of this horror." Alec looked down. Shadows from the fire were flickering across his hands. Absorbed as he was in them, he barely registered his father's disgusted exhalation.

"Parliament needs you far more than Wellington does. Would you risk the earldom's heir? When you know the future I have planned for you? Are you turning your back on your honor? On our legacy?"

"I am trying to be honorable. This is the only way I know how."

"How to what?" his father cried. "How to give up your birthright to Stansley, that pompous fop, who will inherit if you die during this appalling indulgence of your guilt?"

"It is the only way I know how to stay away, Father. Especially now, after all the pain I have caused. And I must stay away. I have sworn it."

Part 2

Chapter 5

April 21, 1812
Nuneaton

Annabelle's left leg was very good at telling her when it had had enough. Enough of horseback riding. Enough of long mornings spent working in the gardens. Enough of walking. It was speaking quite loudly now, come to think of it, sending a sharp pain from her knee up into her hip in a fit of pique. But she decided that she would ignore it. It had tried far too often in the past to dictate what she did. Not to mention those terrifying months when it had refused to work at all, and she had wondered if she would ever walk again. She would never take the luxury of putting one foot in front of the other for granted.

Of course, she hadn't planned on hiking so far. She took a long walk each morning, but today she'd gone all the way to Arbury Hall, with its tall spires gleaming in the early light. She'd always loved the beautiful Elizabethan mansion, which was surrounded by lakes and lush parkland. In the distance, she could just make out the grazing fields for the estate's famous Southdown sheep, but the Hall itself was shuttered, its windows and doors draped in mourning cloth. She had read the black-bordered announcement in the news sheets. Lord Dorset, Alec's father, had died suddenly. She was very sorry for Lady Dorset, whom she remembered with fondness.

She refused to feel any sympathy for her son.

Annabelle had no memory of Gareth's accident, nor of how she had come to be in the carriage with him. Even the dark days that had followed were lost, and perhaps God had been kind in that. But there was one thing that she did know. She'd never really known Alec Carstairs. The Alec she'd believed him to be would never have watched his oldest friend die, only to leave for London before Gareth was even buried in the ground. He would never have abandoned her, bloodied and delirious, no matter how rash her behavior. And she feared it had been catastrophically rash, with consequences she could not bear to consider.

He alone could speak to the role she had played. But he had never replied to the many letters she'd sent, begging for answers, or even for some indication that he cared if she lived or died. After the accident, he'd made his excuses to her distraught mother, insisting that he had to leave before the scandal touched his family. Upon his return to London, he'd gone off to fight in the Peninsular Wars, no doubt to put even more distance between them, and she'd never heard from him again.

He'd once claimed she was like a sister to him. Until they had kissed, of course. And he'd told her that she was beautiful. After the accident, she had not been so pretty, had she? He'd left her behind, like a broken toy he no longer wanted to play with.

Mother had been right. He'd never really cared at all.

Enough about Alec Carstairs. Some memories should simply stay in the past, where they belonged.

She cast a final, lingering look at the shrouded Hall. She was so tired of death! First Gareth, and then her mother only two years later, although that had not been completely unexpected. A large part of Mother had died with her only son, and Annabelle knew that she'd spent her remaining years waiting for the other part to hurry up and end her misery. What a sad, wraithlike creature she'd become.

When Annabelle was a child, Astley Castle had been filled with laughter and light—a charmed existence by anyone's measure. The Layton family had been blissfully unaware that life could hold unpleasant surprises, like tragedy and suffering. It had learned otherwise.

Tragedy took your measure. It tested you, to see what you were capable of. Annabelle had learned that she was capable of more than she'd thought possible. She'd learned to walk again, despite it having been a painful and lonely process. She'd learned to be self-reliant and not to miss—too much—the friends who no longer came to call. And if men no longer sprouted like spring flowers when she was near, she could accept that. She had no use for them either. Her scars had healed. Even some of the ones on the inside.

She turned away abruptly, and headed back towards home. No doubt Cousin Estrella, who had lived with them since Mother's death, was wondering where she had gotten to. If she was discovered in her hiking attire—a well-worn pair of old riding breeches, a warm wool vest over an oversized linen shirt, and a pair of serviceable leather boots—a lecture was sure to follow, and Annabelle was already running behind.

With luck, she'd be able to avoid both Estrella and her son, Augustus, who also lived at the castle as her father's heir. He had grown from a boy whom she had barely tolerated into a man she actively disliked, with florid waistcoats, and leering eyes, and wandering hands.

• • •

Once back at the castle, she slipped through the servant's entrance and pulled off her weathered sun hat, unleashing a long braid that fell more than halfway down her back. Cook didn't like hats in her kitchen, after all. Flashing a conspiratorial grin at Elizabeth, one of the downstairs maids, she sneaked a biscuit still warm from the oven, and headed toward the back stairway. Rounding the first flight of steps, she was on her way up the second when she heard an unfamiliar voice, mellifluous and faintly imperious. Did they have a visitor? No one ever came here. During the long year of her rehabilitation, Mother had refused all callers, and after that, people had simply stayed away, on the off chance grief and madness might be catching.

Torn between her need for haste and a powerful sense of curiosity, she crept back down the steps, and crossed over to a service door that opened onto the main hall. She could hear Estrella, who was obviously agitated. "As I said, Lady Marchmain, Annabelle will be sad to have missed you. However, she's hardly well enough for your visit, which comes as such a surprise, after all."

Lady Marchmain? She didn't know anyone by that name. And why would Estrella say she was unwell? She was perfectly healthy.

"Mrs. Simperton, I did send a letter." The stranger's voice was heavy with impatience.

"But my lady, your letter did not arrive until this morning. I'd hardly finished reading it when your coach turned up the drive."

"I should like to know why you were reading the letter to begin with. It was not addressed to you. It was addressed to Annabelle."

"Yes … well," Estrella faltered. "I read all of the girl's correspondence, such as it is. Her mind has never fully recovered from the tragedy. She's quite simple, really." Annabelle drew back in affront. There was nothing at all wrong with her mind! Why would Estrella say there was? After all, who corrected the house accounts once Augustus had finished them? Time and again, she'd had to move expenses and earnings into their proper columns, and fix a stunning array of computational errors.

"Simple, you say? I'll make that determination. Now step aside, Mrs. Simperton, and have someone unload my trunks. Outside of her father, I'm the girl's closest living relative. I may be late in claiming her, but claim her I shall."

The only relative Annabelle could claim—living or dead—was her mother's sister, but she lived abroad and they'd never met. Her first name was Sophia, but the lady had been married so many times, Annabelle had lost track of her surname. In any case,

Mother had never really gotten along with her. Whatever meager correspondence they'd kept up over the years had ended shortly after Gareth's death.

So many things had been buried with him.

No longer able to control her curiosity, she pulled open the door and walked into the hall. Both women turned, obviously surprised by the intrusion. Estrella looked particularly pained, as if she'd been caught ogling a piece of the family silver—a not uncommon occurrence—but it was the lady beside her who drew Annabelle's gaze.

A trim and elegant woman, she was dressed in a dove grey gown, with a short purple pelisse worn over a petticoat of the same, fitted tightly with a stomacher buttoned with amethyst clasps. With pale blue eyes and dark blond hair beneath her feather-trimmed hat, her features—high cheekbones, slanted brows, and a slim, straight nose—were achingly familiar. For a moment, Annabelle felt faint.

"You're so like my mother," she whispered.

The woman stepped forward, her face wreathed in an approving smile as Annabelle dropped into an awkward curtsey.

"I am Lady Sophia Middleton, the Countess of Marchmain, and your late mother's sister, but you may call me Aunt Sophia, my dear."

Words had deserted her. Annabelle tried to smile, but it was difficult when she felt like crying and falling at the woman's feet like a child who wanted to be held. Her aunt didn't seem to notice. She gave Annabelle a frank and thorough perusal, sweeping her from head to toe. "I'm sure you have a perfectly logical reason for being dressed like a boy," she said. "You are shockingly lovely all the same. And you can't know how relieved I am to discover that you don't suffer from any noxious infirmities, as I was led to believe." She shot Estrella a fierce look of disapproval before returning her attention to Annabelle.

"I can hardly wait to get you to London for the Season. What a time we shall have of it. Thank goodness you're a grown woman, not an infant with grubby, sticky fingers. I wouldn't be here if you were, I can promise you that."

• • •

"Tell me all about yourself," Aunt Sophia said. "There's quite a bit to catch up on." They were sitting together on a settee in the Rose Famille Bedroom, which Mother had named for the fanciful Chinese porcelain she'd loved to collect. It was a feminine chamber done up in pinks, greens, and golds, and it complemented her aunt, who was sophisticated and stylish and all the things Annabelle had forgotten how to be. If only she'd taken more care with her attire this morning. Her former maid, Mary, wouldn't have let her out looking like this, but Mary had left shortly after the accident to care for her grandmother.

"We live a quiet life here, but I'm very happy to meet you," she said. "Mother told me so much about you when I was younger."

"Really? What sorts of things did she say?"

"That you were beautiful and headstrong," Annabelle said after a brief hesitation. "She also said you appreciated a well-turned leg on a man, although I recall wondering what that meant."

Her aunt smiled broadly. "Despite our differences, she certainly understood my nature."

And in that moment, the countess reminded her so much of her mother—at least as she'd once been—that Annabelle had to swallow past a sudden lump in her throat. "I know in later years, she regretted not having a regular correspondence with you."

"Your mother and I grew apart," Aunt Sophia said, waving her hands as if that would dispel the memory of it. "Perhaps we were too much in competition with each other."

"What do you mean?"

"I made a spectacular debut in the spring of 1780. Even Prince George was a beau. He was quite handsome back then, with such a stylish flair. Who knew he would tend to fat the way he has?" She shook her head, as if disappointed. "In any case, I was universally admired. But when Charlotte made her debut two years later, several of my suitors defected to her retinue. I didn't enjoy that at all. You might even say I was jealous." The admission seemed to pain her. "There. I have said it, and I refuse to retract it. It's tiresome in the extreme when people second- guess what they say."

"I am sorry, Aunt Sophia. I don't think Mother ever knew."

"Well, it was a silly enough excuse for staying away. When I met my dearest Carlos, the Marques de Vallado—he was my first husband and a delicious man—we married and left England for Spain. Outside of attending your mother's wedding to your father, I was abroad for a number of years, and rarely looked back. Meeting you now," she said with a smile, "I'm convinced I should have come home sooner."

Annabelle bit her lip against the urge to say too much too soon, lest she scare her aunt away. "You are very kind to say it, but I'm afraid you'll find things rather somber here."

"We'll simply change that. And I am so pleased to find you well. Your mother's last letter, rambling though it was, painted a very dire picture. So did her solicitors, once they were able to reach me with the news of her passing."

Annabelle took a deep breath. "During the carriage accident, I suffered a head injury and several cracked ribs. My leg was broken, the thigh bone forced through the skin—"

Aunt Sophia held up her hand in protest. "I shall insist on a strong drink before I hear the gory particulars."

"I am sorry," she replied, embarrassed now. "I'm not often in polite company."

"But how are you walking so well? I thought to find you incapacitated."

"I was lucky to have been discovered quickly. The person who found me took very good care of my wounds until the doctor arrived." Dr. Chessher had said that Alec's care probably saved her life. Yet he'd abandoned her the next day.

"And who was that person?"

"Alec Carstairs, the Earl of Dorset. He was a childhood friend."

"Carstairs … I remember that name. Charlotte wrote that he was responsible for the whole of it."

"There are many things Alec can be blamed for," she said, looking down at her hands. "But my brother's death is not one of them."

"Where is this Lord Dorset now?"

"He has been fighting on the Peninsula for several years, but his father passed recently. No doubt he'll return to England to take over the title and its duties." They were the only things, in the end, that he truly cared about.

"And are you happy he will return? You must have been close once."

"I don't care if I ever see Alec Carstairs again." She could hear the bitterness in her voice. "Alec made it quite clear following the accident that he wanted nothing to do with the Layton family."

"How very odd," Aunt Sophia mused.

"The true hero of my recovery was Dr. Chessher. He developed a special splint for my leg, and wouldn't let me move from my bed for several months, so things could heal properly."

"Several months! I should never have managed it."

"Actually, it took almost a year to heal completely, but he gave me exercises to improve my mobility, and over time, with lots of work, I was able to walk again. It still pains me on occasion when I am overtired, but I consider myself blessed." Even though during the long months of her recovery, she'd wanted the earth to swallow her whole, and pound her broken bones to dust.

"What a marvelously brave girl. I wish your mother could see how resilient you are."

She swallowed, her throat suddenly thick. "I'm so happy you are here, Aunt, and that I've met you at last."

"Yes. Well, enough about that. I shall ruin my cosmetics if we don't change the subject immediately. Tell me, how is your father? It's been far too long."

Father! How could she have forgotten? "I'm sorry, Aunt Sophia," she said with a quick glance at the mantel clock. "He doesn't do well when his schedule is disordered. I shall explain later!" She fled from the room.

• • •

Annabelle changed as quickly as she could and ran outside to her father's workshop. During her early childhood, Father's lepidopterology collection had been located in a sitting room off of the library. However, when stacks of boxes with pinned butterflies and moths made passage through the room impossible, Mother had exiled him to the stable block, a Gothic revival structure that had housed horses and carriages in the last century. With its arched tracery windows, it offered an abundance of natural light.

Breathless, she arrived as the ornate grandfather clock tucked inside of the doorway struck noon. Father was seated at his desk, surrounded by mahogany display cases. The supplies they would need were organized precisely, in the order of their use, along the top of the desk's old oak surface. Absorbed in readjusting a quill that had slipped slightly, he hadn't yet noticed her, and she felt a familiar surge of sympathy and love. "Good morning, Father."

"Good morning, my dear," he replied, looking up with a boyish grin. When he saw what she was wearing, though, it faded, aging him instantly. "I have mixed up the days, haven't I?" She followed his eyes to her dress. In her haste, she'd put on the lavender muslin. How could she have been so careless?

"Look at the time I've wasted," he said sadly. "You are wearing lavender, which means it must be Thursday, and not Tuesday as I'd supposed. I thought it was Tuesday, so I've laid out the quills and the papers for cataloging our finds." He was becoming increasingly agitated. "I can see now I should have pulled out our boards, our glues, and brushes. I'm so sorry." Muttering, he ran the fingers of his left hand through his graying hair, catching them in a knot. He'd forgotten to comb it properly this morning. It was standing in a series of odd tufts, full of tangles.

He had always been eccentric, but since the deaths of Gareth and Mother, even the smallest adjustments in his routine were upsetting. And he'd abandoned any role in preserving their estate. Annabelle had tried her best to manage things, but the signs of benign neglect were obvious. The castle's heavy sixteenth-century doors were sagging on their hinges. Several of the ancient mullioned windows that ran along the north face had sashes infected with dry rot, and the formal gardens that had once been Astley's glory were sadly overgrown. There was no longer any money to repair them.

She walked forward, and gently reached for his hand, pulling it from his hair. "Father, let me comb that for you," she said, her voice hitching in her throat. "You're not blame for the mix-up today. I've worn the wrong dress, you see. We have a visitor. Can you imagine? And I was in a rush. You are right, perfectly right. I should be wearing my peach dress. It is Tuesday, after all."

"Are you certain, Annabelle? If it is indeed Tuesday, I must get the boards and glues. I must get this right. I am haunted by my mistakes."

"Father, the mistake was mine. Please don't upset yourself. Today, we shall simply be daring. It's an adventure, is it not, to wear the wrong thing, and to do the unexpected?"

She could tell from his sad, perplexed expression he didn't think so.

Once he was settled, the afternoon passed with relentless predictability. Father wrote out tags featuring both the vernacular and Latin names for each new specimen, and then Annabelle laboriously copied them, because two sets were always better than one. They ate their customary luncheon—yeast rolls, cold meats and cheeses, sliced fruit, and tea—and then cataloged the tags by family, genus, and species. Just as they had for two years' worth of Tuesdays.

• • •

Over the course of the next several days, Annabelle learned a number of things about her aunt. First, Sophia Middleton was a remarkably tenacious woman; you wasted time and breath standing in her way. Second, her aunt saw no point in spending time with people whom she did not like, which was why the Laytons and the Simpertons now dined separately. Estrella and Augustus had failed to impress. That wasn't to say, thirdly, that she was without kindness or sympathy. If Father had initially been discomfited by her arrival, lapsing into prolonged silences when she was near, Aunt Sophia had slowly won him over with a well-feigned interest in lepidopterology. She'd also indulged Annabelle's relentless questions about her mother's childhood, and even ordered up a special poultice when she overheard Thompson, their footman, complaining of muscle spasms.

The poultice incident underscored Annabelle's fourth observation. Aunt Sophia had an abiding weakness for handsome men. Fifth, even a handsome man was not a good enough reason to rusticate indefinitely. Aunt Sophia was most assuredly unsuited to country living.

Which was why, three weeks after her arrival, she rushed into Father's workshop in a flurry of green taffeta and lace and made a declaration.

"Annabelle, we're bound for the Continent. How soon do you think you can be ready?"

She laughed in response, sure that her aunt's outburst was prompted by another unpleasant interlude with Estrella. "You know I can't leave Father," she said with a quick glance behind her. He was at his desk, absorbed in mounting a silver-spotted skipper on a specimen board, oblivious to the conversation.

"My dear girl, you are young. You're beyond beautiful. Allow yourself, for once, to be self-indulgent. It's past time that you should see more of the world, and the London Season won't be in full swing for at least another month."

"Do you really think I'm beautiful, Aunt Sophia?" she asked, even as she cringed at her own insecurity. Every painful and agonizing step of her rehabilitation had taken her farther away from the girl she'd once been—carefree and overconfident in her beauty. "The truth is I am awkward, and I limp when I'm overtired. I don't know enough about what goes on in the outside world to offer much in the way of sophisticated discourse. I've forgotten how to behave in the company of others. You can't sugarcoat it."

"Never doubt you are beautiful, my dear. And if you were any of those other things, I'd have left this backwater weeks ago. My duty—too long overlooked—is to make you live the life you were born to. I'll be grossly offended if you continue to waste it by hiding out in Nuneaton."

"But Father will never leave his collections."

"Annabelle, your father is grieving, and to an unhealthy degree, I might add. You've assumed so many of his responsibilities that he has never had to move beyond that grief. Trust me when I tell you this. I'm an expert in dealing with death. I've buried three husbands, after all."

Could it be true? All she'd ever wanted to do was to give him time to heal.

"But Augustus and Estrella have a strong suspicion of foreigners." Annabelle was caught up in the notion of a trip, despite herself. She missed the wider world. She missed her old self and her old life.

"Your cousins are hardly invited. A more encroaching woman than Mrs. Simperton, I've yet to meet, and Augustus? Such dreadful clothes, with a personality devoid of wit or humor. As for your father, if he chooses not to travel with us, it will offer him an opportunity to reassert his control over Astley Castle."

"It's not so as easy as that, Aunt Sophia. And even if I could go, I'm afraid I don't have the funds to undertake a prolonged journey."

"I have more money than is conscionable, and a strong desire to return to Valladolid in Castile-Leon, where I lived with my darling Carlos. I still have an estate there. We could drink Spanish brandy in the shade of my olive orchard."

"I don't believe I have ever had brandy," Annabelle said wistfully. Could they travel for just a short while? Surely, she could muster the courage for that? She'd been practically fearless once.

"No brandy?" Aunt Sophia asked, thoroughly shocked. "Well, we'll have to remedy that. And did I mention that Spanish men are marvelous dancers? It will be wonderful practice for the Season."

How tempted she was. She could not spend the whole of her life hiding away. She'd done enough of that already. Just this once, she wanted to be carefree again, full of promise and possibility.

"I would love to drink brandy with you in the shade of an olive tree."

Aunt Sophia smiled broadly. "Leave it to me."

Chapter 6

May 20, 1812
London

Back in London for less than a month and already Alec's new title had settled like a yoke upon his shoulders. He was the ninth Earl of Dorset. His father had raised him for this, not only to handle the many obligations of their estates but also to further their position in society. To proudly represent the Carstairs name.

What was the point of it? During the war, the traditions of the aristocracy had seemed petty when men were dying all around him.

His final battle had been at Badajoz in Spain. He'd fought in the trenches, but after his father's unexpected death, the military sent him home, a privilege of the peerage, it seemed. He'd been tasked with giving Whitehall an overview of the victory there, distilling a grisly, gut-wrenching battle into a bloodless accounting of what had been lost and gained.

Afterward, he'd returned here to Dorset House with only his soldier's trunk and a small satchel filled with journals and private correspondence. He'd forgotten how beautiful the house was, with its immense proportions, its antiques and heirlooms, but he'd never felt more out of place. Apparently, four years was more than enough time to grow uncomfortable in one's own skin.

As he looked around his father's private office—his, now—his mind was racing. He needed to see to his mother's care. Despite a few streaks of gray, she looked much the same as she had when he'd left. But she was not the same. Something vital had gone out of her.

He also needed to take up his seat in the House of Lords, to argue that Parliament's hesitations were undermining the war effort on the Peninsula. There, at least, he could make a difference.

And he needed to visit his father's grave in the chapel at Arbury Hall to say goodbye.

Arbury Hall. So close to Astley Castle and Annabelle. All that he had left behind. He'd fought hard not to think of her once he'd learned that her leg, thank God, had been saved. But there had only been that one letter from Mary, her maid, when she'd promised more. And reports from Nuneaton said that Annabelle was no longer seen in the village there.

Not knowing how she fared was haunting. As haunting as his dreams of her in the night. But he did not take vows lightly.

A sudden knock on the door distracted him from his thoughts. "My lord," his butler intoned as he stood in the doorway. "Are you at home to visitors? Lord Marworth would like to speak with you."

Benjamin Alden, the fourth Viscount Marworth, was always welcome at Dorset House, but Edmunds strictly enforced the rules of etiquette. No doubt he'd have old King George himself cool his heels in the hallway. Not that Marworth was the sort to cool his heels anywhere. Tall, with a ready smile and golden good looks, he was one of the leading lights of the ton.

"Of course, Lord Dorset is at home," Benjamin said, slipping past Edmunds. "Despite my best efforts to get you out on the town these past several weeks, you're always here, wading through that sea of correspondence. I wouldn't be surprised if your ass had grown roots in that chair."

Alec rose and came around his desk with a smile, as the butler raised his nose a notch higher and swept from the room. "Some of us actually bother to answer their correspondence." He gave his friend's hand a warm shake.

"Unless Claudette has sent an invitation to call, my personal secretary can handle the mundane matter of organizing my schedule and keeping the duns from my door. You really need one of those, you know. A secretary. Come to think of it," Marworth continued, "you could use a mistress, too. Claudette has several appealing friends."

"You know I've never been one for mistresses." He still hadn't gotten over the shame of the last time he'd purchased a woman's affections. She'd had long blond hair and blue eyes. Just like Annabelle.

"Don't you ever tire of being so respectable? I make it a point to do something irresponsible each and every day. It makes for a world of fun."

"If only I could be more like you." Alec smiled. "But I am leaving for Arbury Hall tomorrow, and I've a number of things to settle."

"Off to Nuneaton so soon upon your return? I'd thought you'd forsaken it."

How he wished he could. There were too many painful memories there. "The estate must be seen to. I can hardly ignore it."

Marworth considered him from a long moment. "Then your visit has nothing to do with Annabelle Layton?"

"You know that it cannot," he said, picking up a sheaf of papers from his desk, and making a great show of studying them. Anything to distract Marworth from his question.

"I had wondered, with Lady Layton's death, if your position had changed."

The papers suddenly slipped from his hands, scattering onto the floor. He'd had no idea. "When did she die?"

"Two years ago. There was a notice in the paper. I wrote to Miss Layton to express my regrets. I've always had a soft spot for that girl, miracle of beauty that she is."

Alec felt as if the room was spinning. "Did she write you back?"

"She did. She thanked me very prettily for my condolences."

His first, irrational spurt of jealousy was replaced by a dawning sense of hope. Was she well, then? Had she recovered? If she was writing correspondence, would she welcome a letter from him?

"Have you seen her?"

"I have not. I've heard that the Laytons no longer welcome visitors. But you are an old friend. No doubt they'll make an exception for the hero of Badajoz."

"That designation is patently ridiculous," Alec said, raking a hand through his hair, his voice sharper than he'd intended. "The heroes of that battle are still there, dead in the ground."

Two years, Lady Layton had been gone. Why hadn't Annabelle tried to reach him? Did she despise him, as her mother had vowed she would?

Marworth quirked a brow. "I'm only quoting *The Times*."

"Well, it should never have been printed," he said, welcoming the distraction of the subject, if only to keep his thoughts from spinning. "The men I fought with came from some of the poorest segments of society. They sacrificed their lives knowing their families wouldn't be provided for. What did I sacrifice?"

"Several years of your life, I'd say."

"Even if I hadn't survived the war, my mother would still have been taken care of. Very few of the soldiers I fought with had that consolation." Here Alec sat, surrounded by every luxury. Living the life of his father. Missing a woman he might have been able to love. How had it come to this?

"For the love of God!" Benjamin groaned. "Do you have advantages that others don't share? Of course you do, in the same way you bear responsibilities that others are free from. God knows your father drilled *that* into you. So propose a bill on the subject when you take your seat in the Lords. But for now, put aside your work and join me for a drink. You've made me thirsty. I feel like I'm at a sermon on Sunday."

• • •

Never, never, ever again. As he and his mother bounced across the rutted roads outside of London, their carriage heavily laden with trunks and other baggage, Alec renewed his vow to never again let Marworth take him out on the town. His head felt as if a blacksmith had set up a shop inside it. A blacksmith with a very heavy hammer. His tongue was dry and cracked, and his eyes seemed to have swollen inside of their sockets to twice their normal size. If there was any whiskey left in England following last night's extravagant immaturity, he'd be surprised.

"If you will forgive me, dear, you are hardly looking your best. I haven't seen you that particular shade of green since you were a child," his mother observed anxiously. "Remember those egg creams at the county fair in Dorset? You'd had two before we realized they'd spoiled in the summer heat."

"Mother, I love you dearly, but you mustn't mention the egg creams again." His stomach was roiling at the memory. God, he'd never been so sick in his life. Then again, the day was still young.

"One can never be too safe when one eats out," she continued. "Why, just last week, Lady Doncaster was quite alarmingly ill following a meal at Grillons Hotel. She insisted on several helpings of their mussels in garlic cream, which are deliciously addictive, but so rich, even in small doses. She cast up her accounts right at the table, sending her dinner companions scattering in alarm."

The mention of creamed mussels did nothing to calm his nausea. Blessedly, however, Mother moved on to a protracted and one-sided conversation about the infamous Lady Doncaster. He closed his eyes to block out a vision of mussel shells swimming in whiskey.

He and Marworth had started out at Watier's club last night, where the cuisine was truly outstanding—a marked improvement over the food served up at White's. If only they'd limited themselves to dinner there, instead of making the fateful decision to sample their way through the club's excellent cellars.

The entire evening, in retrospect, had been rather juvenile. Nor had it made him any less apprehensive about what lay ahead in Nuneaton.

Had Annabelle forgiven him?

Whenever the horrors of war had threatened to overwhelm, he'd picked up a quill and written to her, secure in the knowledge that he could reveal his greatest fears and hopes without embarrassment. After all, he had packed the letters away in his soldier's trunk, knowing full well that they would never be sent.

But now there was the very real chance he would see her again. In fact, he would insist on it. He had kept his promise to her mother, and with it, an unspoken vow to his own father. He had kept his distance in spades. There was every chance that Annabelle needed someone to care for her.

"Alec?" His mother's voice interrupted his thoughts. "Have you heard a word I've said this past hour?"

"I apologize." He had just enough energy to feel chastened. "My thoughts were elsewhere."

"I can tell from your face that they were hardly pleasant thoughts, so here's something to cheer you. We have stopped for lunch. Remember The Bull's End, that marvelous little inn on the way to Nuneaton? It was one of your father's favorites. One of their steak-and-kidney pies will make you feel better."

His stomach turned over in protest, but Alec forced a smile. As he led his mother from the carriage, a hot, sticky rush of early summer heat enveloped them both. He hoped that he would make it through lunch without causing a scene to rival Lady Doncaster's.

• • •

Annabelle and Aunt Sophia wouldn't be traveling abroad, after all. In her aunt's words, "that nasty little Corsican" had effectively put a halt to all pleasure travel on the Continent, and not even her tenacious will could change the fact that Valladolid had been a French stronghold in Spain since 1809.

That didn't mean, however, that they would stay in Nuneaton. Over the course of the past week, they'd settled upon a visit to Bath, which would be less crowded than Brighton this time of year.

After Bath, they would travel onto London to prepare for Annabelle's debut. Her aunt had even persuaded Dr. Chessher's wife, Henrietta, to watch over Father in their absence. When she'd made a fuss over a pair of Poplar Hawk-moths—two of his newest specimens—Annabelle knew he'd be well taken care of.

Their boxes and trunks were already loaded into her aunt's glossy black carriage, ready to leave Nuneaton with its memories and ghosts behind. Aunt Sophia was comfortably ensconced on the fluffy squabs within. The only thing left for Annabelle to do was climb into the carriage so that they could be under way.

And so she did, absolutely terrified.

As the horses started, pulling them forward, she knew that she was worst sort of coward. Her head was pounding and her palms were sweaty. Her serviceable dress became more unfashionable and uncomfortable with each passing mile. The neck in particular shrank by several sizes, constricting every breath. Soon now, her buttons would start flying off of her bodice, threatening her aunt with bodily injury, or she'd faint for lack of air, right here in the carriage.

"Annabelle, are you quite all right?" Aunt Sophia asked solicitously. "You're very quiet."

"I've been worried that if I opened my mouth, I would start screaming."

"Oh, dear. Surely it's not as bad as that?"

"I know I should not be so anxious," she replied, picking at a sleeve with restless fingers. "After all, we'll have a wonderful time, and even if I say or do the wrong thing, no one will notice. Even if I trip over my feet, it's not as if people will be watching us."

"Actually, everyone will be watching us. We're a very pretty pair."

"Please, Aunt Sophia. What if we visit the Assembly Rooms, and a gentleman asks me to dance, and I don't remember how?"

"Then you will laugh about it, and he will be completely charmed. And then all of the other girls will forget how to dance, because you've made it the style to do so. And very soon afterward, orchestras across Bath will be silent, because no one will want to dance anymore."

She smiled briefly at that absurdity, before settling back into her panic. "I think it far more likely the gentleman will simply ask someone else, and that I shall be an outcast."

"You have lovely manners and an innate grace, Annabelle. Circumstances have kept you out of society, but you'll shine there. You will remember how to dance."

"I hope you are right. I hope I don't make a fool of myself." In the choking confines of the carriage, however, it seemed the only likely outcome. "Will we stop soon, do you think? A cold glass of water might settle my nerves."

Aunt Sophia gave her an appraising look. "Wine is always the better choice, my dear, but we will stop at The Bull's End. It lies up ahead."

· · ·

So far, so good. Despite the strong aromas filling the small dining room, his stomach was behaving as it should. Always happy to accommodate the Carstairs family, the innkeeper had showed them to his best table, a linen-topped affair tucked into a corner between two windows. With the casements thrown open, a welcome breeze offered respite from the heat of the day. Alec sipped on a pint of the house ale—a suggestion from the innkeeper, who made much of its restorative powers—while Mother enjoyed a small glass of ratafia. As at any busy hostelry, there was a constant flurry of activity. He listened as a carriage rolled into the courtyard. He could hear the stable hands rush forward to water and feed its horses. Moments later, he watched the innkeeper move toward the main door, wiping his hands on his apron, eager to welcome his newest customers.

When the door opened, a striking, middle-aged woman walked in. She was clad in an elegant lavender traveling gown, and in the line of her cheek and the shape of her eyes, there were hints of someone he knew. As if sensing his regard, she turned, her head tilted faintly, and he caught his breath. "Surely that is not Lady Layton," he said in an undertone, a chill coursing down his spine.

"Why, it must be Sophia, Lady Layton's sister," his mother replied. "I haven't seen her since our coming out a lifetime ago."

He was no longer listening. A willowy figure had followed the older woman into the inn. Dressed in a simple blue traveling gown, her face was obscured by the wide brim of an unfashionably weathered hat, but he could see her hair gathered in a soft knot at the side of her neck—honey shades, shot throughout with strands of blond corn silk. She moved hesitantly, as if she was self-conscious, and Alec felt a prickling awareness. She turned to survey the room, and as she angled toward him, he could see pale skin rising above a demure neckline. A long, graceful neck. Full lips and high cheekbones. Cornflower blue eyes.

All of the air in the room left in a vacuum. In his befuddled state, was he imagining this? The last time he'd seen Annabelle, she was in and out of consciousness, and in terrible pain. Yet here she was. In a fantastical confluence of chance and circumstance. Walking and whole.

He heard a clatter behind him, and was surprised to realize that he'd stood quite suddenly, sending his chair in a crash to the floor. Even in the busy dining room, the sound of it was jarring, and she looked directly at him. Her eyes went wide with shock, and he smiled slowly, unsure of what to do. But she didn't smile back. Her face went white, as pale as a moonstone. Her mouth dropped open. She seemed to be struggling for breath, and even though he rushed toward her at a sprint, he barely caught her before she fainted dead away.

In that instant, Annabelle was cradled in his arms, the room around them nebulous and indistinct. It was as if she were sleeping, her thick lashes casting soft shadows. He gently pulled one hand from beneath her, and used his teeth to tug at the fingers of his glove, wrenching it off. He touched his bare hand to her forehead. There were no signs of fever, and he felt a rush of relief.

How unlike Annabelle to faint. It was a hot day, though, and the room was too close, and she would be weaker now, because of all she'd suffered. He felt absurdly protective. He couldn't bring himself to lay her down on the floor of the common room. Nor could he stop staring. It seemed impossible that she was here.

"I appreciate your help, young man, but perhaps you could loosen your hold on my niece. One does need air to breathe, after all." He looked up, surprised to see her aunt standing beside him. Noticing that a crowd had gathered, drawn by the commotion, he loosened his arms fractionally.

"That one's a beauty," a young man whispered reverently.

"Wish I'd caught her myself," another groused, prompting an angry shove from the woman beside him.

"'Twas the heat," warned an elderly woman. "It were too much for the angel."

"Alec, bring her here." His mother was standing at the door of one of the inn's side rooms. He lifted Annabelle as gently as he could, careful to keep her head against his chest. She seemed to weigh nothing at all. He could carry her all day if she needed him to. Angling through the doorway, he moved beside a small feather bed and laid her down carefully on its white cotton coverlet. He smoothed her hair, untying the ribbons at the throat of her traveling gown.

"I'm sure I can handle that on my own." Annabelle's aunt had swept into the room, closing the door behind her.

He flushed with embarrassment. "My apologies. I forgot myself in my concern for Miss Layton."

She looked at him in surprise. "Do you know my niece?"

"I am Alec Carstairs, Earl of Dorset. I was a close friend of the Layton children when we were young, although it has been many years since I've seen Annabelle."

"How interesting." Her eyes seemed to miss nothing. "I am Sophia Middleton, Countess of Marchmain, and Annabelle's maternal aunt. Perhaps you could leave us for a few moments?"

"Of course." Had he forgotten all of his manners? "I'll wait just outside the door."

• • •

Annabelle felt a cool cloth on her forehead and opened her eyes to see Aunt Sophia and Lady Dorset standing above her. Oh God, Lady Dorset! And she had fainted. She never fainted! She sat up, self-conscious. Somehow during this debacle, she'd lost her hat. "Don't worry, my dear," her aunt said. "We will hardly judge your appearance."

Everything came flooding back. The stifling carriage ride. The stuffy dining room. Alec Carstairs. She felt a spurt of anger. How ironic that his return to Nuneaton, so long overdue, had coincided with her departure. Had he hoped to sneak back home unnoticed? Now that she'd found him out, did he think he could smile his way through her defenses?

"I am so glad to see you recovered, Miss Layton," Lady Dorset said. "You gave us quite a scare."

His mother had always been very kind to her, but Annabelle could see enough of Alec in her features that she struggled to keep her voice calm. "Thank you, my lady. I was very sorry to hear of Lord Dorset's passing."

Lady Dorset lost her smile then, her eyes growing misty. "Yes, well … it was very sudden. But at least my son has returned safe from the war. Alec will be so glad to know you are better. I'll go and fetch him so he can offer his felicitations."

"No!" Annabelle cried, surprising even herself. "Please don't." She could not see him now. Not when she was still so unsettled and angry. There was every chance she'd rush at him, fists flying. She'd worshipped him as a child. Had foolishly thought she loved him. How embarrassing to remember it.

"Oh, my dear, of course, you'll need a few minutes. Let me leave you to the care of your aunt, whom I've not seen in such an age. I will secure a private room so we can all reacquaint ourselves." With that, Lady Dorset walked out, closing the door securely behind her.

Annabelle lowered her head into her hands. "I cannot see him," she said, her voice tense. "I simply cannot."

"I know you are still angry with Lord Dorset," Aunt Sophia said. "But you must learn to put the past behind you. Why, I'd have very few people to speak with if I avoided everyone who gave offense."

"He abandoned me four years ago. I wrote to him, and he ignored me still. I can hardly make small talk and pretend he didn't hurt me terribly."

"I can't claim to know what his motives were, Annabelle. There may be things about that time you do not know. But he carried you in here as if you were precious to him."

"Oh, he can play the role of a gentleman to perfection. He's a great one for honor and nobility when it suits him." Would her letters have been so terribly difficult to answer? Surely, he could have sent word to explain what had happened? Why he and Gareth had raced? Why she'd been in the carriage? Why, after kissing her, he'd gone away and never returned?

"He caught you when you fell, which is worth something. You must thank him for that, at the very least. And you never told me he was so handsome."

There was no denying it. Her heart had lurched at the sight of him. Ridiculous girl! But then all of those painful months of rehabilitation, and all those years of being alone and unwanted had rushed back, choking the breath from her body. How she hated that she'd shown any weakness in front of him. She'd been impossibly naive where he was concerned, but no longer.

"Perhaps you are right," Annabelle said with sudden determination. "Perhaps I can speak to him after all." She would never let him know how much his blatant disregard had pained her. He'd made himself a stranger in these past four years, and strangers they would remain.

• • •

"Alec, you are pacing the floor like an awkward schoolboy," his mother admonished. He felt like one, too, but that didn't mean he could stop himself. He'd known he would call on Annabelle when he returned to Nuneaton, but he hadn't yet planned the things he would say. There had been the very real possibility, after all, that she would be feeble and infirm—a devastating reminder of all he had cost her. How could he have begged forgiveness for that?

Shockingly, though, Annabelle had recovered. She walked without hesitation. Her beauty—if possible—was even more staggering. God had decided that she should not suffer for his sins, and Alec was profoundly grateful. Humbled, even.

As if summoned by his thoughts, she walked into the small room, trailing her aunt.

"Miss Layton." His mother smiled, rising from a small settee in the room. "You are the picture of good health."

"Thank you again for your assistance, Lady Dorset," Annabelle replied with a pretty curtsey. There was only the slightest hesitation in her movements, and her cheeks were flushed with color. Was it possible that she, too, was nervous?

"Lady Marchmain," his mother said, "perhaps you and I can step into the corridor for a few moments, and catch up on these many years we've missed?"

"That would be marvelous, Lady Dorset," her aunt replied. "Leave the door open a crack for propriety's sake, won't you, my lord?" And with that, the two older ladies left the room.

Annabelle took a deep breath, turning to face him. "I apologize for my earlier weakness, Lord Dorset," she said without preamble. "It was no doubt the heat."

What an odd thing to say, after so many years apart. Was she embarrassed to have fainted? She shouldn't be. The shock of seeing her had nearly felled him. He took a step forward, hoping to put her at ease, but she moved behind the settee in an obvious effort to avoid him. The hands he'd reached out fell awkwardly back to his sides. Whatever he'd expected, it was not this. Annabelle was distant, almost haughty. A different person entirely from the woman who'd once kissed him so passionately.

"This is quite an unexpected surprise," she continued. "It has been a very long time."

"I'm happy to see you again, Annabelle. I am so relieved you are well."

Her eyes glittered at that—in the same way they had when she was furious as a child—but when she spoke, her voice was impassive. "And are you well, my lord?" she asked, looking past him to the open window.

"I suppose I am. I have just returned from the war on the Peninsula."

"Yes, I know. Please accept my condolences on the passing of your father."

"May I offer the same for your mother? I only learned of it recently. I was going to stop at Astley Castle when we reached Nuneaton."

"Really? How thoughtful."

It was obvious she didn't believe him, but she was trying hard to remain calm. This new Annabelle, who measured her words and actions, was almost a stranger. He was suddenly desperate to ease the strain between them.

"I have missed you and our friendship. After the accident, I was so worried you wouldn't recover."

"Were you indeed, Alec?" He could hear the disdain in her voice.

"Of course I was. You can't know how often you've been in my thoughts since that terrible day."

She was truly angry now. He could see it in every line of her body. "Is that the excuse you've given yourself? That a thought now and then was good enough for the friends you'd left behind—one of them broken, one of them dead?"

He'd almost forgotten it in the shock of seeing her. She had every right to be angry.

"I have wanted to ask for your forgiveness. I know what my carelessness brought about. I know the horrible pain I've caused you. I am more sorry than I can say."

"All I know is that I woke up one morning to find that my brother was dead and my leg half-ripped from my body," she replied coldly. "My poor mother, she'd very nearly gone mad. Father was not far behind. And you were gone."

He was stung by her bitterness. And it was unfair she blamed him for leaving. Blame him for the accident, yes. Blame him for wanting her, yes. But not for being forced to leave. That had been her mother's doing. "You know I had no choice, Annabelle, though I wish it had been otherwise.

"I'm not interested in your excuses," she said. "Mother shared them with me long ago. You did what you thought you had to do, and it seems silly to dwell on a past that can't be righted, no matter how much one might wish it."

"You don't seem to understand." How could the vow he'd made be considered an excuse?

"There is nothing to understand. I was hurt, of course, when you left without a word," she said offhandedly. "But after all, there were battles to fight a thousand miles from home."

Something was not right. "Annabelle, despite what happened, I did leave word. I left a letter behind. I even bribed one of the footmen—he was new, I think—to deliver it. In it, I tried to explain—"

"There was never any letter," she cut in dismissively.

How could she not believe him? And why was she quibbling over a letter, in the face of all they'd been through? "I swear to you as a gentleman that I left one for you. You know the position that I was in. I had no choice but to leave. I've always cared about your welfare. I have missed you very much."

She took a long moment before replying. Her bright blue eyes flickered. "I don't believe you, Lord Dorset."

Surely, he'd not heard her correctly. "I do not lie, Annabelle. You know what sort of man I am, the sort I was raised to be."

"Ah yes, the honorable Alec Carstairs. Noble and pedigreed, a proud reflection of his father." Her voice was deliberate and edged with ice. "But it is all a facade, because you are not the man I thought you were."

Her words struck him like a blow to the gut. It was the gravest of insults. No one had ever doubted his honor. She had known him for a lifetime. When she was so gravely injured, he'd wiped her brow and sat beside her as she writhed in pain!

She must know how hard it had been for him to leave the Layton family behind. Gareth had been his oldest friend. She'd been his friend, as well. And something more, too, no matter how unwise. The day he left, he'd felt like he was severing a limb to leave her there, barely recovered, because her mother demanded it. Yet she had no faith in him.

Deep inside, he felt something shrivel, like parchment curling to black in a flame.

God, how stupid he now felt. All of those letters he'd written to her during the war, the ones he'd kept safely hidden in his satchel, as if they were a lifeline to sanity. He had damn well spent the past four years in exile, all to fulfill a promise he made to Lady Layton. He'd even defied his own father, and he could never take that back now. He could never make amends for it, or thank him for not sending Mother away. The earl had been right about Annabelle all along, about the dangers she presented. How dare she question his honor?

"It is unfortunate, then, that our paths crossed today." His voice was cold and hard. "It's obvious that anything we shared in the past is best forgotten."

"It appears so, Lord Dorset. How lucky that my aunt and I are traveling to Bath for an extended visit. It's unlikely we will have to suffer another chance encounter between us."

"I will not bother you again," he said. "Whatever you may think, I am a man of my word." He turned sharply on his heel, and left the room.

Without explanation, he ushered his mother from the inn, tossing the innkeeper a sovereign for the expenses they'd incurred. With a quick snap of his fingers, their carriage pulled up to the doorway, and he helped his mother into it, climbing in after her and slamming the door behind him, to the surprise of the inn's stable boy. She tried to ask him what had happened with Annabelle, but he didn't trust himself to answer without speaking harshly.

On the long ride home to Arbury Hall, she regarded him with wary eyes, because he said nothing. Not a word.

• • •

For a few long moments after his departure, Annabelle could not move. It felt as if a cold wind—completely at odds with the warmth of the afternoon—had swept in to surround her, cloaking her in ice. She'd never purposefully hurt anyone until today. She shivered with the shame of it.

Wasn't that a small sin, though, when measured against the pain he'd caused her? He had left her behind to protect his precious reputation. He had not even bothered to offer her a better excuse, merely claiming that he'd had no choice. As if Napoleon himself had swept into Nuneaton, dragging him off to the war.

Anger was a good substitute for pain. She'd relied on it every time it had hurt too much to put one leg in front of the other. Every time she'd wanted to give up. And she would use it now to prove she hadn't been broken after all. She would go to Bath. She would dance and laugh and see what she'd missed of the world.

If only this lingering sadness would go away. If only it were easier to reconcile the man she'd once believed him to be with the incontrovertible truth of what he'd become. All those years, for God knows what reason, he had been humoring her, pretending some sort of deep and lasting bond. As if she didn't know the truth when he said things like, "I have always cared about your welfare. I have missed you very much." He had never really cared for her, no matter what she'd thought had sparked between them, and the death of that illusion was something to be mourned.

Perhaps that was why, when Aunt Sophia hurried back into the room in a rush of silken skirts, Annabelle wrapped her in a desperate hug and burst into tears.

Chapter 7

June 21, 1812
London

Decisions, decisions, decisions. Alec had a particularly important one to make and a rare hesitancy to do so. Since the death of his father several months ago, he'd increasingly felt the need to secure his family's line. In other words, he needed an heir. Which meant that he needed a wife.

Jane Fitzsimmons, whom Father had approved of, was a wise choice for the post. The earl had expected him to be responsible and productive, to bear his duties with alacrity, and she seemed to be much the same. She, too, was an only child, the daughter of Lord Reginald Fitzsimmons, who was a powerful figure in the House of Lords despite his reputed weakness for cards. Alec's new soldiers' bill would benefit immeasurably from his support.

Furthermore, Jane was more than passably attractive—beautiful, even—especially when she smiled. Not that he put much store in beauty. It was the measure of nothing. And what did it matter if the thought of bedding her brought on a faint feeling of unease? Surely she was capable of something resembling passion? Her smiles were rare, although he would hardly call her humorless. Merely serious. Perhaps excessively so. But she would be a dutiful and faithful wife.

A sudden burst of commotion sounded in the hall. Rousing himself from one of the club's capacious leather chairs, he went to see what was causing the stir, only to nearly collide with Marworth himself. "Dorset! God's blood, I've been looking for you everywhere. Come with me straight away." Benjamin turned toward the entrance hall.

"Is anything the matter?" he called out. "Where are we going?" The racket—unheard of in the hallowed confines of White's—was rapidly escalating.

"We're off to Hatchard's," Benjamin replied over his shoulder, naming the popular bookseller on Piccadilly. "You'll understand when we get there." Crossing into the hall, Alec was surprised by the sight of more than a dozen members demanding their coats from harried staff.

"Get a move on, my good man!" exclaimed William, Lord Alvanley, one of Prinny's great cronies, as he waved his hands impatiently at a house steward. "She'll be there in mere moments."

"Surely it was Gunter's first, and then Hatchard's?" Arthur Gormley, also known as Baron Asquith, asked. "We'll make it in time if she has stopped at Gunter's first."

"Who is she?" someone else called out. "And why are we chasing after her?"

"Only the greatest beauty since the Gunning sisters," gushed Percy Billingsly, the second son of the Marquis of Brimley.

"The Gunning sisters came out with my grandmother. I prefer living, breathing chits myself." That had come from Charles, Viscount Petersham. This must be an event indeed if it had roused Petersham, who was rarely seen before the late afternoon.

"Beauty don't last!" cried Lord Archibald Higgins. In his mid-sixties, Higgins was one of the ton's more decrepit roués. He had already buried three wives and was said to be on the hunt for another. "I'd rather see what her dowry looks like."

Billingsly, who was a self-styled romantic, took offense. "You may either come with us to Hatchard's, or stay here and read *The Times*. I hardly care. All I know is that the Regent himself is agog over the girl. He was at her presentation to the Queen Mother the other day, and he has declared her the most glorious thing in all of Britannia." He was shouting to be heard over the din. "Prinny vowed that if he were twenty years younger, he would throw over Princess Caroline herself to marry the girl."

That comment brought several derisive snickers. "That's hardly a ringing endorsement," Alvanley laughed. "He'd marry you to be rid of Princess Caroline." The Regent's marriage was famously miserable. The future King George fell in love as often as he fell into debt, and his wife had been carrying on notorious affairs abroad for years.

Alec, though, was losing patience with the entire exchange. Didn't any of these gentlemen have more pressing concerns? He had no interest in debutantes, no matter how beautiful. He'd made his choice. But then someone else called out, begging for the girl's name, and Benjamin turned toward him, his expression mischievous, which was never a good sign.

"Her name is Annabelle," Marworth said. "Annabelle Layton."

But of course.

"I've no interest in joining you," Alec said, his tone uncharacteristically short as he waved aside a footman who'd hurried forward with his top coat, hat, and gloves.

"Really? Still smarting, are we?"

"Don't be ridiculous." He'd put the entire episode at The Bull's End last month behind him.

"Do you know something about the girl we don't?" Asquith interrupted.

Alec sent him a shuttered look. "She was a childhood acquaintance, nothing more." And he had put away childish things.

"Well, then," Benjamin announced with a smile. "I'm off without you. I'm eager to see the luminous Miss Layton again. I have met her before, as you'll recall."

At that, several of the other gentlemen came forward, anxious for more information, and Marworth led them out of White's, like Goethe's Pied Piper.

...

"Don't I remember a library at Astley Castle?" Aunt Sophia asked idly, as she admired one of the jaunty new hats that had just been delivered from Mrs. Bell's millinery shop on Upper King Street. There were boxes all over her aunt's elegant boudoir.

"Yes, but it is filled with Father's books on lepidoptera, and one can only read so much of that," Annabelle replied. "At Hatchard's, there were books on culture and history, geography, and the sciences. I've never seen so many volumes. And I was very surprised to see so many fashionable men wandering among the stacks. Several of them were discussing Mrs. Radcliffe's novels."

"That sounds suspicious," Aunt Sophia said, turning from her hat. "None of them approached you, I hope, while Lisette waited outside?"

"Only Lord Marworth, but we have been introduced. He was one of Gareth's friends from Oxford."

"Ah, Marworth … I'm tempted to forgive him anything."

Annabelle could guess why. With blond hair, the brightest of blue eyes, and perfectly symmetrical features, he was perhaps the second most handsome man she'd ever seen. Unfortunately, he'd shared some unpleasant news with her. "Lord Marworth mentioned that Lord Dorset is staying here in London for the Season. Do you think it will be possible to avoid seeing him?"

"London is far smaller than you suspect, my dear, at least the part we will frequent. Do you really wish to miss any of it?"

"I suppose not." London was far too glorious. She'd enjoyed their time in Bath, but it couldn't compare to the capital, which coursed with life and vibrance. And of course, they'd gone shopping. Repeatedly. She had been measured and fitted by Madame Boucheron, the ton's most exclusive modiste. They'd gone to Harding Howell & Co. for gloves, R. Willis for shoes, Grafton House for parasols and silk stockings, Mr. Arpthorp's shop on High Holborn Street for delicate underthings. She had so many beautiful new gowns on order that a separate bedchamber here at Marchmain House would be needed to hold them all.

The house itself was no less beautiful. A large Georgian structure looking out over Grovesnor Square, it was such an impressive residence that Annabelle was just now becoming accustomed to it.

"I don't know how I can ever thank you, Aunt Sophia, for all that you have done. You have incurred so many expenses on my behalf. I've written to Cousin Estrella asking about my allowance, but she has not written back."

"Don't mention that woman's name. I find it impossible not to frown when I hear it, and I refuse to wrinkle on her account. Don't concern yourself with funds. I need something to spend my money on, and I'm having the most marvelous time. Your presentation at St. James Palace was a triumph." She'd made her formal debut just a few days ago in an elaborate gown encrusted with tiny seed pearls and delicate crystal beads. The enormous skirts and long train required for court dress had been a challenge, and the deep and prolonged curtsy she'd made to the queen had taxed her leg, which still occasionally weakened under a direct assault. Annabelle had been convinced that her fanciful headdress of ostrich feathers would list under its own weight, possibly taking her head along with it.

"Thanks to Lisette, my coiffure would have held fast in a hurricane."

"My maid is a marvel, but with the Season upon us, you will need your own lady's maid. I've taken the liberty of hiring one for you. I would have done so in Bath, but I had a very specific person in mind, and it has only just been arranged. She will be arriving here tomorrow. I hope she will prove a pleasant surprise."

With a mysterious smile, Aunt Sophia returned her attention to the boxes from Mrs. Bell's shop.

• • •

They were sitting together in the breakfast room the following morning when Canby announced the arrival of Miss Mary
Stevens, formerly of Nuneaton. Following close behind him was
a diminutive figure with bright red hair beneath her mobcap and
familiar green eyes.

"Mary!" Annabelle gave her aunt a grateful smile before
standing up to grasp Mary's hands warmly.

"Miss Annabelle, I hope you're not upset to see me. When I
received Lady Marchmain's note through the placement service
for ladies maids, I could hardly believe my eyes."

"I'm thrilled to see you. How could you believe me to be
anything else?"

"But I left under such an awful cloud. You'd barely recovered
from that terrible accident."

"Your grandmother needed your help, Mary. I've always been
glad you were able to go and care for her. I hope she's well?"

"My grandmother, miss?"

"I know you were urgently needed. Mrs. Fritchens said it was
an attack of pleurisy. Oh dear ... she did recover, didn't she?"

Mary flushed. "She is well, Miss Annabelle. I thank you for
asking."

"That's wonderful news. I have so missed your company, and
this is such a wonderful surprise. Will you mind working with me
again?"

"I never wanted to leave. I'm so glad to see you recovered."

She grinned at that. "I'm happy for it, too."

As the afternoon continued, and Mary settled into Marchmain
House, Annabelle was indeed happy. Granted, she was nervous
about the upcoming Season, and about whether or not she would
make a fool of herself, but she was beginning to regain a measure

of her confidence. A number of men had asked her to dance at the Assembly Rooms in Bath. And time and again, she'd danced.

• • •

The next afternoon, Aunt Sophia sat beside her, sublimely elegant in a pale green and light sarsnet riding dress that was the first stare of fashion. Annabelle was also turned out in the latest of styles, as the coachman turned the sumptuous Marchmain barouche onto the crowded bridle path known as Rotten Row in Hyde Park. She wore a white jaconet muslin dress with a short jacket in sky blue and a white willow bonnet ornamented with a wreath of flowers. She also wore matching sky-blue gloves and half boots. With her Boucheron creation and Mary's help, she'd never felt more elegant.

The Row was a scene unto itself. Conveyances of every size and shape lumbered along the route, while men on horseback rode alongside, pausing occasionally to greet friends and acquaintances. From dowagers to debutantes, not to mention soldiers in their showy uniforms, there were people everywhere, smiling and bobbing their heads to the left and to the right, as if they were participants in a puppet parade.

"In many ways, this will be your first introduction to the haute ton. I'm eager to see their faces when they catch a glimpse of you." Aunt Sophia briefly bowed her head and smiled as an elaborate open carriage carrying two women rolled by. The women reciprocated, and then turned to look rather fixedly at Annabelle. She smiled demurely, as Aunt Sophia had mentioned she must. The moment passed, and they moved on.

"Lady Jersey and the Princess Lieven are supercilious snobs, but unfortunately, we must cozy up to them. They are patronesses at Almack's, and we'll need to secure you a voucher. I'm rather surprised to see them together, actually. The princess cannot abide Lady Jersey. The woman never stops talking. And don't let Lady

Jersey's haughty demeanor fool you. Her mother is scandalous, and a former mistress of the regent to boot."

"You are up on the latest gossip, Aunt Sophia, despite our brief time here. I'm very impressed."

"If you look discreetly to your left, you'll see Viscount Petersham in all his glory." The most astonishing high-perch phaeton was rolling by. It was a study in unrelieved brown from the carriage to its matched horses and livery, even down to the clothes of the man who drove it. He was wearing a brown top hat; a brown coat, vest, and gloves; and rather fantastical trousers that ballooned out about his legs, only to nip back into his boots. They, too, were brown, like his eyes, which were watching her with a shocked expression. Annabelle quickly looked away. Ladies she must smile at, but not men she didn't know.

"The viscount is trying to gain the favor of a certain widow, a Mrs. Mary Browne."

"No doubt he has her attention," Annabelle said, caught somewhere between awe and amusement. "He certainly must be given high marks for creativity."

"Now quickly, to your right, you'll see George Brummell and Lord Alvanley. Brummell—the one with the elaborate cravat—is the undisputed arbiter of fashion in society. He'd rather hang than be seen in Petersham's get-up." Aunt Sophia smiled in acknowledgment to both of them, as Mr. Brummell raised an elaborate quizzing glass and gazed intently at Annabelle. Eyes wide, he tipped his hat before moving on. "I hear he is on the outs with the prince regent. Not a good place to be when you have expensive tastes but empty pockets."

"I've never seen anything like this. I feel like we're all on display."

"Indeed, you are. I must say things are going even better than I expected, and I had very high expectations."

"But all we have done is ride through the park and look decorous." The ways of the ton would take some getting used to.

"You must trust me, my dear. The young women coming out this Season are suddenly far less sanguine about their prospects. And that's a good thing. Jealousy, at least when you have inspired it, can be marvelously invigorating." Aunt Sophia leaned toward her, lowering her voice. "By the way, unless I am mistaken, Lord Dorset is heading toward us."

Annabelle's breath caught in her throat. She'd prepared to be polite and nothing more, but she couldn't help but remember the angry and dismissive words he had last spoken to her. And of course, she'd said much in the same vein.

He was less than forty feet away, handling the reins of a phaeton with ease as he spoke to a lovely brunette who sat beside him. The woman was neatly attired in a rose-colored riding suit, and while Annabelle found herself unaccountably curious about the stranger, she found it even more difficult to look away from Alec. He wore a bottle-green jacket fitted to showcase the breadth of his shoulders. Handsome, traitorous man.

As if sensing her gaze, he glanced up, and even at this distance, she could see his jaw clench. His eyes were flat as he studied her, and then he turned away, speaking to his companion. Irrationally, she felt a stab of disappointment. "I don't believe Lord Dorset will acknowledge us, Aunt Sophia." She'd looked forward to showing him how very little she cared about being in his good graces.

"Nonsense. He is a gentleman, and you must stifle your resentment. It will do you good to be seen in his company. The Carstairs are haute ton, the very best kind."

• • •

This was the very worst sort of surprise. Had he known she would be here, Alec would never have come. As it was, a perfectly satisfactory afternoon was about to be spoiled. A carriage carrying Annabelle and her aunt was headed this way.

He'd learned quite a bit about Lady Marchmain since his return to London in the last few weeks. After all, how better to avoid someone—or her niece, for that matter—than to learn her habits and haunts? He'd made discreet inquiries, only to find there was almost nothing discreet about the woman. She'd lived abroad any number of years, changing husbands as often as most women changed their bonnets. To be fair, each of the men had died unexpectedly, but that only made the countess more scandalous. She lived precisely as she pleased, answering to no one. And now Annabelle was her protégé.

"My dear Miss Fitzsimmons," he said. "The sister of an old friend is approaching in the next carriage. I should stop to offer my greetings."

"Of course," Jane replied easily. "I am always eager to meet your friends."

Within minutes, the carriages had pulled up alongside each other. "Lord Dorset," Lady Marchmain said. "How nice to see you on this lovely day."

"Lady Marchmain, Miss Layton, what a surprise." It went without saying he thought it a poor one. "May I present you to Miss Jane Fitzsimmons? Miss Fitzsimmons, allow me to introduce Lady Sophia Middleton, the Countess of Marchmain, and her niece, Miss Annabelle Layton. Miss Layton is a neighbor from Nuneaton."

He didn't make eye contact with Annabelle, focusing his attention instead on Jane, who inclined her head and gave the other ladies an austere smile. She really was a pretty woman, with an appealing softness to her face and form. Even better, she never troubled his dreams in the night. Or stole the breath from his body.

"Miss Fitzsimmons," Lady Marchmain said, "are you related by chance to Lord Reginald Fitzsimmons?"

"I am indeed. I am his only child."

"He's quite outspoken in the House of Lords. I have seen his speeches in *The Times*."

"Father takes his responsibilities very seriously. He is working with Lord Dorset on an important bill regarding soldiers' benefits. We're hopeful it will be well supported."

As Jane explained the details of the legislation, Alec risked a quick glance at Annabelle. She appeared to be listening intently, but he could tell by the soft blush on her cheeks that she was nervous. The fact that she was also dazzlingly beautiful did not signify. Because really, what had she to be nervous about? Her success in the ton was assured. All around them, men were practically falling off of their horses to get a look at her. And there she sat, pretending not to notice, radiating the sort of innocence that roused a man's protective instincts. Surely, she'd studied the effect. Only look at how her head was tilted in order to highlight the perfection of her profile.

"You must be very proud of your father's efforts, Miss Fitzsimmons," Annabelle said when Jane had finished.

At that, his gaze narrowed on her exclusively. One did not wish to draw attention to one's own efforts, but she'd intentionally ignored his role. "I'm the author of the bill, Miss Layton."

"Yes." Her eyes were suddenly fixed on him, and something fluttered uncomfortably in his chest. "But I already know how proud you are. I would never wish to be redundant." Her smile was innocent, but there was no doubt she was mocking him.

"Proud of my fellow soldiers, Miss Layton, and of their valor in battle," he insisted coldly. "I mean to honor their sacrifices."

"Of course you do." She turned to Jane. "Lord Dorset can always be counted on to remember the people he has left behind, even though years may pass before he has the opportunity to do so."

Lord, but she was impertinent! Just as he was about to offer a retort, a familiar voice interrupted them.

"Dorset, you're a thorn among these beautiful roses." Benjamin was beside the two carriages on horseback, flashing a smile.

"You've always been a master of the bon mot, Marworth," Alec replied, surprised by a sudden flash of annoyance. No doubt he'd been tracking Annabelle ever since she had entered Hyde Park.

Benjamin turned first to Jane. "Miss Fitzsimmons," he said, touching a gloved hand to the brim of his hat. "Just this morning, my mother was praising your work at the Society for Indigent Children. She's most impressed by the seriousness and sobriety of your demeanor."

"Thank you, my lord."

"And how are the children faring?" he continued, even though it was obvious his attention had already moved on to Annabelle.

"They are still poor, Lord Marworth. I am certain your mother has mentioned it."

"Yes ... quite." At least he had the grace to look embarrassed. He turned to Annabelle and her aunt. "Lady Marchmain, how nice it is to see you back in London. And Miss Layton, how happy I am to see you again. It was such a lucky surprise to find you at Hatchard's."

Of course, Hatchard's had been no surprise at all. The man had hunted her there.

"Are you enjoying that volume of poetry, Lord Marworth?" Annabelle asked. Alec knew full well that Benjamin didn't even like poetry. He used it to seduce women.

"Surely you were my inspiration for its selection, Miss Layton. May I say that 'the violet in her greenwood bower may no longer boast itself the fairest flower ...'"

Alec fought the urge to groan aloud, and Jane seemed equally unimpressed by that tepid attempt at gallantry. "Sir Walter Scott, Lord Marworth?" she said. "How surprising. His poems are too ponderous and sentimental for my tastes."

Benjamin looked back at her with a smile. "How curious, then, that you know his words by heart." At that, Jane pressed her lips together, and made a great show of rearranging her skirts.

"Lord Marworth," Lady Marchmain said. "We'd like to welcome you to Grovesnor Square one afternoon this week. I know Annabelle would enjoy hearing about your time with my late nephew at Oxford."

"I will look forward to it," he replied, "although the tales of our schoolboy antics will have to be appropriately expurgated. Until then, will you allow me to introduce a few of my acquaintances? They're most eager to meet you both."

With a sweep of his hand, Benjamin pointed to several gentlemen waiting on horseback nearby. Among them were Alvanley and Asquith, Billingsly, Hertford—he was an unrepentant rake—and a host of other fops. What a disaster. Alec grimaced as Annabelle greeted each gentleman, tilting that head again just so.

At last, Lady Marchmain intervened. "Annabelle, we've brought traffic to a standstill. We really must be going." So they had. The Row was crowded with carriages that couldn't move.

"Ladies, it was an unexpected surprise," Alec said with a quick nod, eager for the chance to escape. "Miss Fitzsimmons, shall we be off?" Jane, who had gone unusually quiet, merely nodded. They said their final goodbyes, and continued on their way until Annabelle's carriage was a mere speck when he looked over his shoulder to watch her.

Chapter 8

Alec looked down at the note in his hand, and then again down the long marble hall of Marchmain House. He had no interest in being here, but he had no choice. The countess had sent a summons yesterday afternoon requesting this meeting. As a gentleman, he couldn't refuse.

He hoped Annabelle would not be at home. He didn't want to see her again after successfully exorcising her from his thoughts. He didn't miss her at all. But for the past three days, White's had been filled with talk about her. So had Brook's and Boodle's and Watier's and Tattersalls. And of course, there had been the spectacle on Rotten Row yesterday. If Alec heard one more man compare her to the damned Gunning sisters, or Botticelli's *Venus*, or Helen of Troy, he'd surely strike him. On second thought, perhaps the Helen appellation was mildly appropriate. After all, Annabelle's face had launched a thousand fools.

All too soon, the butler who had gone to announce his arrival returned, and Alec followed him to a drawing room a short distance away. With a bow, the man opened the doors wide, and Alec briefly took note of a pretty room with tall casement windows, corded silk hangings, and lots of flowers. He couldn't help but notice the flowers. Arrangements covered nearly every surface, spilling over with a profusion of roses and lilies, morning glories and apple blossoms, tulips, and azaleas, and more. There were enough to rival the damned Botanic Gardens. He turned to a particularly effusive display and noticed Marworth's card perched beside it.

He shouldn't be surprised. Benjamin never had been one for subtlety.

Then he remembered his manners. Lady Marchmain sat in the midst of the blooms on a blue and white pinstriped settee, striking in an emerald silk gown with long fitted sleeves. She rose to greet him as he walked forward and extended his bow.

"Lord Dorset, it was kind of you to come here at my request."

"It seemed a rather urgent matter, Lady Marchmain," he replied. "I hope all is well."

"I have something to ask of you, but first allow me to ring for some refreshments." She gave a gentle tug on the bell pull beside the settee. Almost immediately, the butler returned. "Would you be so good as to bring a bottle of my favorite Gran Riserva, Canby, along with two snifters? And don't forget a few almond cakes." Turning back toward him, she said, "Surely we can dispense with tea? Brandy is superior in every way."

"Certainly, Lady Marchmain."

"I developed a fondness for Gran Riserva while I was married to my first husband, Carlos. We were blissfully happy, until the terrible accident that took his life." She sat gracefully upon her settee, indicating he should sit on the plum-colored fauteuil beside her.

"I'm sorry for your loss, Lady Marchmain."

"Thank you, Lord Dorset. His death was the first great shock of my life, because he knew better than to mix strong spirits with bull fighting. Were it not for the solace of my darling Stephano, whom I met in Capri, I should never have recovered."

Thankfully, Canby returned with the tea cakes and brandy. Taking advantage of the conversation's sudden lull, she prepared a plate for Lord Dorset, and poured them each a generous measure of liqueur. After a long sip, she began again. "Stephano is one of the reasons why I was so late in meeting Annabelle. He died suddenly in the spring of 1792, when she was born. I was in no mood for travel."

"Another tragic loss. I'm sorry to hear of it." He was completely befuddled as to the point of this conversation. Why had she asked him here?

"It was the second great shock of my life," she said, sad for a moment in what he supposed was reflection. "Beware of oysters past their prime, my lord. Stephano believed they boosted his virility, but poof! A bad batch, and two days later he was dead."

"I'll take that warning to heart," he replied. "And may I also offer my sympathies on the death of Lord Marchmain, while we speak of such sad things?"

"Dearest Edward. My third husband. At least his death and that year in black bombazine brought me to Annabelle."

"I am sure she's very happy for your company," he said. "Perhaps we can speak about why you've asked me here?" And perhaps insanity ran in the Layton family, as Father had suspected.

"Of course. I only tell you my history so that you can understand the relationship I have with my niece. We get along so well because we've both known great tragedy." She let that last word hang in the air.

"You are speaking of Gareth's death, which was devastating to all of us. I have the utmost sympathy for Miss Layton in that regard."

"That's why I feel certain you will offer me your assistance," she replied. "I have brought Annabelle here to London to enjoy the Season, but I have an eccentric reputation, one that might not see her invited to all the best events. I need an eminently respectable family to help me launch her into society. You were once close friends. Will you do it?"

What an appalling suggestion. They were no longer friends, or acquaintances even. They had no place in each other's lives. "Lady Marchmain, I hardly know how I can help."

"I need your help to find her a husband."

Now he was shocked. "Does Miss Layton know of your plans, Countess? I hardly think she'd approve."

"I'm only doing what I believe is best for Annabelle."

He hesitated. He liked to think that he would help Annabelle in any way that he could, but she'd made it quite clear that she no longer needed him. "I'm sorry, Lady Marchmain, but Miss Layton barely tolerates my company. If you'll forgive me, I have another appointment." He stood abruptly, offering her a respectful bow, and turned to depart.

"Lord Dorset?"

He turned back after the slightest hesitation.

"If Gareth was alive, I would not need your help."

"No, you would not," he replied, his voice low. "I can't help but acknowledge my role in his death."

"Did you know that Annabelle was bedridden for months after the accident, that it took her more than a year to walk without a noticeable limp?"

"I did not," he admitted, his hands clasped together tightly.

"Annabelle's recovery was extraordinarily painful, of course. But even after she'd healed, Charlotte, my sister, was terrified that something else would happen to her. She wouldn't let her venture into town. She wouldn't let friends visit, for fear of contagion. She made Annabelle believe that the world, at large, forgot her very existence."

"But what of her father?" He couldn't prevent the stern set to his jawline. "Why didn't he intervene?"

"Since my sister's death, Sir Frederick is increasingly unstable. His heir, Augustus Simperton, has moved into Astley Castle with his mother, and the two of them are trying to force a match on Annabelle. They're after her dowry, you may be assured of it."

"I'm sorry that Miss Layton has had so many difficulties," he said quietly. He curled his left hand around the back of his neck, and squeezed it, if only to stop himself from a less than gentlemanly impulse, which involved turning around and walking out the door. Instead, after a long pause, he walked toward her and sat back down upon the fauteuil.

"I can't help but admire my niece," she continued. "She's had to overcome many challenges. Were it not for that terrible day, she'd no doubt be settled now, secure in the love of a husband and a family. Instead, she faces an uncertain future without your help."

She spoke the truth, of course. He'd robbed Annabelle of so many things when he'd allowed that race to go forward, when he'd left her behind at the behest of a woman who quite probably had been mad with grief.

After a long silence, he cleared his throat. "My mother has always been fond of Miss Layton. Moreover, she has just arrived in town for the start of the Season."

"I hope her trip was an easy one."

"I know she'll be eager to help your efforts. I will send a note straight away. And I can escort both you and Miss Layton to her home on Park Lane tomorrow. Would that be convenient?"

"That will be perfect. Annabelle will enjoy renewing her friendship with the countess. And I must thank you, Lord Dorset. You're doing the right thing."

"Somehow I doubt that Miss Layton will share your opinion."

• • •

As they sat down to tea in the small boudoir off of her bedchamber—an elegant room with Sheridan furnishings and chinoiserie paper—Annabelle couldn't conceal her anxiety.

"Please tell me that you did not do it. Surely, you are jesting, Aunt Sophia." She and Mary had returned from a long walk in the past hour, only to discover that her aunt had been busy making plans for their time in London. Plans involving Alec Carstairs.

"Lord Dorset can hardly have an interest in squiring me about the Season."

"My dear, he was more than happy to offer his assistance, and that of his mother."

It was shocking, really. She could find no reason why he'd wish to involve himself. Then suspicion dawned. "Aunt Sophia? What specifically did you say to Lord Dorset?"

Her aunt smiled mysteriously. "I may have inadvertently told him about the many struggles you've faced since the accident."

"Oh, you did not!" she said softly. "Why should he even care?"

"My dear, surely you cannot be so naive? Do you not see yourself when you look in the mirror?"

She could not deny that men were once again sprouting up around her like flowers, but Alec Carstairs would never be counted among them. She'd learned that long ago.

"Beauty makes things so much easier," Aunt Sophia continued. "Not to mention more fun. You have allowed an old infirmity to color your view of yourself. You have no idea of the power you could yield, if you so choose."

"Alec has no interest in me," she said . "He has made that abundantly clear."

"Then we must settle for allowing him to help you, my dear. Your brother would have wanted you well settled. The Carstairs family has the influence to show you off to your best advantage. I've been too much abroad these many years to offer the same."

"I have always admired Lady Dorset, but whatever am I to say to her son? We can barely stand the sight of each other. Surely you saw that in the park?"

"You'll come up with something. Besides," Aunt Sophia smiled wickedly, "he was looking tremendously attractive. One must always appreciate tight trousers on a man like that."

In the past, Annabelle might have blushed over such a comment, but it was difficult to preserve one's naiveté around

Aunt Sophia. There had been that morning in Bath, after all, when she'd stumbled upon her aunt and Thompson, the footman, wrapped in a heated embrace. She hadn't even known garters came in that color.

"Do you still have feelings for Lord Dorset?" her aunt asked. "It's obvious you once did."

Annabelle looked down at the tea cup in her hands. "I once thought I loved him. Not that he is to blame for that. We were friends of convenience, it seems, and nothing more.

"But I can and do blame him for leaving me when any friend would have stayed," she continued. "No one would tell me the full details of what had happened. I don't even know why they raced that day. At the very least, Lord Dorset could have told me that before he vanished."

"My dear, you will be much in each other's company in these coming weeks. Perhaps, at last, you'll have an opportunity to pose those questions to him yourself."

Alec was the one person who could speak about the accident. If she was brave enough to ask, would he tell her the truth? Was she to blame for the whole of it? Was the anger she directed at him better directed at herself?

Chapter 9

Marchmain's

Back once more in the front hall of Marchmain House, Alec tried not to let his annoyance show. The countess had manipulated him quite thoroughly yesterday; he could see that now. But he also knew she was right. He had come to that realization during a long and mostly sleepless night. This was a duty he owed to Gareth, who would have seen to it that Annabelle married well, if he'd lived long enough to grow out of his dissipations.

He was still angry with Annabelle. Perhaps he always would be. He did not like the person she'd become—cold, haughty, and distant—but she had suffered terribly. He must remember she had been as much a victim that day as her brother, even though she'd recovered physically, as far as he could tell.

Her aunt came alone down the staircase to greet him. She was clad in a jonquil morning dress with a cream underskirt that rustled as she walked. "Lady Marchmain, will Miss Layton not be joining us?"

"She is already waiting in the small sitting room. Canby, our butler, will show you the way. I have just a few things to collect before we visit your mother."

The ever-solicitous Canby was immediately at his right, and with a faint nod, he led Alec toward the sitting room door, only to open it a fraction and then step aside. With a deep breath, Alec knocked gently and walked in. At first glance, the room was empty. The day was a gray one, and the room was limned in shadow. It seemed melancholy. Yet there she was, a slender figure in silk, as she stared out of the bow window that faced the street.

"Miss Layton?"

She slowly turned, and he realized again how very beautiful she was. For some reason, that particularly rankled this morning. She was wearing a fitted blue spencer with a high winged collar and plush cuffs, over a lemon muslin underskirt. She hadn't yet donned her hat. Her blond hair was parted down the center, and pulled back. On another woman, the style would have been too severe, but on Annabelle, it only served to highlight the rare symmetry of her features, and the intense blue of those bewitching eyes.

There it was again. That curious sensation, fluttering in his chest. It was most unpleasant.

"Lord Dorset," Annabelle said. "I want to thank you for offering your assistance this Season."

She was very nervous. He hardly wanted that. He wasn't a beast, after all. Just because they were no longer friends didn't mean he wanted her to be uncomfortable. He felt enough discomfort for the two of them. "Miss Layton," he replied carefully. "For Gareth's sake, I'm happy to help in any way I can." Of course, he was not happy, and he didn't do this for Gareth alone. He did it for himself, as well. The sooner she was married and gone from London, the better.

She flushed, but whether in anger or because of something else, he couldn't say. There was a long and awkward pause. It was deathly quiet in the room. "How was your trip to Bath?"

"I enjoyed it very much."

"Did you see any of the sights? Did you visit the Assembly Rooms?"

"We did," she said with a half smile. "Aunt Sophia and I went to a number of the evening soirees there, and we both loved the dancing. It's been such a very long time since I danced."

"I am glad you enjoyed yourself." He was determined to be pleasant. "Your mother used to despair that you'd ever learn to dance. If I recall, tree climbing was more to your taste."

"That was because all of my dance masters were old and humorless," she said, taking a step toward the fireplace, as if to warm herself. "They creaked and smelled of liniment, and badgered me about my posture."

He didn't know if he should laugh at that or take offense. "I taught you a number of dances, and I've never used liniment."

"No," she admitted, turning again toward him. "You rather made dancing fun. Aunt Sophia is quite a dancer, as well. She has been trying to show me the waltz, but it's difficult to learn when one only knows the woman's part."

"I hope she didn't do so in public. The waltz is still considered forward, and you'll need the permission of the Almack patronesses before you attempt it."

"Surely, that is one of society's sillier rules. One would think they could find a better use for their time."

"All the same, here in London, certain proprieties must be adhered to if you want to be accepted in the best circles."

"Both Aunt Sophia and I are cognizant of polite behavior, Lord Dorset," she said, frowning now.

"I'm certain you are." Even if that had not always been the case. He ruthlessly suppressed an unbidden image of Annabelle in the fountain. "However, Lady Marchmain asked for my family's help because she's concerned that her eccentricities—her reputation, if you will—might be a burden to you. My role in this is to help steer you in the proper manner."

"The insinuation being, of course, that I am incapable of behaving myself. I must be steered, rather like a pushcart."

"Miss Layton, you are putting words into my mouth. You've been sequestered in the country these past several years—no matter the circumstances—and it's to be expected that you will need some guidance."

"So you are offering me your advice," she said, her voice rising slowly in volume. He'd obviously angered her. She walked deliberately closer, eyes narrowed, skirts swishing about her long legs. "I have some questions, then, concerning our activities in Bath. May I ask you about them? I should hate to think I've behaved improperly."

"I'm happy to help, if I can."

"When we danced in the Assembly Rooms, I drank champagne, and found it wonderful and well worth drinking again. Is that acceptable?"

"Only if the serving is very small, Miss Layton. A woman must never appear to be inebriated."

She was directly in front of him now, and he wished that she would take a step back. She was too distracting. He could smell the subtle hints of her soap. It was no longer honeysuckle, but a spring-like scent with the faint hint of French lilac.

"What about whiskey? Aunt Sophia had me try some in Bath."

"Most definitely not. Whiskey consumption by a woman is an appalling breach of etiquette."

"That's a relief, then. It burned on the way down, and I promptly spit it back up into my glass. I shall never touch it again, per your strong recommendation."

"One does not mention bodily functions of any kind in society," he said, faintly alarmed. "Surely you remember?"

"Perhaps I'd forgotten. Let me see, what else. Oh yes, I was kissed by a man one evening outside of the Assembly Rooms. Aunt Sophia was there, but she did not immediately see me. Was that appropriate?"

"Damn and blast, Annabelle! What has gotten into you? You can't run about casting lures at men." She hadn't lost her audacity, had she? "Let me warn you, I'll not allow you to do anything to embarrass the Carstairs name while you're here in London. I value its good reputation, even if you do not."

She watched him for a long moment. "It has finally happened, hasn't it?" she said, her voice tight. "You have turned into your father."

The observation made him uncomfortable, but instead he said, "He taught me the value of restraint and propriety, two things for which you have regularly evinced disdain."

That remark hit home. Her eyes were flashing dangerously as she raised a long, elegant finger and jabbed him in the shoulder. "Let me tell you what I know about proper behavior, Lord Dorset. I know that it's inappropriate to say things like 'damn and blast' in front of a woman."

Of course, she was right.

"I know that it's impossibly rude to use a woman's given name when you have not been granted permission to do so."

There was that, as well, he realized with an accompanying flare of discomfort.

"And," she said as she flattened both of her hands against his chest, "it's beyond rude to impugn a woman's character because you have made assumptions about her. I'll have you know the kiss was not freely given. Aunt Sophia fell just a short way behind us, and the man took advantage. I fended him off until she arrived."

She pushed at him with such force that he fell back a step. Quickly bracing himself, he grasped her upper arms and held them tight against her sides. He'd hardly give her the chance to push him again. She struggled briefly, but as they stood there and she stared up at him, eyes mutinous, he realized several things. First, that she had goaded him deliberately, and in the most unladylike way. Second, that she was hardly a cold woman; she was practically breathing fire. And third—that holding her was a very bad idea. Because he wanted all of that forbidden passion. He always had. He wanted to lean down, trap her mouth beneath his own, and run his hands over her exquisite body. He'd never forgotten the feel of her.

Instead, Alec pulled his hands away, and took a step back, because he was no better than that beast outside of the Assembly Rooms. "Annabelle ... Miss Layton," he said after a deep breath. "I am sorry you were subjected to such an unfortunate experience." He wanted to say more, but at that precise moment, Lady Marchmain entered the room in a rustle of jonquil skirts.

"Is your carriage ready, my lord?" She didn't seem to notice that he'd been standing far too close to Annabelle. "I, for one, am eager to renew my acquaintance with your mother. It was most kind of her to offer her help."

"Indeed, it was, Lord Dorset," Annabelle said, quickly moving away from him.

They exchanged trivial comments as they walked out onto the steps of Marchmain House. The countess wondered aloud if they would see rain later in the day. Annabelle commented again on his mother's kindness, acting as if nothing untoward had happened. Alec, for his part, hardly knew what inanities he spouted. His thoughts were in disarray.

He should never have touched her. It was far easier to ignore her beauty when there was an impersonal distance between them. In the park the other day, for example, he'd done quite a good job of remaining immune both to it and to her. She'd reminded him of one of the Dresden figurines in his mother's collection room. Undeniably beautiful, but all brittle gloss, cold and unfeeling. That image, though, had just been shattered. His hands still pulsed with the warm feel of her.

• • •

As she watched Alec help Aunt Sophia into his waiting barouche, her heart would not stop racing. Annabelle could still see the expression on his face when she'd pushed him. His eyes had gone wide with shock, and then with something more visceral.

She hadn't planned such behavior. Waiting for him this morning, she'd been ready to lay her bitterness aside. She would not get the answers she sought if she did not placate him. For a brief time, they had even managed to be cordial, but then he'd turned into a terrible snob, dismissive and eager to criticize. Just like his father. It was as if the man who'd laughed with her and teased her so long ago had never existed. So she'd goaded him, eager to see some spark of passion, something to indicate that he could still feel anything besides self-righteousness.

When he'd grasped her by the arms, his eyes glittering darkly, she'd gotten her answer. Strong emotions waged within him. Anger, frustration, and something else. There was so much unsaid between them.

After she settled into the carriage, Alec climbed in behind her, taking the backward-facing seat across from her and Aunt Sophia. Then he rapped his knuckles against the side of the exquisitely appointed vehicle, indicating to his driver that they were ready to be off. Quite suddenly they were, riding smoothly down the street toward Dorset House, where the ladies would meet with Lady Elaine Carstairs.

• • •

After an hour spent poring over accounts at his bachelor's lodgings, Alec returned to Dorset House to collect Annabelle and her aunt. Both were chatting so happily in the carriage that they hardly took notice of his presence, and though that offered him a perfect opportunity to look out the window, he found it difficult to turn his attention from Annabelle. She seemed determined to ignore both him and their earlier confrontation, as she laughed at something Lady Marchmain said. Such a lovely, musical sound. He'd always loved her laugh.

How had he been talked into this farce? Her sudden reappearance in his life was untenable. He was a man like any other, and Annabelle Layton was a distraction, with her flashing eyes and her ridiculous beauty. Surely her sole purpose was to torture him. He owed Jane Fitzsimmons his attention now. Indeed, it was past time for him to make an appointment to see her father, to offer his proposal, and get the whole thing over and done with. He needed to focus on getting his soldiers' bill before the House of Lords.

After they pulled up to the front of Lady Marchmain's home, Alex saw both ladies safely to their door. Eager to learn what had been planned and how quickly it could be set into motion, he sped back to Dorset House and raced up his mother's marble steps. She had obviously expected him, because he'd hardly knocked before Edmunds pulled open the black lacquered door. "She's waiting for you in the library, my lord." And indeed she was, looking lovely and quite pleased with herself in a wing chair by the fireplace. Mother had more color in her cheeks then he'd seen in a long while. He might have something to thank Annabelle and her meddlesome aunt for after all.

"How long will it take?" he asked.

"I am not sure much will be required beyond introducing her to society. I will secure a voucher at Almack's. We'll plan a ball in her honor. The usual first steps for any debutante."

"Is she eager to start?"

"She is excited about the prospect of friends. And what girl does not look forward to all of the parties and those beautiful gowns? She does, though, appear to be self-conscious about your involvement. She is perhaps nervous about the whole of it."

Nervous. There was that word again. It was never one that he'd have associated with Annabelle growing up. "She has no reason to feel that way, Mother. Her beauty makes things absurdly easy for her."

She tilted her head, as if surprised by his comment. "Beauty like that makes you a target, my dear. And you must remember that Annabelle has had little interaction with others these past several years. The attention will be relentless, and anyone would lack confidence in those circumstances."

He didn't like to think of her as vulnerable. Not when it was easier to think of her as a conniving Jezebel.

"Have you spoken with Miss Fitzsimmons about befriending Annabelle during the Season?"

"I have. She is always willing to devote herself to a cause."

"That is very kind," his mother replied, with just a touch less enthusiasm than Alec would have preferred. He still couldn't tell if she approved of his intended fiancée.

"Miss Layton's beauty, of course, has generated a tremendous amount of interest," he admitted. "There are an appalling number of floral tributes at Marchmain House."

"You must help us vet every suitor. She has a very generous annuity from her mother's side of the family, and that always attracts the wrong sort. I think a trip to the opera next week would be appropriate. I'd also like to plan an outing with several young people, perhaps at Hampstead Heath. I feel certain that Lady Hertford will invite Annabelle to her annual Summer Ball. It is always a fantastic crush. And then, of course, I will help plan her come-out party at Marchmain House. In the meantime, the two of you must spend some time reacquainting yourselves. It will do no good if people sense there is tension between you."

He would be almost constantly in Annabelle's company, which meant that the next few weeks would be excruciating. They'd have to find a way to get along, but what would happen if he couldn't keep her at arm's length? He could still feel the press of her hands against his chest, where they had laid heavy and close to his heart.

• • •

"I thought I'd find you here, Dorset," Marworth drawled later that same afternoon, as he dropped himself into a chair beside Alec in the dining room at White's. He motioned to one of the house stewards, clad soberly in a gray morning suit. "I'll have whatever my good friend here is having, and you may charge my meal to his account." He returned his attention to Alec. "It's no more than you deserve. You've been keeping secrets from me."

"I don't have the slightest idea what you are talking about, as is so often the case between us. What have I done now?"

"The Carstairs family is helping to launch the divine Miss Layton this Season. Yet you've given me every impression that you wanted nothing to do with her."

"The Countess of Marchmain reminded me that I have a responsibility to see Gareth's sister well settled," he said. "But she is a distraction I don't need."

"I can hardly think of a more pleasant distraction. She's stunning."

Alec eyed Benjamin warily. "Granted, but that doesn't change the history between us."

"The vast majority of that history was positive. You were great friends once. In fact, as you grew older, you visited Astley Castle to see Annabelle, rather than Gareth."

Alec shifted under the weight of that uncomfortable observation. "That was before I moved to London to study with my father. And well before she insulted my honor."

"Ah, yes, your honor." Benjamin flicked an imaginary fluff of dust from his immaculate blue jacket. "You've been pouting over that slight ever since you returned from Nuneaton last month."

"I have not been pouting!" Where had Marworth gotten that idea?

"Have you asked yourself why she felt that you could no longer be trusted?"

Alec shook his head. "I can only assume that she holds me responsible for the accident that day. After all, the failure of my carriage directly contributed to Gareth's death, not to mention her own injuries." He could never forget that.

"I've never understood how all of that came to pass. Surely the grooms at Arbury Hall cleaned and checked your carriage before you set out for the castle that evening? After all, you'd just journeyed in from London."

"I'm certain they did, but it's an unassailable truth that I did not do so." He would always bear the ultimate responsibility. "The broken wheel had a linchpin that failed. They were still trying to find its pieces among the wreckage when I departed for the city."

"Do you still employ the same manager?" Benjamin asked, drumming his fingers on the table top, as if absorbed in the thought of something.

"He's been with our family for more than a generation, as was his father before him."

"You should ask if those pieces were ever found."

"I will do that, but it won't change Miss Layton's opinion of me. Do you know she tried to push me down today?"

"Really? Beauty and high spirits are such a seductive combination. What happened?"

As the waiter returned with their lunch—beefsteaks, boiled fowl with oysters, and apple tarts—Alec admitted to himself that he was not proud of the way that he'd acted this morning. Upon reflection, it was easy to see that he'd insulted Annabelle. He'd jumped to conclusions, and that was not fair. There was so little trust between them.

"I said several ill-advised things, and may have insinuated that she was not all that she should be."

Benjamin paused between bites of beefsteak, his fork suspended midway between his plate and his mouth. "That is so unlike you, I'm nearly speechless."

"I know. And it's no excuse that she goaded me with all sorts of insinuations. Annabelle has always had a rare ability to manipulate me."

"How will you make it through the Season if you cannot ease your estrangement?"

"I've just realized that apologies might be required."

"Without a doubt. I've never known you to be so ungentlemanly."

Alec stared down at his fast-cooling luncheon. "Something about Annabelle Layton makes me behave irrationally."

"I wonder what that could be," Benjamin said, before returning to his lunch with a great show of enthusiasm.

Chapter 10

As she waited for Alec to arrive the following morning, Annabelle glanced at one of the large gold-leaf mirrors that hung on either side of Aunt Sophia's hallway, each of them centered above a matching set of Louis XIV credenzas. She looked well enough, if a trifle unsettled. After all, she had no idea what he was about.

Alec had sent a note yesterday evening, requesting her company this morning on a ride in Hyde Park. Indeed, he was due at any moment, though it was barely past the breakfast hour. The park would be empty, save for ostlers exercising their horses, which meant that this was hardly a social call. She'd dressed with care in a cream-colored riding habit with black braided cording, gold buttons, and cuffs embroidered à la militaire. With matching half boots and a small tasseled riding hat, she was the picture of stylish propriety; but she almost wished that she'd worn something outrageous, cut low across the chest, and in a color that couldn't be missed. After all, he had already made all sorts of assumptions about her. She didn't wish to disappoint.

At nine o'clock precisely, a quick rap sounded at the door, and Canby opened it to welcome Alec, who looked every inch a peer of the realm. He was dressed in a flawless brown buckskin coat and matching vest over a white linen shirt, with riding breeches and glossy black Hessians. His eyes flared briefly when he saw her, taking in her attire with a swift glance before he came forward and offered his bow.

That glance surprised her. It made no sense coming from Alec. Other men looked at her that way, but he did not desire her. He didn't even like her.

"Miss Layton, thank you for agreeing to ride with me this morning. Will your aunt be joining us?"

"I'm afraid not, my lord. She appreciated the invitation, but not the hour." According to Aunt Sophia, the only reason to be up this early was so that you could slip from a lover's bed without the risk of detection. But she could hardly repeat that.

"I see. Let's be off then." He indicated that she should precede him through the open doorway, and a moment later, they were standing in the bright morning sunshine. Thompson was waiting with a sweet-tempered mare that she'd ridden on several occasions, but her breath caught when she saw the glorious black stallion Alec brought with him.

"What a handsome animal. Wherever did you find him?"

"He's the grandson of my father's favorite horse, Lucifer. Perhaps you remember him from Arbury Hall?"

"How could I forget? I was desperate to ride him when I was a child."

"You barely reached his flanks at the time," he said, seemingly amused by the memory. "We'd have needed a set of stairs to get you into the saddle."

"He was the biggest horse I'd ever seen."

Alec reached up and affectionately stroked the stallion's mane. "Mars here may not have his size, but he has his heart."

"Mars? After the god of war?"

"He was born when I was away on the Peninsula. Father trained him personally, and planned him as a gift upon my return."

"He must have been very proud of your decision to fight." The earl hadn't been given to displays of generosity or affection.

"On the contrary. He said it was one of the worst decisions I ever made." As Annabelle tried to hide her surprise, he walked over to inspect her mount, his face unreadable. "A sidesaddle, Miss Layton? At long last? That is decidedly proper of you."

"It's far more uncomfortable than riding astride, I can tell you that," she said. "But I've been warned not to wear breeches in London, so the sidesaddle it must be."

Had his mouth quirked in a smile? She'd swear that it had, but he was already leaning down, joining his hands to offer a foothold. Bracing one arm on his broad shoulders, she placed her right foot into his upturned palms as he boosted her gently into the saddle. She wasn't heavy but she was tall, and his strength seemed effortless. It was most annoying, not to mention distracting.

A heartbeat later, Alec swung up on Mars, and they set out for the park. "Miss Layton, your ensemble is far more beautiful than breeches would be," he said. "If I'm not mistaken, it's in the new military style."

"Yes," she replied, surprised by his unexpected compliment. "I thought it an appropriate choice, since we invariably fight in each other's company."

"I hope to change that this morning," he said. "After all, we can hardly spend the entire Season at odds with one another."

"Is that what this is about, then? Are we to chat happily about horses and fashions, and admire the weather, and forget all that happened between us?" She didn't like the bitter tone in her voice. She sounded childish.

"We can't change the past," he said, his voice sober and serious. "No matter how we might wish it."

It was a quote, almost verbatim, from their conversation at The Bull's End inn. "How clever you are, Lord Dorset, speaking my own words back to me. I can hardly contradict them that way."

Alec chose not to respond, and they rode on in silence. Why had he deliberately disappointed his father, when he'd spent his childhood craving the earl's approval? But it wasn't a question she could ask. There was no longer any closeness between them. The silence stretched on, until Alec pulled Mars in front of her horse, effectively halting their progress. "Miss Layton, I didn't ask you to ride with me today to gloss over our differences. Although you are predisposed not to trust me, please believe me in that."

While she watched him suspiciously, he continued. "I merely wanted to apologize for my behavior yesterday." The shock of that nearly knocked her off her saddle. "It was wrong of me to jump to conclusions."

"I take it that you're referring to lures and my willingness to cast them?"

He flushed at that, and Annabelle found his reaction oddly—endearing. Until she remembered she no longer liked him.

"I wish I could have saved you from that experience in Bath. Such men should be beaten to within an inch of their lives."

"I appreciate the thought," she said. "But you may rest assured Aunt Sophia and I made him regret his behavior."

"Let me guess." He tilted his head to one side, his eyes contemplative. "You had a pistol hidden in your reticule."

"No," she said with a hesitant smile. "But silver-tipped parasols have their uses."

"I'm very glad to hear it." And then he paused, growing serious again. "Please know I didn't mean to offend you yesterday, or infer that you are lacking in some way."

"I've not been in the company of many people these past several years, and I will make missteps," she said, her smile fading. "But I'd never intentionally embarrass you or your mother. I wish you would believe that."

"I do. You were certainly a hoyden as a child. In fact, it was one of the things I liked best about you. But you've grown up, and thrived in difficult circumstances. And while I may like to pretend otherwise, you don't need lessons on behavior from me."

She regarded him suspiciously. "You are overdoing your compliments."

"No, I'm being honest. I thought quite a bit about this yesterday. I have been trying, I think, to make you into something you are not."

"Why would you wish to do that?"

He looked into her eyes. "Because it's far easier to be angry with you."

"I don't understand."

He continued to watch her. "In the absence of that emotion, we will be forced to find out what feelings remain between us." Then he pulled away suddenly, urging Mars forward. "We seem to have Rotten Row to ourselves," he called over his shoulder. "Shall we let the horses run?"

In an instant, they were both galloping down the path. Alec opened an immediate and sizable lead, and she had no hopes of catching his horse on this troublesome saddle. But it was better that way. She needed a moment to think, because if she didn't have anger to color her feelings, she wasn't quite sure how she felt about Alec Carstairs.

● ● ●

After slowing their horses, they rode for an hour or more, and Alec was happy to see some of the distance between them fade. For the most part, they discussed any topic that Annabelle suggested. She'd always been inquisitive, and her curiosity hadn't dimmed during the many years she had stayed close by Astley Castle, injured and alone.

It was a remarkable trait, he thought, watching her eyes follow a flock of geese that had settled on the Serpentine Lake at the center of the park, their wings stirring ripples in its shallow waters. In spite of the challenges she had faced, the losses she'd suffered, Annabelle was remarkably resilient. He could not help but admire that.

There were many things he admired about her.

Like the way her lips, lush and pink, opened on a quick intake of breath when something angered her. The way her eyes softened and her head tilted to the side when she saw something that surprised her, as if an angled view offered an especially interesting perspective on it. The way she'd looked at him when he'd said he was sorry, as if he had finally become the man she'd thought he could be.

Sirens calling to lost sailors from their rocks were less dangerous.

Annabelle sparked thoughts that were disloyal to Jane Fitzsimmons, and if he'd any sense, he'd put as much distance between them as he could. But when she smiled up at him, it was difficult to turn away, and even more difficult to remember why he should. By the time they returned to Marchmain House just before noon, he had offered to escort her to the British Museum the following day. He'd even promised to teach her the waltz.

So much for keeping his distance.

• • •

"One must always appreciate the Greeks' sense of proportion," Aunt Sophia said, sighing as she studied a large statue of Apollo in the British Museum's collection. Whether she was admiring the sculpture's classical allusions or its rendering of the nude male form, Annabelle couldn't say. She was too busy trying to ignore the god's more manly attributes.

She heard Alec cough discreetly behind her, and turned toward him with such obvious relief that she was certain his lips twitched with amusement. "Would you like me to show you some of the other sculptures in the collection? The Townley Marbles are quite famous."

"Yes. I'd enjoy that very much," she said, trying to will away her embarrassment. She'd had a sudden and distracting vision of Alec's body, slick with lake water.

As Aunt Sophia gave them a distracted nod of approval, he took her gently by the elbow, his hand warm and steady as he led her toward a grouping of smaller statues that lined the walls of the oversized chamber. "Perhaps *The Cannibal* will be more to your liking," Alec said, pointing to the sculpture of a boy biting into a disembodied human leg. At least the boy had his nether regions discreetly covered by a cloth. "Roman, possibly from the first century B.C.," he announced, reading the small sign mounted beside the piece.

"If one wants to eat a leg," she said, "one should remove the sandal from its foot first."

"I don't think the sculpture depicts a cannibal at all. I think the leg belongs to the boy's opponent in a game of astragali, and the rest of his body did not survive the journey here from antiquity. Do you see those small, elongated pieces that are chiseled beside him?"

She looked more closely. "They appear to be bones of some sort."

"They're knucklebones from a cloven-hoofed animal, like a sheep or a goat. In ancient Rome, children played with them. They'd assign number values to the different sides of each bone and roll them like dice."

"The prize being a pound of flesh? I think I'd have preferred a quiet game of cards," she said.

"I think our young friend here simply did not like being bested. I'm well acquainted with the type."

"You are referring to that incident when we played ducks and drakes all of those summers ago. It's most ungentlemanly to mention it."

"That rock took quite a skip off of the lake, didn't it?" he said with a grin. "One might almost say it defied the laws of physics."

"I never meant to hurt you, Alec."

"There I was, with an enormous lump on my brow, and Gareth was doubled over with laughter, tears streaming down his face."

Annabelle wanted to smile as she remembered it, but suddenly she couldn't, because Gareth was as cold and still now as that marble boy. And even though she suspected Alec would understand what she was feeling, her truce with him was too new and untried. She cleared her throat, and moved toward the other sculptures in the gallery. "So who was this Mr. Townley?"

"He was a famous antiquarian who fell in love with Greco-Roman relics while on the first of his Grand Tours," Alec replied, falling in step beside her. "He bought so much statuary, he had to build a mansion on Park Street to house it all. When he died there in 1805, the trustees of this museum bought his collection for 20,000 pounds."

"That's an enormous amount."

"Yet it's probably half of what he spent to amass the whole of it. No doubt his family was happy to recoup at least some of the monies he spent during his travels."

"I can only imagine the trouble my father would get into if he had to buy his specimens, rather than collect them in the wild."

"You don't share his passion for collecting?"

"I'm glad to help my father display his butterflies once he has caught them," she said after a long pause. "He finds them soothing."

"That doesn't answer my question, though."

"The butterflies and the moths he collects are such beautiful creatures," she said, surprising herself with her reply. "It's sad that the beauty which makes them so desirable is also the thing that traps them. There is a terrible irony to it."

He stopped short and looked down at her, his head tilted.

"Father surrounds himself with them, and they look like they are alive, but of course, they're not." She met his eyes. "Sometimes I feel like I'm living among the dead."

"Oh, Annabelle," Alec said gently, his striking eyes serious. "You sparkle with life. You always have. But your past, difficult as it has been, is behind you now. Your life is your own to lead." He spoke with such sincerity that her breath caught, and if the welling in her throat was any indication, she needed a distraction. Otherwise, she would start crying right here in the middle of the British Museum.

She looked about quickly, her eyes landing on a statue of Aphrodite crouching beside a water jar. The goddess was shielding her body, as if a stranger had surprised her during her bath, but her hands barely covered the swell of her breasts, and the angle of her body accentuated her femininity. Instead of hiding her nakedness, Aphrodite was using it to tantalize the stranger. "The clothes have fallen off of the statues again," Annabelle said, feeling a warm rush of embarrassment. She remembered her own absurd efforts to tantalize Alec when she was younger. She'd practiced swaying her hips just so.

As if that could attract someone like Alec.

Still, he was playing remarkably close attention to the naked Aphrodite. He didn't try to mask his appreciation. His eyes touched on all of the places that hers shied away from. "*The Goddess of Beauty, second-century B.C.*," he read. "To think the Greeks managed this while we Britons were still running around in bearskins."

"Aphrodite might have preferred a bearskin, if only to hide herself from so many prying eyes," Annabelle said primly. But she could hear the envy in her voice.

• • •

Once again, Alec had allowed himself to be talked into something unpleasant. Lady Marchmain, Annabelle, and his mother were shopping for opera gloves to wear to the King's Theatre tomorrow, and he'd been asked to escort them. Of course, he had more important things to do. He'd spent the morning mired in his business accounts, dreading the planned trip. He was spending far too much time in Annabelle's tempting company.

The day was bright and warm, though, and as they walked down Bond Street—Annabelle on his arm, the other ladies walking just behind, his carriage and driver following at a discreet distance—he couldn't help but admire how the sun cast dappled shadows through the overhanging trees. There was a breeze stirring the air, carrying the scent of lilacs on the wind. In truth, this wasn't such an unpleasant duty after all.

Annabelle was dazzling in a bright green walking dress with a Circassian wrapper in the palest lemon cream. Her matching bonnet, tied beneath her chin, featured a cluster of pink flowers, and she wore lavender kid boots and gloves. The sun caught her hair where it peeked from beneath her hat, illuminating her face like a halo. She looked like a study in the colors of spring.

Unfortunately, he wasn't the only man who noticed. More than one buffoon tripped over his feet as their small party walked past, and Alec wondered again if Annabelle could be unaware of the effect she had on others. Wherever she went, one's eyes could not help but follow, in the same way that it was difficult to turn away from a rainbow arching across the sky, because it shimmered and surprised.

She took such delight in her surroundings. The people bustling by, the bright colors and textures on display in the shop windows, the street vendors hawking their wares in rhyme. When he'd first returned to London, he'd been hard pressed to notice the life and vibrancy of the city. He'd been haunted by men—including Gareth—who could no longer enjoy a breeze on their faces, or the laughter of a lovely woman.

God help him, though. He took pleasure in Annabelle's company, and not just because of her beauty. There was no doubt she still suffered pain from her injury, but she didn't allow it to define her. And right now, as she walked beside him, her hand resting on his forearm, he felt at home, at long last. He liked hearing the rustle of her skirts beside him, and the steady intake and release of her breath. Even though it did odd things to his cadenced heartbeat.

"Annabelle, look at that adorable pair of gloves in the window," Lady Marchmain called out as they passed by yet another shop devoted to fripperies. "White leather with two full inches of gold trim, the very style that Napoleon's Josephine is said to favor."

Alec welcomed the distraction of that comment. Did the woman not know England was at war with the French? Who gave a damn what their empress was wearing?

"All the more reason for us to find another style, Aunt Sophia," Annabelle replied, even as she cast a quick covetous glance at the offending gloves. He supposed they did have a certain panache.

"If only the men would be done with it," Lady Marchmain complained. "Everyone knows French-made gloves are the finest to be had. Not to mention that we've suffered the loss of their gowns and their wines. I think I miss the wines most of all."

"These wars have stretched on interminably," his mother added. "Will we ever be at peace again, Alec?"

"Wellington is doing his best," he replied. "I am certain victory will be ours in the end." Even though the cost would be terrible. It was already terrible.

"I shouldn't doubt it, my dear," Mother said. "Not when men like you have been fighting for us." She turned toward Annabelle and her aunt. "Alec has a commendation from the great general himself. I know the army would love to have him back, but I say that he has done enough."

"I bet you were dashing in your uniform, Lord Dorset," Lady Marchmain said with a sly smile. "I wouldn't doubt it if the French ladies fought their men for you."

This wasn't a conversation he wanted to have—most especially with Annabelle's aunt—so instead of answering her directly, he made a great show of peering into the adjacent shop's window. "What a smashing set of gloves. I don't believe I've seen the like."

The two older ladies hurried to stand beside them. "How clever! I love the way the crystals along each cuff catch the sunlight," Lady Marchmain exclaimed. "Let's take a peek inside, Annabelle. Those will be beautiful with your opera gown."

"You go ahead, Aunt Sophia. You and Lady Dorset know what will be best. I'll wait out here and keep Lord Dorset company." After casting a quick look at each other, the two ladies agreed, and rushed in to meet the eager shopkeeper who'd spied them through the window. "It was kind of you to join us," Annabelle said. "This can hardly be what you'd planned for your afternoon."

Alec smiled at her sympathetic expression. "All the same, I am happy to escort you."

"I think you're more happy to have foiled a stylistic assault by the Empress Josephine."

"That is merely an added bonus."

"If you'd not been forced to join us—though it was for the good of king and country, mind you—what would you have done today?"

"Spent more time spent on my account books, I suppose. We finished shearing the sheep at Arbury Hall a few weeks ago, and I've been reviewing reports about how the wool is faring at market."

"I remember wanting one of them for my pillow when I was little. They were always so fluffy this time of year."

"The problem was that you wouldn't make do with their wool. You wanted a live sheep bleating around your bedchamber."

"I can see now that it wouldn't have worked out particularly well. You were wise to deny me."

"I've always had your best interests at heart, Annabelle."

Her smile suddenly dimmed, like the sun hiding its brilliance behind a cloud. Because he'd forgotten, for just a moment, the doubt still between them, and the separate lives they were destined to lead. He cleared his throat. "I would also have spent more time on the bill that I've been working on. I'm hoping to have it presented before the House of Lords."

"The one Miss Fitzsimmons spoke about in the park?"

Dear Lord. He hadn't seen Jane since that carriage ride on Rotten Row. Surely, she'd expected that he would call. "The very same."

"It is very important to you, isn't it?" She looked up at him expectantly.

Was she pretending polite interest? Few people liked to be reminded of the hardships others faced. "Something must be done to help the men and their families," he said. "They've not had a wage increase since the colonies' revolt, yet prices have hardly remained stable, and the soldiers are serving longer now, with little relief. With wars on both the Peninsula and in America, our forces are stretched too thin."

"I can't imagine the stress of fighting each day, never knowing when your enemy will appear."

"Or if the next day will be your last. For many soldiers I knew, it was."

"You're proposing this measure because they can no longer fight for themselves."

His eyes searched hers. Of course, she understood. She was no stranger to pain, or suffering, or death.

"I'm sorry for their loss," she said quietly. "But I am happy that you've come home."

He resisted the terrible urge to run his fingers along her cheek, as if the mere fact of touching her would make the hurt of what he'd seen and done go away. But he had lost the right to reach out to her. He'd never really had it, and he was tired of wounds that scarred over but never healed.

Just then, Lady Marchmain and his mother reappeared, eager to show off what they claimed was the most stylish set of gloves ever found on either side of the Continent. Annabelle laughed over their girlish enthusiasm.

He regretted he'd ever hurt her. He didn't like to think of the pain that he'd inflicted on others. If anything, during the war, he would have gone mad if he pondered it. It had been a brutal and violent existence, where the value of a human life was only considered once it was lost.

Was it the same way with friendship? Did you miss it most after you'd cast it aside? He would do almost anything to reclaim the easy camaraderie he and Annabelle once shared, but he worried that friendship would never be enough. When he dreamed of her at night, it was not as a friend.

• • •

There was a small garden behind Marchmain House, hidden from neighboring homes by a high stone wall covered with dark-green ivy. It was filled with spring flowers—peonies and bearded iris, blooming azaleas and fragrant roses—all tucked into beds that fanned out from a small marble fountain at the center of the garden. Secluded in one corner, set in the shade of an ornamental tree, was a carved marble bench, and Annabelle had a habit of coming here in the early morning hours, when the household was just coming to life, and Cook had baked the first of her sweet rolls for the day.

In the still quiet of this morning, wrapped in a soft blue kerseymere shawl over a pink morning dress, she watched as a handful of butterflies danced among the flowers. She couldn't see butterflies without thinking of her father. She wished with a sudden desperation that he was here.

She and Aunt Sophia had received a letter from Mrs. Chessher yesterday, who'd said their plans were well under way for traveling here in two weeks' time. Cousin Estrella and Augustus would come in the Laytons' only carriage, while Father would arrive a day later with Dr. Chessher and his wife, who would then travel on to Dover. Mrs. Chessher had worked miracles if she'd convinced Father to travel here during the height of the spawning season, when the butterflies and moths were just emerging from their cocoons to take flight for the first time.

But he had promised to come for her ball. Perhaps this trip to the city would show Father what he was missing in the wider world. It had certainly done as much for her. She marveled at the new path in her life, even as she tried to understand the feelings she had for Alec Carstairs.

Over the past several days, she and Alec had often been together. He'd twice taken her to Gunter's for their marvelous ices; she adored the tart lemon flavor in particular. They'd gone riding with Aunt Sophia in Hyde Park, where he'd introduced them to a number of his friends and acquaintances. And he'd followed through on his promise to teach her the waltz.

During the lonely early days of her recovery, before her heart had turned against him, she'd sometimes pretended she was in his arms again, the sole focus of his attention. The reality of it, though, had left her breathless. While Aunt Sophia kept tune for them on a pianoforte, playing with surprising skill, Alec had walked her through the dance, his hand warm against the flat of her back. Even though she'd made several missteps at the start, he'd been patient and encouraging, like the man she'd spun fantasies about long ago.

They had danced, circling each other and spinning about the room so smoothly, she'd fought the urge to laugh out loud with delight. Instead, she'd smiled while looking into his eyes, feeling affection well up within her like bubbles in champagne.

For a moment in that music room, she'd been eighteen again, an innocent, with little knowledge of suffering or betrayal. It was easy to forget he had once abandoned her.

In the quiet of the garden, though, she only had her thoughts and feelings to confront. She wondered if the time had come, if not to forget, then to forgive. She'd let anger keep her mired in the past for too long. At the time of the accident, Alec had been just a few years older than she was now, and she still felt the need to run from problems she couldn't solve and experiences that might hurt her. Perhaps he'd left Nuneaton with every intention of returning, once the scandal of the accident had died down. With each passing day, though, that would have become more difficult, as distance pulled their lives apart, and hurt dug a cavernous divide.

Her life was cracked into two distinct pieces, the before of the accident and the after. She fervently hoped she could build a bridge between the two, so that some of the good from before could find a place in the present.

Chapter 11

The home of Lord Reginald Fitzsimmons in Mayfair

"Miss Layton, Lord Dorset has told me any number of amusing stories about your childhood together," Jane Fitzsimmons said with a tight smile as they waited for Aunt Sophia, Lady Elaine, and Alec to join them in the drawing room before the opera. And while others might think it an innocuous comment, Annabelle knew better. Jane was insinuating that she shared an affectionate familiarity with Alec. Did she consider her a rival for his attentions? That was a promising development.

"Indeed, we were often in each other's company, Miss Fitzsimmons," she replied sweetly. "And often in trouble." Annabelle would let her guess as to which sort.

"I'm sure it was nothing too damning. I've never known Lord Dorset to be anything less than the perfect gentleman. Wouldn't you agree?"

In other words, Alec had been neither affectionate nor familiar with Miss Fitzsimmons. Annabelle couldn't help but smile broadly.

"He would never dare to be otherwise in your company," she said. "You have an enviable reputation for all that is proper." She would not add boring, because it seemed unfair to judge the girl on such short acquaintance. Still, anyone who belonged to The Ladies' Auxiliary to Improve Manners and Morals had to be viewed with suspicion.

"How kind of you to say it," Jane replied. "Lord Dorset has asked me to help introduce you to other like-minded ladies. And while I hesitate to say so, the ton will readily accept you once it's known that I approve of your company."

Surely the girl could not be as pompous as she sounded? It would make for a long night at the opera if she were. She was very pretty, with bright brown eyes, lustrous hair, and elegant features, but her mouth was pinched, as if she'd swallowed something sour. Perhaps she simply felt unwell?

"Thank you for offering your guidance, then," Annabelle said. "I am a bit nervous about meeting so many new people."

"I'll not allow you to embarrass yourself, so have no fear. Please call me Jane, and I shall call you Annabelle. Should we seek out the others?"

Instead, the others took that moment to find them, crossing through the doorway in a companionable cluster. "It's unfortunate that Lord Fitzsimmons is unable to join us for this evening's performance," Alec said, coming to a standstill beside them, "But I am lucky indeed to have such lovely ladies all to myself. I shall be the envy of every man at the opera."

"Be on guard," Jane said, grinning up at him. "Men will say the most shamelessly flattering things. Do not believe a word they say if you wish to preserve your modesty."

"May I let you in on a small secret, Miss Fitzsimmons?" Aunt Sophia asked, her eyes dancing.

"But of course. I am eager to hear it."

"Modesty is overrated."

Annabelle giggled inappropriately. It was almost a snort, really, and decidedly unladylike. Alec was hiding a smile behind his gloved hand, but Jane was stiff with disapproval. "We should set out for the theater," she said. "There's a chill in the air, and we don't want to be stranded in the carriage, battling the crowds."

Crowds or no, the air in the drawing room had already turned frosty.

...

Annabelle sighed with delight as the famed opera singer Angelica Catalani hit the final notes of her aria, and the curtain of the King's Theatre in Haymarket descended. She had never been so entranced. According to her program, an intermission was scheduled between Acts III and IV to give the opera's patrons a chance to mingle, but she wanted nothing so much as to see the performance begin again.

Of course, she'd not understood a single word of Mozart's *Le Nozze di Figaro*. The entirety of it had been conducted in Italian, a language her beleaguered governesses had never even bothered to attempt. Somehow, though, the actors, with their voices and their expressions, communicated all that she needed to know.

As the gaslights were turned up, Annabelle gazed around the theater. It was a glorious space, with an enormous velvet curtain masking the set, and a painted ceiling with allegorical panels presiding high above. The pit seats lay in front of the stage, while five floors of private boxes ringed the theater like a horseshoe, separated by pairs of crimson silk partitions. The Dorset box offered one of the finest views.

"Jane," she said, continuing to look about her. "Isn't this marvelous?" Miss Fitzsimmons, who was seated beside her, had been silent for most of the performance, no doubt transfixed. When she made no reply, however, Annabelle looked at her, and gave a cry of alarm.

Jane was as pale as one of the Townley Marbles at the British Museum. Her face glistened with a sheen of sweat, and she appeared to be in terrible pain, her breath wheezing in labored pants. "Jane, are you all right?" Annabelle asked. "Lord Dorset, something is happening to Miss Fitzsimmons."

Alec, who was standing at the back of the box with his mother and Aunt Sophia, turned first to her, and then to Jane, his features stark with concern. As all three rushed forward, Jane winced, turning toward her.

"Please," Jane said haltingly, as she covered her eyes with a shaking hand. "I have a headache, nothing more. I've suffered severe megrims since I was a small child."

"May I get you a cold cloth?" she asked. "Is it the light that bothers you?"

"Could someone ... see me home? I don't wish to be a bother, but I cannot stay."

"We'll get you home as quickly as possible," Alec said gently, clasping her hand. "Ladies, I'm sorry that our evening must be cut short, but we need to get Miss Fitzsimmons into her father's care."

A butler entered the box with refreshments, and Alec asked him to gather the ladies' wraps and notify their coachman that they would be departing. At that, his mother spoke up. "Alec, my dear, if you help me escort Miss Fitzsimmons to the carriage, I will see her home. She should lie down for the duration of the journey, but she can hardly unbend and be made comfortable if you come along."

Jane nodded weakly, so Alec agreed, and together they helped her to stand. "Lady Marchmain, Miss Layton, please make yourselves comfortable. I'm sorry to leave you unescorted, but I will ask the steward to stand by the door and turn away any curious onlookers. I'll return as soon as I am able."

"We understand, Lord Dorset," Aunt Sophia replied. "We will hope for Miss Fitzsimmons' quick recovery." He returned his attention to Jane and carefully escorted her from the box, his mother fluttering anxiously behind them.

• • •

This evening was an exercise in frustration. Alec had returned to the theater with Act IV well under way—the opera was a bravura performance if the response of the crowd was anything to go by—but he'd barely glanced at the stage. He couldn't seem to look away from Annabelle, who now sat beside him. She glowed with joy, and like some pathetic creature locked outside on a bitter night, he craved her warmth.

She'd always been that way. Even as a child, he'd been drawn to her vitality, but now that she was a grown woman, it was an insidious thing. He was increasingly helpless in the face of it. He remembered the feel of her when they'd danced in Lady Marchmain's music room, her body smooth and supple as it moved with his. He could see the compassion in her eyes when he'd spoken of the war.

When the opera was done, Alec fought to keep them moving through the crowds in the lobby. Everyone and their mother wanted an introduction to Annabelle, and he was hardly interested in watching people make simpering fools of themselves. When Lady Marchmain spotted a friend and wandered off into the throng, he was able to maneuver Annabelle outside, but they waited by the carriage for what seemed like an eternity. He was intensely aware of her all the while. The curve of her back. The rhythmic tapping of her feet. The sway of her body as she hummed a song from *Figaro*. And when finally, at long last, a steward arrived with a note from the countess, he wanted to curse out loud. Lady Marchmain wanted him to return Annabelle to Grovesnor Square.

Insufferable woman. One didn't abandon an unescorted debutante. She was the very worst of chaperones! Didn't she realize that being alone with her niece in closed quarters would be torture? He helped Annabelle into the Dorset carriage and quickly climbed in behind her, calling out to the coachman to be off. The fewer people who saw them together and alone, the better.

...

"Alec, I can't thank you enough for bringing me to the opera," Annabelle said as soon he settled onto the squabs across from her. "Signora Catalani has the most magnificent voice."

"I'm glad you enjoyed it." Even in his acutely frustrated state, he couldn't help but smile. "Napoleon himself was so captivated when she visited France that he refused to let her leave. She had to disguise herself as a nun to escape the country."

"Well, that is yet another reason to dislike Emperor Bonaparte," she said emphatically. "Tell me, how is Miss Fitzsimmons? Was she any better as she left?"

"She was in a great deal of discomfort. I'm eager to get an update on her condition."

He stared at his hands in his lap; in all truth, he hadn't thought about Jane since returning to the theater. It was not something he was proud of.

"I only wish she'd said something earlier. I'm afraid she could see how much I was enjoying the opera, and did not wish to draw attention. She was suffering terribly."

"She has offered to help with your debut, and she didn't wish to falter in any way."

"You seem to like her a great deal."

He looked up. Her eyes were focused intently upon him. "Yes, of course. She is in all ways admirable." And she was. He must remember that.

"She's very pretty."

He gave a wry smile. "Coming from you, I know she would appreciate the compliment."

Annabelle looked out the window. They were well away from the theater now, threading a path along the dark streets of London. "Do you remember when the three of us would act out the stories I had written?" she asked quietly. "You and me and Gareth?"

"I remember you invariably gave me the most embarrassing role."

"That is unfair. You were always the hero. Gareth had to play the villain in every piece, while I was the distressed damsel."

"You should have played the villain, for all of the things you made me say and do."

"Leaving you to play the damsel, I suppose?"

"Absolutely not." He chuckled. "You could have played both. Indeed, you had enough enthusiasm to play all the roles simultaneously."

"After you both went away, that's what I was reduced to. It was not nearly so much fun."

No. It was never so much fun again.

As the streets continued to roll past, her face became pensive, and it grew very quiet in the carriage. There was only the sound of the horses clip-clopping on the cobblestones beneath them. "I still miss him every day," she whispered at last.

"Annabelle … I have never told you how very sorry I am that Gareth died so tragically. I will always regret the role I played."

Those blue, blue eyes were on him again. "Mother blamed you, you know."

His gut clenched. "It was a terrible accident. You must believe me."

"I have never thought you responsible, Alec. I may have blamed you for other things, but never that."

She could not have surprised him more if she'd leaned over and kissed him. "Thank you," he said, his throat suddenly tight. "That means a great deal."

She looked down, seemingly absorbed by a shaft of moonlight on the floor of the carriage. "I think Mother blamed you for the accident, because the alternative was too difficult to bear."

"What do you mean, Annabelle? What alternative?"

"I was in the carriage with Gareth, although I don't remember why. Perhaps I was hiding, like I used to do when we were children and you would not let me race with you. Perhaps I distracted him ..."

"You don't remember?"

"Nothing of the accident, nor of the first days that followed. Dr. Chessher told me it was not uncommon, given the head wound I suffered, but he expected my memories would come back. I only remember the night of the dance and the fight with that stranger from London. I remember this horrible sense of foreboding." She was on the verge of tears, trying not to let them fall. "Then the whole world ripped apart."

To think that she'd regained consciousness, alone and in agony, only to find she had no recollection of how she'd come to be that way. No idea of the horrors lying in wait.

He had been angry after the accident because she'd put herself in harm's way. The sight of her there, so desperately injured, had nearly torn his heart out. But he'd never dreamed that she might blame herself for the whole of it.

"Perhaps you thought that you could help," he said, wondering what he could possibly say. "You were always the better driver."

"But he was a grown man, and I was nearly grown. I would never have wanted to embarrass him. I must have startled him in some way." She took a deep, shuddering breath. "I must have drawn his attention from the road."

"Oh, Annabelle. You weren't in any way responsible."

Her tears began in earnest then, coursing down her cheeks in trails that looked silver in the moonlight. Suddenly, it seemed like the most natural thing in the world to move across the rocking carriage to where she sat, to pull her into his arms and hold her close, as he had done so often when she was a child.

As one arm held her, he withdrew his other hand from its glove, and rubbed her back in an effort to calm her, while he tried to ignore the shape of her through her cloak. He kept whispering her name as she sobbed, because he didn't know what else to say, other than she was not to blame, and he was so very sorry she had suffered. He could feel her heart pounding against him.

Slowly, as the carriage swayed, her crying ebbed, and then stopped all together. Still, he held her. Somewhere in the back of his mind, an alarm bell sounded, but he was merely offering comfort. Even though her body, nestled against his, was soft and lushly curved. Her head was tucked against his shoulder, her breath fanning his neck. He reached into his pocket to withdraw a handkerchief and touched his hand to her chin, so that he could tilt her face up toward his. Her eyes glistened as he dried her tears, smoothing the handkerchief down her cheeks and along her jaw.

Her skin was a marvel, silky and lustrous, like trailing one's fingertips through a bowl of cream. And that mouth. Unthinking, he let the handkerchief drop between them and touched a forefinger to her lips, slowly tracing their outline, utterly fascinated. She caught her breath in surprise, her lips parting slightly. He'd never seen anything so tempting in his entire life, and before he could ponder the innumerable reasons why he shouldn't, he tilted his head, and leaned in to kiss her.

It had been so long. The feel of her lips on his was indescribable, her mouth warm and plump beneath his own. He lightly touched his tongue along the fullness of her lower lip, marveling at the sensations that it aroused. When he drew her lip into his mouth, sucking slightly, she opened her mouth with a gasp.

This was so wrong in every way, despite the fact that he'd never wanted anything more. But then she leaned into him, her hands reaching up and curling into his hair, as she tentatively touched her own tongue to his mouth. Its hot, wet stroke evaporated his self-control, and suddenly, he couldn't get enough of her. He ran his hands along her shoulders and up into her hair, pulling at its pins until it fell in great waves about them, its lilac scent filling the carriage. He brought his hands back down to pull her even closer, his mouth still entwined with hers. The feel of her breasts pressed against him inspired all sorts of carnal images. He imagined pulling her dress from her shoulders, exposing those breasts, and taking them into his mouth.

He trailed his lips down the long column of her throat, to the soft swell of her décolletage, and ran his hands along the curve of her breasts, his fingers gently tracing their shape, caressing the exposed flesh just above her neckline. And because the temptation was simply too great, he dipped a thumb into her bodice, and rubbed it across the nipple of one breast until she moaned, and then he tucked a forefinger in as well, squeezing the nipple until she writhed beneath his hands.

This was madness! He had to end this before there was no going back for either one of them. Somehow, he pulled away, disengaging his hands, and moved back to the other side of the carriage. The vehicle had stopped.

Dear God. How long had they been outside of Marchmain House?

Annabelle's face was flushed, her lips faintly swollen. Her breath was coming in pants, soft and quick, as if she had been running very fast. He imagined her naked above him, her breath hitching with those short, hot gasps as she rode his body.

And he was the worst sort of degenerate. He put his head into his hands, trying to will his painful arousal away. At the inn, she'd said she no longer trusted him, and he had been so mortally offended, so willing to judge her. But she'd been right. He did not deserve her trust. Because nothing could come of this.

"Alec?" Her eyes had never seemed so wide and bright. Would he see his own dark heart reflected in their depths if he looked deeply enough? "Why did you kiss me?"

"Annabelle, I am sorry."

"You did not answer my question," she replied, her voice still slightly breathless as she made an effort to put her hair back in order and straighten her clothing. The movement highlighted the curve of her breasts, and he nearly groaned.

"I'm not sure you want to hear the truth, Annabelle."

"I am stronger than you think I am. But I need to know how to act when I see you again. I need to know why this happened."

She wasn't afraid to ask difficult questions, was she?

"Annabelle ... you are unbearably tempting. But that cannot happen again. I don't have that right."

Her eyelashes lowered, and before he knew what she was about, she gathered her things and sprang from the carriage. The butler must have spied the coach from a window, because before he could even make a start at running after her, the door of Marchmain House opened and shut, tucking Annabelle safely inside.

• • •

How odd that she could still perform mundane tasks, as if nothing had happened and her world had not been upended. If Canby noticed Annabelle's disheveled appearance when she barreled through the front door, flushed and agitated, he didn't say anything. He asked after the performance. She replied politely that the opera had been marvelous, and that her aunt would not be home until late in the evening. She walked up the long marble staircase to her room with its soothing patterns and colors, and Mary helped her change out of her evening attire. She'd already laid out Annabelle's bedclothes.

"This will need airing out and ironing, Miss Annabelle." Mary glanced dubiously at the heavy wrinkles across the bodice of the dress. "Let me take it to my room, and I'll be right back."

Annabelle put on her nightgown. Walking to her nightstand, she rinsed her hands and her face, and freshened her mouth with tooth powder. In drying herself off with a small hand towel, she was wiping away all traces of her encounter with Alec. But of course, that was not true. She could still feel his lips on hers, feel his hands pressing against her body and caressing her breasts. She doubted she would ever forget those sensations. They'd been even more powerful than before, when he had kissed her so long ago. She had not wanted him to stop. She'd wanted to feel his hands all over her.

Even when they were at odds with each other, he was still the most handsome man she'd ever seen. But when he was kind and gentle, as he'd been at the museum and in the carriage when she'd lost her composure, he turned back into the man she'd worshipped for so long. The man she had loved.

What in the world did he want from her? He'd said he had no right, but what did rights or even wrongs have to do with any of it? It was entirely possible that if she let him, he would break her heart all over again.

She walked over to her dressing table and sat down, ready to brush out her hair for the evening. "Let me do that for you, Miss Annabelle," Mary said, coming up behind her. "It's a proper bird's nest, after all. Who knows what you did to make it so?"

She blushed. A part of Annabelle wanted to tell her. Mary had known all about her feelings from before, had mailed her letters to Alec, after all, and waited with her for the responses that never came. Mary had seen her through the worst of those early days. Yet Annabelle held her tongue. Since her return, neither of them had spoken of that time, as if the subject was best left in the past, in the hopes that its pain would stay there as well.

A silly notion, now that she thought about it.

"You must be more careful with your hair and your dress," Mary admonished, watching her closely in the dressing table mirror as she ran the brush through her curls. "They reflect on your reputation."

"I will try, Mary. It was very windy this evening, and I tripped at the theater."

They were plausible excuses. Any more lies, though, and Mary might guess at the real cause of her dishevelment. If she hadn't already.

Chapter 12

After a sleepless night at his bachelor lodgings, Alec climbed the stairs to his mother's house, wondering if his perfidy was obvious for the world to see. He'd shamed Annabelle. He had not meant to, of course, but that wasn't an excuse.

He would have taken her innocence, right there in the carriage.

It hadn't been the behavior he owed to Gareth, and certainly not to Annabelle. He would have to go to Marchmain House today, much as he dreaded the notion. He would make his heartfelt apologies, and continue on the path that had been set. He owed it to his father. He would see Annabelle well settled, even though giving her into the care of another man might prove to be the most difficult thing he had ever done.

He gave a quick rap on the door, and Edmunds answered it promptly. "My lord, your mother will be happy to know that you are here. She is in the drawing room with her guests." It was the heart of the day, when society paid its visits and gossiped about its members. Perhaps a few of her friends had stopped by. When he crossed through the doors of the drawing room, however, Alec was shocked by the number of people there. More than a dozen were in attendance, a suspicious mixture of young men and their mothers.

"Alec, my dear," she called out when she spotted him. "Come in and see so many of your old friends." She was being too kind. Surely he'd been away at school when these infants were still in short pants? Yet there were older gentlemen, as well. Cartwright, and that fop Petersham, and Marworth.

Damnation, he should have guessed it before now. They were here because of Annabelle, trying to ferret out information from his mother before planning their pursuit.

At least they had the good sense, upon gauging his mood, to scatter. Benjamin, for his part, made quite a show of begging his mother's indulgence for his abrupt departure before announcing that he was off to pay his respects at Marchmain House. At the mention of it, the room's other occupants also took their leave, and in short order, he and his mother were alone. "I seem to have cleared the room," he said. "Am I dressed to offend? Potter won't be happy to hear it."

"No, Alec, although you do look as if you are out for blood sport this morning."

He could hardly tell her why. "I only hope that you weren't put out by so many visitors."

"It's far better to have visitors than to be left alone," Mother said, smiling as she sat back against her toile-covered fauteuil. "When your father died, I had legions of people who paid their respects. They wanted to know if I missed him, if I'd been well provided for, if I was worried I'd lose you to the war. All sorts of disrespectful questions, actually. Then rather suddenly, they stopped coming. After all, nothing is more depressing than a widow in her weeds, and they'd done their duty."

"I am sorry, Mother." When had it become easier for him to stay away than to return?

"Don't be sorry on my account. I daresay Annabelle has made me fashionable again."

"About Miss Layton ... how are your plans progressing?"

"They couldn't be better. After the opera last night, she's the talk of London, although there have been more than a few complaints that you barred the door to our box at intermission. A number of people were queuing up to meet her. Others claim you were stingy with introductions following the performance."

"I was in no mood to make small talk. Do you know that Lady Marchmain had the audacity to leave Annabelle alone in my care? She saw an old friend and wandered off."

"That was unfortunate, but she knows that you're not a threat to her niece's reputation. It was like leaving Annabelle with a brother."

He felt his jaw tighten. "I am not her brother. It was not well done."

"By all appearances, my dear, you won't have to play the chaperone for long. Several eligible gentlemen are already interested. Indeed, I think Marworth is among them, and he can hardly be faulted."

"His faults are legion! And he's abominably flippant."

"Alec, what is the matter? You're not yourself today. It's obvious to me you want no part in this."

"That is not true. I am committed to helping Miss Layton, but she shouldn't be pushed at the first eligible suitor." Certainly not at Marworth. Or any of the others either. All of them were wrong for her in one way or another.

"I thought you were eager for her to be settled, so you could refocus on important duties."

"I am. But before she marries, Annabelle could use some measure of happiness. She hasn't had much of it these past few years."

"You do know that marriage and happiness aren't meant to be mutually exclusive? I certainly hope you expect more from Miss Fitzsimmons than a political alliance. That is, if she is still in your sights."

He looked down at the floor. "She is. I expect we will deal quite well together."

"Yet you haven't even asked me about our ride home together last night."

"Was she feeling any better? I've thought of little else since the morning." And he had just lied to his mother. What kind of man was he turning into?

"She will be fine after a day or so. She was very embarrassed by the episode."

Jane was not the one who should be embarrassed. She deserved far better. "I will wait then to pay her a call."

"Perhaps I shouldn't pry, Alec, but about Miss Fitzsimmons … she is a lovely girl, but I've seen little evidence of any real affection between you." He looked up to find that she was watching him, her face serious and sober. "Why do you wish to make her your wife?"

"Miss Fitzsimmons is a fine woman from a respected family, and she has a pristine reputation," he replied. He had been over her qualifications any number of times. "She's a skilled hostess, which will be an asset as I move forward in Parliament. She will value our family's name and its legacy."

"I recognize that logic." His mother sighed. "Those are the same assets your father sought to gain when he married me."

"Which validates their worth, don't you think?" he asked, smiling gently, hoping to coax away the sadness that had settled over her.

"I only know that at the time, I wanted to be loved. I wanted to be desired for myself, rather than for what I could bring to a marriage. I tried to be a good wife. Eventually, I grew to love him, but I'm not sure he ever felt the same way."

"Of course he loved you. How could he not?" They had grown closer when he was away during the war, hadn't they? Hadn't they loved each other in the end? "You were a wonderful wife. You are a wonderful mother."

"I have no doubt that your father bore me some affection after all of our years together, but it took time. You see, he was in love with someone else when we married."

Alec felt as if the world had just shifted dangerously, leaving him standing on unsteady ground. "Why do you say that, Mother?"

"I'll not bother with the details of who she was. I will only say that she was unsuitable, and your grandfather was a severe and demanding person. He had great expectations for his only son. He would not let Henry follow his heart. You are familiar, of course, with the type."

Alec swallowed past the sudden lump in his throat. "I didn't know any of this."

"It wasn't necessary for you to know. And he was happy when you were born at last, even if he wanted a child with her and not with me. He loved you, although I don't think he knew how to show it."

No. He had never had.

"I'm sorry I was not here for you, Mother. You should not have had to bury him alone."

"You did what you needed to do at the time, Alec. You served your country with distinction. And Henry seemed so healthy."

He'd always exuded such an air of invincibility, but of course, no one was invincible.

"You are your father's son and mine as well. Above all else, though, you are your own man. You shouldn't be made to live a life someone else planned for you. Henry did that already, and once is more than enough. I merely want you to be happy. I hope you will remember that."

• • •

"Lord Marworth, thank you for suggesting this stroll. It's a lovely day, and it was exceedingly warm in my aunt's drawing room." Annabelle had barely been able to breathe.

"Between all of those flowers and eager swains, there was hardly any air in the room. I could hardly stand by and watch you expire from an excess of adulation." He flashed perfectly straight, white teeth.

What an excessively beautiful man he was, like an angel from a Renaissance-era painting. Not one of the effeminate ones, but the kind who battled dragons and devils in a full suit of armor. Then again, weren't angels supposed to be saintly? She doubted Lord Marworth had a pious bone in his handsome body.

"Thank you, as well, for the flowers you sent. They are most impressive."

"Impressive is too kind a word, Miss Layton. I was appalled when I saw them in your drawing room."

"The florist was paying a tribute to your patronage." His arrangement had been very pretty, after all. It had just been very large, with two footmen needed to carry it into the house.

"Perhaps my florist should stick to neckcloths and waistcoats."

"Lord Marworth," she said. "That comment fairly screams for an explanation."

"My valet is a creative sort. When I mentioned that I wished to send you flowers, he took it upon himself to create the arrangement. My family enjoys a large garden behind our home here in London."

"That was very thoughtful."

"Yes, but he managed to denude nearly all of my mother's flower beds in the process."

"Was she very disappointed?"

"I doubt it. Withers is a marvelous eccentric. He keeps things interesting."

"I understand completely, my lord. My father defines eccentricity."

"I remember meeting Sir Layton several years ago. A charming man, and a great fan of butterflies and moths, as I recall."

"You have a gift for understatement."

They walked companionably for a few moments, enjoying the afternoon sunshine as Mary followed a short distance behind, acting as chaperone. "Are you enjoying London, Miss Layton? It's quite a bit busier than Nuneaton."

"There is that gift you have, on display again. And yes, I'm enjoying it very much. Now I know why Gareth found it so difficult to leave."

"Gareth ran with a rather unsavory crowd here. To be honest, more time spent in Nuneaton would have served him well."

"Did you often see him in the city?"

"I always enjoyed his company, of course, but in that last year or two, he was more interested in gambling than in meeting up with old classmates." He suddenly turned toward her. "I'm sorry. That was poorly said. I didn't mean to dishonor your brother's memory."

"You have not said anything I didn't already know. He and my father argued about money whenever he returned home."

"Gareth fell in with a man who made him risk far more than he could afford."

"Are you referring to Mr. Digby? I met him the night before Gareth died." She shuddered at the memory. "He was a very unsettling man."

"He was a cheat and a dangerous character. At least Dorset made sure it would be a long while before he could get his hooks into anyone again."

It was her turn to stop suddenly. "What do you mean?"

"I am sorry, Miss Layton. My tongue is running away with me today, spouting things I've no business discussing."

"Please tell me. I have no memory of the events surrounding my brother's death. All I know is that a race between Lord Dorset, Gareth, and Mr. Digby went horribly wrong."

"I think Alec's role haunts him this day."

She could see that now. Perhaps it was why he'd first offered to help her this season. But surely something else was blossoming between them? Something that might help them both to heal?

"We all make decisions that we regret," she said after a long moment. "And I know how hard he worked for his father's respect. Even though I am still struggling with Alec's reasons for leaving, I understand the pressure he must have felt."

"My apologies again," Lord Marworth replied. "I'm afraid I'm not following you."

"Alec left after the race in order to limit the damage to his family's reputation. That was why he could not wait to see Gareth buried. Or even to see if I would recover."

"Miss Layton, who told you such a thing?" He was clearly dumbfounded. "You are mistaken."

"My mother told me. I wouldn't believe her at first, that Alec could abandon us for so shallow a reason. She blamed him for Gareth's death, after all.

"But then all of my letters to him went unanswered," she continued. "He made no effort to contact me. Perhaps it was too painful for him to remember his part in that day. Perhaps I reminded him too much of my brother."

She fell silent then. She had been over it in her mind so many times. She didn't know why she expected to come up with new answers now. Her heart and her head no longer seemed to be working in concert with each other. And after last night, her heart was making all of her important decisions.

Lord Marworth opened his mouth as if to contradict her, but then he seemed to think the better of it. He appeared shocked by what she had told him. As they walked on, Annabelle heard Mary call her name. When she turned, her maid was ashen-faced.

"Mary, are you all right? Has something upset you?"

"I'm fine, Miss Annabelle," she said, looking away quickly. "But the sun is setting. We should return to the house."

"I shall hate to relinquish your company, Miss Layton. I may even need to observe a period of mourning before setting out to my evening appointments."

She laughed, charmed despite her pensive mood. "Do you find it difficult, Lord Marworth? Swallowing past that silver tongue?"

His eyes swept her with ill-disguised interest before settling on her face.

"My dear Miss Layton, how you wound me. If only you would offer me the slightest encouragement …"

"According to my aunt, you are very busy keeping up with the many ladies who encourage you. I should hate to burden you further."

When he flashed another of his wicked smiles, she was tempted to return it. Were it not for Alec, she'd be very tempted indeed.

Chapter 13

Why couldn't she learn a lesson once and be done with it? Three full days had passed since that night in the carriage, when Alec had kissed her.

On the first day, she'd gone on a series of morning calls to meet Aunt Sophia's acquaintances and friends. In the late afternoon—because those morning calls were euphemistically termed—they'd received a flattering number of visitors at Marchmain House. Lord Alvanley had paid her an additional visit, bringing several gentlemen with him. He was an exceptionally witty man, with a dry sense of humor and preposterous compliments. Viscount Petersham, the mysterious man in brown from the park, had also come to call. By all accounts, he had a scandalous reputation, but Annabelle was amused by his studied, lisping manner. She'd also enjoyed her walk with devilish Lord Marworth, who was so handsome.

But when Alec had not called by the second day, she'd turned anxious. She kept hoping for a note to explain why he'd been detained. As of this morning, though, there had been no visit or note. No word at all. Which meant he wanted nothing to do with her. It was why he'd apologized. He had kissed her because he was a man with needs. Wasn't that what the oaf at the Assembly Rooms in Bath had called it? She was to blame, of course, for assuming that his actions had meant something—not so much the kissing, because that was separate and apart—but the kindness and the sympathy and the affection.

The kissing had swayed her good judgment. She'd known for any number of years the kind of person he was. He abandoned his friends when things became difficult. He appeared steadfast yet was anything but. And he played with people's emotions, just like the other night in the carriage, when his kiss reawakened so many feelings. She'd felt desired, hoping he was as caught up in those wondrous sensations as she was, but he'd fooled her again.

• • •

The last several days hadn't gone at all as Alec had planned. He was sitting in the Dorset carriage with his mother, Lady Marchmain, Miss Fitzsimmons, her father, and Annabelle. They were on their way to Hampstead Heath, a vast parkland set on one of the highest spots in the city, where an elaborate picnic had been set up for them by his family's efficient staff. Marworth would meet them there, along with several other young ladies and gentlemen, all properly chaperoned, of course. The picnic was intended to introduce Annabelle to a wider circle of friends, and at least the weather was agreeable today.

He couldn't say the same about Annabelle.

She sat across from him, implacable and silent. Not that he could blame her. He hadn't seen her since the night at the opera. He'd stopped by Marchmain House after speaking with his mother that next day, but she'd been out on a walk with Benjamin. An unpleasant discovery, since it meant Marworth might be pursuing her in earnest. Rather childishly, he had decided not to leave his card.

But then he'd been unable to return. He'd learned the House of Lords would begin debate on his bill within the week, and he'd locked himself away in the library at Dorset House, fine-tuning his proposal. Not even Marworth had made it past Edmunds, although he'd tried several times. Indeed, Alec had ventured out on only one occasion, meeting with Lord Fitzsimmons at his home, where he learned that Jane was much recovered.

Yet it was unconscionable that he had not spoken with Annabelle. Did she think he'd forgotten that night? Nothing could be further from the truth. Outside of the soldiers' bill, he'd thought of little else. A small part of him could admit, though, that he hadn't known what to say to her, or how to express his feelings, which suddenly felt immense and uncomfortable. He didn't like to think he was a coward, but there was hardly another excuse for his actions. He had been battling the two sides of himself: the one that wanted to honor his father's wishes, and the one that wanted to decide his own future.

His father had spurned the woman he loved in order to satisfy his sire. And Alec, like a puppet on a string, had let his father's beliefs about Annabelle dictate his own. He'd pursued the very suitable Miss Fitzsimmons, taken up his seat in Parliament, and authored legislation that would have a lasting legacy. How pleased his father would be. Yet there was no pleasing a dead man. Any choices were now his to make. Why had it taken so long for him to recognize it?

He stole a surreptitious glance at Annabelle, but she was staring fixedly at him, along with everyone else in the carriage. "My apologies," he said. "Have I missed something?"

"Distracted, are you, my boy?" Lord Fitzsimmons boomed in that distinctive voice of his, oddly high and squeaky despite its impressive volume. "Lord Dorset is no doubt thinking about the fight ahead, my ladies," he continued. "We have been hard at work this week on the soldiers' bill. Dorset, myself, and my darling Jane. We make a formidable team, don't we?"

"Father, please don't overstate my contributions," Jane said, her face flushed with color.

"Nonsense! My Jane is sharp as a whip. I am deuced proud of her, although she's only a woman, with too many tender sensibilities. If she were a man, she'd be a fine addition to our government. As it is, though, she'll have to trust her ideas to me, and perhaps to Dorset going forward, eh?" Fitzsimmons laughed at that, and nudged Jane, who looked as if she wanted to leap from the carriage. "They make quite a pair. Yes, they do."

Lord, this was awkward. Alec stole another look at Annabelle, but she was staring out of the window. Her beautiful eyes were hidden from his view, but by her stiff posture and the tense line of her chin, he could tell she was upset. Rightly so. He only hoped he would be able to explain things properly.

"Lord Fitzsimmons," his mother interrupted smoothly. "I saw your treatise on farming innovations in *The Times*. Could you share your ideas with those of us who hadn't the pleasure of reading it?"

Jane's father preened and settled into a long dissertation on the subject. So long, in fact, that no one else spoke for the remainder of the ride out to the Heath.

• • •

"Lord Fitzsimmons is a pedantic boor," Aunt Sophia said once they were finally free of the carriage, and at a distance that encouraged honest discussion. "Why Dorset would wish to align himself with that pompous flap-jaw, let alone his bluestocking daughter, I will never know. They've quite driven me to drink." Spying a wine steward, she slipped away.

They were welcome to him. If Annabelle still harbored any illusions about Alec Carstairs, the ride here effectively shattered them. Why hadn't she guessed it before now? He was on the verge of proposing to Jane. He'd known it when he kissed her.

Which was why she was determined to put him behind her once and for all. She would see him at the Hertford's party tomorrow night, and then at her come-out ball, to be held in a few weeks' time at Marchmain House. Afterward, she need never speak to him again. And if there was a sudden lump in her throat making it difficult for her to swallow, she'd recover. She'd recovered from far more painful things.

Alec's mother had picked one of the most bucolic corners of Hampstead Heath for their picnic. A large white linen tent was set up in the middle of a long sweep of grassy lawn, complete with pennants that fluttered in the soft breeze, like something out of a medieval tournament. She could see several long tables inside, each topped with pristine white linens, and a veritable groaning board of assorted foods. Small seating groups were set up beneath the shady trees that dotted the lawn, and there were perhaps two dozen people in attendance, including Lord Marworth and a number of the gentlemen who had called on her. She didn't know any of the young ladies who sat in a pretty array of pastel gowns with their mothers, but hopefully she would find a friend among them. There would be lots of opportunities today to meet new people. Lady Dorset had planned a series of lawn games and ordered horses brought from the Park Lane mews, in case any of her guests wanted to explore the heath.

Hopefully, Alec would take one of those horses and ride straight into the Thames.

"Miss Layton?"

Lord Marworth was walking toward her with those long strides of his. "Although I told her I wished to keep you all to myself, our hostess has insisted you meet a few of the gentlemen and ladies of my acquaintance. Will you join me?"

Pasting on her brightest smile, she said, "Do you promise that none of them bites? If so, I shall be delighted, Lord Marworth."

"Not a one of them will bite you," he replied with a sly grin. "But I might."

• • •

By all appearances, Annabelle was enjoying herself immensely. All afternoon long, Alec heard her laughter in the distance, as she and the other guests played the lawn games. There were pantomimes, word puzzles, and even an archery contest, during which Annabelle amazed all with her prowess.

But as free as her laughter was, she didn't smile at him. Not once. Indeed, she looked away whenever their eyes met, and he hadn't yet had the opportunity to speak with her. Lord Fitzsimmons had trapped him into a discussion about parliamentary procedures, and he was too old for the games anyway. But they looked like fun. Annabelle enjoyed them, and he wanted to share her joy. He couldn't remember the last time he'd felt as carefree as she seemed today, smiling in the company of her new friends.

"Lord Dorset," Jane interrupted prettily, earning a look of censure from her father. "I hope you won't mind if I return home with Lady Fairbanks and her daughter, Miss Traemore. We are well acquainted through my work with the Society for Indigent Children, and we're all quite fatigued by the afternoon's festivities."

"Not in the least, Miss Fitzsimmons. I've enjoyed your company, and I appreciate your help with Miss Layton." Thankfully, her father decided to join Jane in an early departure. Alec was finding it difficult to think of anything besides his need to speak with Annabelle.

As he looked about, however, she was nowhere to be found. Indeed, most of the guests had disappeared. Had he and Fitzsimmons missed the entire picnic? He vaguely remembered a footman bringing them plates of food, but that had been quite some time ago. After a quick perusal inside the tent, he turned to find Benjamin standing directly behind him. The man was as quiet as a cat.

"Have you seen Miss Layton?" Alec asked.

"I have indeed. She's the sort that makes your eyes linger."

"She's not one of your flirts, Benjamin. Where has she run off to?"

"Miss Layton and her aunt left with your mother several minutes ago. You were distracted by Miss Fitzsimmons."

"I couldn't get away from her father. I wanted to speak with Annabelle privately."

"I've been trying to speak with you privately all week, but you refused to see me."

"I know, and I am sorry. I've been busy preparing my arguments for the bill."

"I wanted to talk to you about Miss Layton," Benjamin said. "I have important news to share."

Alec was suddenly uneasy. "Tell me your intentions toward her. She's no woman to be made a sport of."

"What a prig you are, Alec. I have the upmost respect for Annabelle."

"Are you pursuing her?" he asked, his voice tight because Marworth had used her given name, hinting at something between them. "Do you find her attractive?"

"That's an inherently silly question. She is a remarkably beautiful creature. But I'm not pursuing her."

"You've been doing a fine imitation of it, then. You hardly left her side today."

He could hear the jealousy in his own voice, and when Benjamin grinned widely, Alec wanted to smash his obnoxiously handsome face.

"You have it bad, don't you, Dorset?"

"Don't be absurd." Had Annabelle told Marworth about that night at the opera? He'd not believe it.

"Well, you may rest easy. Annabelle Layton has no interest in me, despite my best efforts to charm her, and I'm far too lazy to expend energy in a pointless pursuit. Furthermore, it's obvious something is between you two."

"You are imagining things. I'm only looking after her as Gareth would have."

Benjamin didn't bother to respond. He merely quirked a brow in disbelief.

"You don't understand," Alec said, suddenly tired of hiding his feelings. "You know Annabelle and I were once very close, but she doesn't trust me. She thinks I abandoned her after Gareth's death. She dismissed my vow to her mother as an excuse."

"That's where you are wrong. Annabelle knows nothing about your vow."

"You're not making any sense," Alec said, shaking his head to clear it.

"Annabelle was told that you left Nuneaton to protect your family's reputation from the scandal of the race."

The words had no bite at first. They were hazy and indistinct. Like that wound at Sabugal that he hadn't felt, until he saw all of the blood soaking through his uniform.

"Lady Layton made me swear I wouldn't contact Annabelle. I could hardly ignore the wishes of a grieving mother. Are you saying Annabelle was never told the truth?"

"You're forgetting that Lady Layton blamed you for the death of her son. Annabelle was told that you wanted nothing to do with her."

God almighty.

"She didn't believe her mother at first. She sent several letters, begging you to return. To this day, she thinks you ignored them because the memories they prompted were too painful."

"I never received any letters. Christ, I'd have crawled back from Spain if I'd known Annabelle needed me." His hands fisted at his sides, but there was no one to rail against. No one alive, anyway.

"Lady Layton must have intercepted the correspondence. After all, how better to turn Annabelle against you than to let her believe those letters had been sent, but you never came?"

He had an almost overpowering urge to sit down, to simply let his legs fall beneath him. A similar feeling had come over him at Badajoz, in that instant when he realized that there was only one way up to the fortress breach, and that it was between the dead bodies of his fellow soldiers. Only later had he let the horror of that sink in. Neither was this a time for hesitation.

"I need one of the horses."

"Your mother asked us to return them to the mews. A few of the footmen have stayed behind to help."

"I'm sorry. I need to find Annabelle." He ran to the closest mount, swung quickly into the saddle, and galloped off toward Grovesnor Square in the fading light of the day.

* * *

After a halfhearted burst of speed at the onset, the mews horse settled into such a lackadaisical trot that Alec could probably have outrun her. Indeed, the mare was so far removed in temperament and ability from Mars, she was surely a different species altogether. When at last, almost an hour and a half later, the horse finally stopped in front of Marchmain House, the sun had long since set in the sky. A wind was kicking up, and the windows of the grand houses around the square were twinkling with candlelight.

He dismounted, tossing a coin to a street lad with instructions to return the horse. He was covered with road dust—a creased and crumpled mess—but waiting any longer to speak with Annabelle was untenable. On the long ride from the Heath, he'd kept revisiting their reunion at The Bull's End, when Annabelle was so cold and distant. Was it any wonder, considering what she'd been told?

Grief made people do terrible, illogical things, but Lady Layton hadn't had the right to keep them apart. He could have been a comfort to Annabelle during her rehabilitation, all those long and painful months when she must have desperately needed a companion. Certainly, he wouldn't have let the woman keep him away with a flimsy excuse about contagions.

Or would he have? He'd already allowed his father to drive a wedge between them.

Had he stayed, would things between them be different? Could they be different now? He rapped on the door, and within moments, Canby welcomed him into the wide marble hall.

"I apologize for interrupting what is most likely the dinner hour. It's urgent that I speak with Miss Layton."

"I am afraid Lady Marchmain and her niece have left for Almack's. Their vouchers were delivered this morning."

Alec withdrew his pocket watch to check the time. It was just after 8:00 P.M. They might be there for hours. He briefly considered rushing home to change into formal attire so that he could meet them there, but they might also return at any time.

"I would like to wait here, if you are amenable."

"Certainly, my lord. May I suggest the library? Lord Marchmain found it a most comfortable room. I will also have a tray sent up, along with some of the countess's favorite libations to keep you company."

Minutes later, he was sitting on a deep-seated Grecian sofa in front of a warm fire. The library was blessedly free of floral tributes for Annabelle. A selection of breads and sliced meats had been placed beside him, and he had a glass of Gran Riserva in hand. What he did not have was patience. He had no way of knowing when she would return. And at the moment, he had little idea of what he would say when she did.

Chapter 14

Hours later, Alec was still in Sophia Middleton's library. The fire in the grate was burning brightly—a footman had come in over the course of the evening to stoke it—but out in the square, all of the neighboring houses had gone dark. A steady rain had begun to fall, and the wind rattled the windows in their frames. He checked his pocket watch. It was past midnight. Voices suddenly sounded in the hall.

"Nasty weather, and it came on so quickly ... A visitor, at this hour?" It was the countess who spoke. "Lord Dorset? How very curious."

The voices moved closer.

"If you don't mind, Aunt Sophia, I will take myself off to bed. I've never danced so much. Thank you for talking my wrap, Canby." Annabelle sounded breathless. Strained.

"If he's out at this hour and in this weather, my dear, Lord Dorset has important news. Let us see what this is about."

"I'd rather not," Annabelle replied, but their footsteps were already headed this way. He stood hastily, brushing at his creased clothing.

"Lord Dorset." The countess swept into the parlor. "I hope nothing is amiss."

"I apologize most sincerely, but it's rather urgent I speak with Miss Layton."

Annabelle walked into the room with a stiffness in her gait he'd not seen before. As beautiful as she was, it was obvious, to him at least, that she was in pain.

"I can't think of anything so pressing, Lord Dorset, that it must be said this evening," Annabelle replied. "You should return home before the weather gets worse. I bid you good night." She turned to leave the room. Was she limping?

"Annabelle, please. I have waited here all evening for you." She stopped at that, squaring her shoulders as if preparing for battle.

"Is that brandy?" Lady Marchmain asked. "How marvelous! Why don't I pour each of us a glass?"

"No, thank you, Aunt Sophia. I am sure this will not take long."

Her aunt looked at Annabelle, and then at Alec, and then back at her niece again. "Come to think of it, I'm desperate for one of the petit fours we enjoyed after dinner. I asked Cook to hide them from me for just this very reason. They are the most delicious things. I must go and ask Canby if he knows what she's done with them." Lady Marchmain swung about, moving toward the hall. "Leave the door open, Lord Dorset," she called over her shoulder.

But as she left the room, she pulled the door shut.

"Annabelle, is your leg bothering you?" He couldn't hide his concern, although he made no move toward her.

"You persist in calling me that, when I would prefer you didn't. It intimates a closeness we obviously don't share."

"Come and sit here by the fire." He gestured toward the large Grecian couch, with its roll-curved ends and bolstered cushions. "It will relieve the pressure on your leg. Does it pain you often? You don't have to hide it from me."

"My leg is none of your concern, but rest assured, it would feel better if I were upstairs, tucked into my bed. That way, neither of us would have to endure this conversation." She made no move to sit down.

God, he was an ass. Annabelle had every right to be angry at him, and not because her mother had spread lies. His misplaced sense of responsibility was the reason she stood before him, distant and aloof. "I'm sorry I haven't apologized before now."

"It's not important," she said, staring directly into his eyes. "None of this is or was." Only when she looked away did he realize she wasn't as composed as she seemed.

"After the other night, I should have come straight here."

"But you've been very busy, after all. At the picnic today, Jane told me how hard you have been working at Fitzsimmons House."

"She was at home when I called on her father. He is a co-sponsor with me."

"I'm glad to see she's feeling better," Annabelle replied, her voice tight. "I'm also doing much better, too, if you are interested to know it. I suffered from an excess of emotion just days ago—a case of histrionics, if you will—but it has passed."

She thought that he'd been toying with her. "Annabelle, if I can just get through the next week, there's a good chance my bill will meet with approval, and I can focus on other things. Important things," he said. "You are very important to me. I am sorry I didn't send a note to explain why I was delayed."

It was hard to find the right words to say. He looked down at the floor. The rain outside was pelting the windows now. "Annabelle, about what happened in the carriage—"

"Please," she said, waving her hands dismissively. "I don't need another apology. It is unnecessary. I found the whole of it quite enlightening. Instructional, even."

His head snapped up at that.

She lifted her chin defiantly and arched one shoulder back, as if to call attention to the swell of her breasts. Either that, or his own lecherous thoughts were running away with any shred of remaining good sense. "The kissing and those other things, the way you touched me. I felt the strangest sensations."

Was she trying to torture him?

"That must be why poets spend so much time writing about what can happen between a man and a woman. I wonder if Lord Marworth would agree. He's very fond of poetry."

He wasn't going to let Benjamin near her. "Annabelle, please listen."

"Oh, but I have been listening," she interrupted, her voice frigid. "It's just that you have so little to say. Really, I am quite tired. Your apology is accepted. I'd like you to leave now."

She was staring at him, eyes cold, but he could see past them to the hurt that he'd caused. He wanted to honor her wishes and walk away, out into the night. But she deserved the truth. It should never have been kept from her. "My apology is overdue, but that's not the only reason I am here. There's something else you must know. There is no easy way to say it."

"You're referring to your impending engagement to Miss Fitzsimmons. You have my congratulations."

"I'm not … that's not what I must tell you. This has to do with what happened after Gareth's death. I'd always thought you knew it. I didn't abandon you, Annabelle."

If possible, her eyes grew even colder. She was standing ramrod straight. "No? Do you have another word for it, then?"

"I had no choice, but it seems you were never told the reason."

"Surely there were several reasons," she said. "Let me see if I can name them for you. Guilt. Cowardice. Even arrogance will do."

"Had anything in our friendship up to that point made you think that I'd leave you in such circumstances?"

"You had all but ignored me for two years," she replied. "But no. I didn't think you'd leave me bloodied and delirious. How naive I was. You were already a world away before I understood what you'd done."

There was no way to soften this. It would be like tearing the bandage from a wound, and splitting it back open. "After Gareth's death, your mother made me swear I would never speak with you again. And I honored that while she lived."

She shook her head in disbelief. "You left after the race, You were afraid that the news of it would upset your father, and harm your reputation. You told my mother so."

"You don't remember it, Annabelle. I stayed by your side at Astley Castle for several days, and cared for you because your mother could not. I only left when she demanded it."

It was as if she had not heard him. She backed away, toward the door, the fading glow of the fire sparking her eyes with an unnatural light, as thunder sounded. "She couldn't have seen how much I missed you and not told me why you were gone."

"It is the truth, Annabelle." How he wished it was not.

"How convenient to blame my dead mother for your guilt, Alec," she said, her voice tortured. "After all, she can hardly contradict you." With that, she rushed from the room, slamming the door behind her. She would be heartbroken when she came to see the truth in what he'd said, and he fought the urge to run after her.

But what if she didn't believe him? Why should she, after all, when his actions over the past several days had done little to inspire trust? He'd shattered the tenuous bond between them. As he walked from the library into the hall toward the front door, he vowed he would see it rebuilt, as thunder rolled again in the distance. This time, he would fight for her.

• • •

She made it to her room before dissolving into tears. How could he say such things? Mother had been ill in her last years, but she'd not been cruel. Still, Annabelle couldn't silence a small voice in her head that said he was telling the truth. His eyes had been so somber and serious. He had tried to be gentle, even though she'd been horribly insulting. It was all too easy to hide her feelings behind anger and blame.

"Miss Annabelle," Mary said, rushing toward her from the doorway of her adjoining chamber. "Why are you crying?" She was in her dressing gown for the evening.

"I'm sorry to wake you, Mary. I will get a hold of myself in short order."

"Wake me? I wasn't sleeping. This storm has me nervous."

She sat down upon the settee and tried to calm herself. "Lord Dorset was waiting for us when we returned from Almack's."

"You've not been right since that trip to the opera. Did he come about that?"

"I suppose so." She sniffed. "He apologized for being busy with a proposal he's preparing for debate, but that's not why I'm so upset. He spoke about the accident, and about what happened afterward."

"Those were terrible times."

"Yes, and he said things that I'm hesitant to believe."

Mary knelt beside her. "I've tried not to bring up those days since my return, because they were so awful. But Lord Dorset is an honest man. He wouldn't lie."

"Surely you remember what he did? The letters you sent for me? He never responded to a one of them. How could he have been so heartless?"

Mary flushed. "I can't speak to the letters, Miss Annabelle. He was traveling, after all. Perhaps they were lost."

"I can believe some may have gone astray, but hardly a dozen."

"Think back on how he cared for you," Mary said. "I thank the Heavens above that he called for Dr. Chessher that day, and he watched over you so well. He saved your leg."

Annabelle straightened, even as tears continued to roll down her cheeks. "But he didn't care enough to stay. He was gone by morning."

"Oh, miss! I've wondered, given the things you have let slip, if you'd forgotten. Lord Dorset stayed with you after the accident and during those few first days. He hardly left your side. Your mother wouldn't let us speak of it later, but I felt sure you knew."

"He stayed with me? But Mother said he went back to London, back to his father."

Mary was twisting her wrapper in her hands. "I don't like to speak ill of the dead, but Lady Layton was not right after that day. I was too afraid of her to tell you."

"Tell me what?"

Mary took a deep, unsteady breath. "This will be upsetting."

"Don't worry," Annabelle said with a weak laugh. "I'm already upset."

"She banished Lord Dorset. He did not even get to see Master Gareth buried."

For several moments, there was silence. "But why?" She could hear the horror in her voice, making her sound faintly hysterical. "Why would she do that?"

"Lady Layton, she was like a wild woman, screaming and ranting. None of the staff was to say his name. When one of the footmen tried to sneak in a letter Lord Dorset wrote to you, your mother found it, and poor Franklin was fired on the spot."

"He left a letter?" she whispered. Her head was throbbing.

Mary nodded, her cheeks wet now with tears. "Your mother burned it in front of us all. I had to hide your letters and pass them to your father to send. I am so sorry." Mary wiped her face with the sleeve of her wrapper. "Lord Dorset wouldn't have left your side if he'd not been forced. She made him promise to leave. Not just then, but forever."

Annabelle felt as if she'd been plunged into a cold lake and held down. She struggled to breathe, the room unbearably close and small. Just like her chamber at Astley Castle, where she'd been trapped for so many months, confined to her bed. Lonely, desperately sad, and in pain.

Chapter 15

Annabelle slept fitfully, tossing and turning so often that her legs and arms twisted in the linen sheets, making her feel like a moth caught in a spider's web, fighting the inevitable. An hour before dawn, she gave into it and got out of bed. It was still dark outside, but the storm that had raged all night had spent its fury, washing the world outside her window so it glittered in the moonlight.

She stumbled toward her armoire, her leg still stiff from last night's exertions, and dug into its recesses for the ivory silk wrap that matched her nightgown. The set had been a gift from Aunt Sophia, who thought high-necked and matronly sleepwear was an abomination.

There was probably nothing so ill advised as a snifter of brandy at this hour of the morning, but that was precisely what Annabelle intended. She would creep down to the library, and with any luck, her aunt's Gran Riserva would still be there, bottle and glass waiting politely on a tray. She would pour herself a small measure, sit on the Grecian sofa, and try not to shy away from last night's revelations. Hopefully, it could be accomplished without tears. There was none left in her to shed. Ironically, there was no doubt that her mother had loved her. She'd practically smothered her with love until Annabelle had no longer been sure where her mother ended and she began. After Gareth's death, she'd perhaps been the only reason why Charlotte Layton hadn't died from her grief outright. Her daughter's terrible injuries had motivated her to rise from her bed and return to some semblance of living.

In turn, Annabelle had tried to protect her parents from the instability that grief revealed in each of them, and in the end it meant she allowed not only her injuries but also other people to define her. She'd hidden within the confines of Astley Castle, only to learn tonight that her mother had schemed to keep her from ever really living at all.

She was the only person who could live her own life, and she could not excuse her culpability in all that had happened. She'd been young at that defining moment, but as she'd grown and matured, what had she done to change the course of things? Little. Perhaps nothing. Instead, she'd stopped pushing beyond the castle to seek a wider world, blaming her scars for setting her apart. She'd spent years hurt by Alec's departure, never truly questioning the story she'd been told.

All this while, he'd been honoring a vow made to a delusional woman, because he was not a man to go back on his word. He had not forgotten her.

Annabelle crept into the library, which was dark with shadow, lit only by the moonlight through its windows and the feeble glow of the candle she carried. The fire in the grate had long since burned itself out, and the room had a coolness that was startling. She pulled the door shut behind her, moving slowly, and almost screamed aloud when she realized that she was not alone. She could hear someone's breathing, slow and steady.

Eyes darting around the library in panic, she saw a man's jacket draped carefully over one of the armchairs that bracketed the fireplace. Was he behind the sofa? Could she make it to the fireplace in time and grab the poker to protect herself? Her heart was racing.

But then her eyes returned to the jacket. It was strangely familiar, and she was suddenly struck by an impossible notion. Unable to stop herself, she crept to the sofa and peered over its edge.

Alec Carstairs. Fast asleep.

His handsome face was angled toward the fireplace. He'd unbuttoned his shirt, and her eyes traveled the length of his neck, down over his collarbone, and lower still, past smooth skin gleaming in the candlelight, to where the ends of his shirt tucked into his pants. It was suddenly hard to breathe.

He looked younger in his sleep, more carefree, and heartbreakingly similar to the young man she'd once adored. She wanted to feather her fingers over the long sweep of his lashes, reveling in their softness. She wanted to run her hands all over him, actually, but so much had happened between them. She knew Alec desired her, but could she have a place in his life, in his heart? Was it was too late to find out?

As if reading her thoughts, Alec opened his eyes and looked straight into her own. "Have you decided?" he asked warily. Startled, she almost dropped her candle on his shirt.

"Decided what?"

"How you're going to kill me? Will it be a fireplace poker through the heart, or will you burn me to death with your candle?"

How mortifying. A hot puddle of wax had fallen between the flaps of his shirt and on to his bare chest. She straightened and moved around the sofa. "How long have you been awake?"

"Since the moment you walked into the room. I became a very light sleeper when I went away to the war."

She settled into one of the chairs beside him, knowing she would never recover from the embarrassment of this. Had he seen her eyeing him up and down, like one of Cook's petit fours? "How did you know it was me?" she asked with a calmness she did not feel.

"The smell of lilacs. Even without it, though, I'd still have known it was you." He sat up, making a brief attempt to straighten his hair. He seemed to have forgotten that his shirt was half off. She watched in fascination as the muscles of his chest flexed with each movement of his hands.

"Why is that?"

"I am strangely attuned to you, Annabelle. I can sense when you are about."

Oh my. That was rather flattering. "I didn't know you were here. I came to borrow a book." That was plausible. "Actually … that's a lie. I wanted a snifter of brandy. I couldn't sleep."

He tilted his head, a smile playing on his lips. "A midnight drinker. I would never have guessed."

"It is well past midnight," she replied needlessly, as she watched him walk over to the side table where Canby had left the libations. He poured a generous glass for her, placing it into her hands before returning to the couch.

"I'm sorry I startled you," he said. "I thought you would scream and bring the house down upon our heads, but you kept yourself together. You always were a brave girl."

She smiled at the compliment, and took a small sip of the Gran Riserva. It was very smooth and faintly sweet, filling her mouth with a pleasant, tingling warmth.

No wonder Aunt Sophia liked it so much.

"I am sorry to still be here," he continued. "I arrived on a mews horse, and it didn't seem fair to wake a stable boy in the middle of the storm. I'm embarrassed to say I drifted off while waiting for it to ease."

"I am sorry not to have known you were here. I could have readied one of the guest bedrooms for you. Mary would have helped me."

His eyes widened at that. "Mary Stevens, your maid from Astley Castle?"

"Aunt Sophia tracked her through an agency and asked her to come work with me."

"I'm happy, then. She was always a good friend to you."

Annabelle set aside her brandy, leaning forward to clasp one of his hands in her own. She did not let it go. "So were you, Alec. I am sorry I didn't believe it for so long."

The room became quiet then, as he watched her steadily, unblinking. He cleared his throat, and when he spoke, his voice seemed deeper. "I am sorry I didn't know you had written. In the letter I left behind, I promised I would come back if you needed me."

"According to Mary, my mother found your letter and destroyed it. No doubt the same thing happened to those I wrote." She was still shocked by that revelation.

"I should have realized your mother was not herself. I should have come back the following morning."

"You would have gotten that poker in your chest if you attempted it. She hated you until the day she died." Annabelle slowly disengaged their hands. "Alec, if I promise not to blame you for things you didn't do, and if I ask very nicely, will you tell me something?"

He smiled, but there was a tension to him. "I suppose it depends on the question."

"Why did the three of you race that day?"

His turned away from her, as if collecting his thoughts. It was obvious he didn't want to answer. "Nobody considered what might happen," he said at last.

"I remember coming downstairs and finding you and Gareth and Mr. Digby in Father's study. You were very angry. I'd never seen you so look so fearsome."

He was watching her carefully now, his expression guarded.

"You said something about the stakes of the race being obscene. What had he risked, to be so desperate?"

"Annabelle, please understand," he replied hesitantly. "I would tell you if I was free to do so, but it would dishonor your brother's memory."

"He is no longer alive to be embarrassed by it. It can't have been so very bad."

"Please. Ask me anything else, and I'll answer. I will be as truthful as I can be."

She felt a surge of disappointment and then anger. What harm could it do to tell her? Why did people always think she must to be protected from the truth? Still, she must learn to trust Alec again. He believed he was honor-bound to keep her brother's secrets. She'd just have to think of a clever way to find them out. And he'd said he would tell her anything else.

Anything.

She took another sip of brandy to calm her nerves. "I have a question, then. And you must be truthful. You've promised it."

"God help me," he replied, though he seemed relieved she would not press him further about the race, at least for now. "Do your worst, then."

"In the carriage the other night," she began, only to realize this was harder to ask a second time, when so many emotions were invested in his answer. "Why did you kiss me?"

His eyes seemed to spark in the candlelight as he tilted his head to one side. He did a slow perusal of her attire, as if noticing for the first time that she was wearing a nightgown and little else. "I kissed you because I could not stop myself," he whispered. "Because I couldn't sit beside you any longer and not touch you." He used one hand to slowly caress her cheek, and then trailed it down her neck to finger a curl of hair that had fallen over the top of one breast. His eyes never left hers. "Because I have thought about kissing you, so often and in so many ways, that the sheer volume of instances would shock you."

Because she couldn't seem to stop herself either, she kissed him.

• • •

When Alec had opened his eyes to see her leaning over him, her unbound hair falling past her shoulder like a gold curtain in the candlelight, it had been all he could do not to pull her against him. Because he'd known then and there. He'd seen it in her eyes, tender and trusting. She believed him.

But he had not expected her kiss, and he was utterly bewitched by the feel of her lips. She tasted faintly of brandy, intoxicating and sweet, as she teased his tongue with her own. Slowly, she brought her hands up, placing them on either side of his head, so she could pull him closer, and he moaned with longing when she edged her mouth from his, tracing soft kisses along his jawline and neck in a tentative exploration, flicking her tongue at the base of his throat.

He moved his hands toward her shoulders to steady himself, only to find that while one hand touched gossamer fabric, the other fell upon bare skin, soft and warm. Her wrap had fallen partly away. A gentleman would pull it closed or avert his eyes, but God in Heaven, that was beyond him. Instead, he pulled back and took in the sight of her, the smooth expanse of her skin, her tousled hair and wet lips. Those incredible eyes watching him.

She slowly stood up and stepped away, but she made no move to leave. It would have broken his heart if she had. Instead, eyes wide, she eased the wrap from both shoulders, letting it fall to the ground, stealing his breath. In the moonlight, she was a goddess. The gown she wore was a filmy thing, a wisp of satin and lace held up by thin straps. It curved smoothly over her high breasts and her waist, caressing her long legs and skimming the tops of her bare feet.

"You are impossibly beautiful, Annabelle," he said quietly. "And that is no debutante's nightgown."

"It was a gift from Aunt Sophia."

"I should have guessed." He hardly recognized his own voice, low and tight with desire. "You can't possibly know what you're doing to me."

"I know one thing," she answered softly. "I want you to touch me again."

She couldn't understand what she was asking. But Alec could no more stop himself than he could stop the sunrise. He pulled her body against his, breathless with wanting, and claimed her mouth beneath his own. She melted into him, her hands reaching around his waist, fingers and palms splayed against his back. Through the fine linen of his shirt, he could feel her breasts push against his chest, loose and unbound, and she moved her hips instinctively against his. Unthinking, he rubbed his hands down her back, running them over the curve of her buttocks and pulling her closer still.

He heard her sharp intake of breath and knew she could feel his arousal. He should loosen his hold, but he'd never felt anything so exquisite. He was almost delirious from the pleasure of it. And then he felt her hands at the small of his back, pulling at the fabric there. With a shudder, he leaned back as she reached up to unbutton his shirt. "I just want to touch you," she said. "Please, don't pull away."

"I couldn't move if a carriage was hurtling toward me."

She glanced at him from beneath her lashes, smiling as if she were just beginning to understand her power over him, and then pulled his shirt from his shoulders, exposing his bare chest to her gaze. She ran her fingers over it, flicking away the wax that had settled, seemingly absorbed in every curve and indentation of muscle. When she found his scars from the war—two larger ones from Badajoz, another from Sabugal, and a network of smaller ridges—she leaned down, kissing each one.

"I worried about you when you were gone," she murmured. Still, she didn't stop, continuing to caress him, smoothing across the swell of his chest. When she ran her thumbs over each nipple, he groaned, reaching up to clasp her hands.

"Annabelle, I am no saint." His breathing was harsh now. "Much more of this, and I don't know if I'll be able to control my responses."

"But I don't want you to control anything."

God above. He felt as if all the blood in his body rushed to his groin, to the hard throbbing there, insistent and urgent. This was impossible. He had no right to her, but neither could he turn away. Just a bit more, for a little while longer. Letting go of her hands, he reached up and gently tugged on the straps of her gown, pulling them over her shoulders until her breasts, creamy white and rose-tipped, were exposed in the moonlight. Then he could no longer think at all, only act.

He dipped his head down and took one breast into his mouth, licking her gently, moaning when her nipple puckered in response. He moved his tongue along the valley between her breasts, and trailed it up to the other one, suckling at it, entranced by the shape and weight of it in his hand. She cried out softly, and just as he worried he had hurt her, she grasped his head with her hands, pulling him closer.

"Alec," she whimpered. "I've never felt anything ..."

So often he'd dreamed of seeing her like this, of feeling her like this. He continued to trail his mouth down her body, falling to his knees so he could kiss along the flat of her belly through the fabric of her gown. He was dazed with need. There was nothing between that fabric and her skin. No underclothes to mask the curve of her body. Just one pull, and all of that beautiful skin was his to touch and taste. The heat of her, so close, just beyond the reach of his lips.

Her breath was coming in short, quick pants above him. And her gown was the only barrier, the only thing stopping him from settling his head between her thighs and taking her with his tongue. Somehow, through the haze of his desire, he knew it was also the last thing saving her from utter ruin.

So he used his hands. He laid his head against her, and bracing her with one arm, he brought a hand to the apex of her thighs, caressing the folds there, using the pressure of one long finger and the soft satin of her gown to rub against the nub between them. Back and forth, in rhythm with the pounding of his heart, until his finger and the fabric were slick with moisture.

When he tucked his finger into the heart of her, tight and warm through the fabric of her gown, she writhed above him, and he imagined spreading her legs, pushing all the way into her, filling her body with the length of him. He was nearly consumed with his need.

But she was so close, and even more than he wanted his own pleasure, he wanted her to come to completion at his hands. His finger moved back to her folds, first one and then two, back and forth, varying in pressure. She was increasingly desperate, arching her hips against his hand. Looking up, he could see her breasts moving with her body, the satin of her gown framing them from below. Her eyes were closed, her face flushed with desire.

Suddenly, she cried out his name, and he could not stop himself from cupping her mound with his mouth, sucking at the wet fabric there, breathing in the heady scent of her. He was desperate to put his tongue inside of her, but it would be too much for him. He'd already gone too far, and was so close himself.

Hands shaking, he lifted her wrap from the floor, and stood up, slowly pulling it over her shoulders. She was watching him with a wonderstruck expression, eyes soft as he gathered her in his arms and held her tight. His heart was pounding so painfully that he worried it would bruise her. If he didn't put more distance between them, he would disgrace himself. So he set her apart from him and fell back upon the couch, breathing heavily, head in his hands so that he could not see the temptation before him.

"Alec, I never knew such a thing could happen."

He kept his gaze fixed firmly on the floor.

"Please look at me," she whispered.

"Annabelle, sweetheart. If I look at you, I'll tear those scraps of clothing off your body and deflower you right here in your aunt's library."

She was silent for a moment, as if considering something. "I rather like the sound of that."

He gave a short, pained laugh, even though he was in agony. "I don't suppose you could sprout a facial wart? Or take on a sudden and marked resemblance to the Prince of Wales? It would make things easier."

"I don't believe so."

"Perhaps we could discuss crop rotation, or algebraic equations, or even lunar cycles."

She laughed. "Well, the sun is just coming up, so that last topic is no longer appropriate."

He looked up, horrified to see its first rays peering through the windows. Hell and damnation. "Annabelle, you have to leave right this moment." He risked a glance at her, his heart constricting at the sight, filling with emotion. She was the most glorious thing he'd ever seen.

"You're probably right," she smiled mischievously. "Even Aunt Sophia might be shocked."

"Quick. Out you go. I'm not yet in a condition to be seen by anyone, and that won't change as long as you are close by."

She looked down at his body, to his arousal. "You will have to show me what that's all about, you know."

"God, Annabelle. Have pity!" he said through clenched teeth.

"Very well, then. But there is one more thing I must tell you."

"What is that?" he asked, keeping his eyes averted.

"That was the most marvelous thing. If I'd known you could do that, I might never have been angry with you." Then she slipped from the room.

Leaving him to the dark realization that he was completely besotted.

Chapter 16

"I'm glad to know you are mortal, after all," Benjamin said as he watched Alec toss back another glass of port. "Something has caused you to abandon your rectitude, and I must applaud it."

"Not something," he said distractedly. "Someone."

He'd slipped quietly from Sophia Middleton's home, walking back to his lodgings on St. James Street in an effort to clear his head. A futile exercise, as it turned out. After changing from last evening's attire and cleaning himself up, he had ridden over to ask Benjamin for advice. Marworth, however, was far more interested in being obnoxious.

"Someone, you say? That's even better." Sipping his own glass of port, Benjamin was still dressed in a brocade morning robe and pajamas. It was barely noon, after all, and he wasn't known to be an early riser. They sat in the privacy of his study, a dark, wood-paneled room choked with ephemera from his extensive travels. Not for the first time, he wondered how any substantive work could be done there.

"I'm going to use my deductive powers, and assume that Annabelle Layton is the root cause of your distress. How did your conversation with her go?"

"I believe we have resolved our differences," Alec said evasively.

"Are you blushing? I hesitate to say so, because it is an unmanly thing, but the proof of it is right there, spreading across your cheeks."

"Benjamin, please!" he interrupted. "I have a difficult situation to resolve, and I don't have the slightest clue about how to proceed."

"And that situation is?"

"Jane Fitzsimmons. I believe her father expects me to ask for her hand."

"Surely, it has not become as serious as that," Marworth said, no longer amused.

"Well, I had resolved to court her—"

"Why didn't you speak to me first? I have seen the bets, of course, in the books at White's. Odds are running three to one you'll make a match of it, but I have placed quite a large wager on the opposite outcome, because it's a preposterous notion."

"Why preposterous?" Alec asked, momentarily taken aback.

"Well, for one, you are not attracted to her."

"Miss Fitzsimmons is a lovely woman."

"I'm the last person who would contradict that."

"And she is intelligent, as well. I value her common sense. She's very knowledgeable about the workings of Parliament."

"Then hire her as your personal secretary. Don't make her your wife."

"That's going too far, Benjamin. We are discussing a lady."

"I am well aware of that."

"Then what are you trying to say?"

"You are too much alike, too serious. Were you to marry, you'd never raise your voices to each other. You'd never have passionate disputes of opinion. And your bed would be as cold and impersonal as your relationship. You need a counterpoint, a spark. I think we both know you've found that in someone else."

"I take it you're referring to Miss Layton?"

Moments ticked by without a response.

"I suppose there's no need to answer that," Alec said, dropping his head into his hands. "But therein lies my problem. The vote on the soldiers' bill is just days away, and that means I will be spending even more time in the company of Jane and her father."

"Go on."

"That will lead to even more speculation about a relationship between us."

"And you worry if you claim a change of heart, Fitzsimmons will think you've been toying with his daughter."

"Perhaps."

"And he will withdraw his support of your bill."

"I hope not, but it is a possibility I can't ignore."

"Are Miss Fitzsimmons's feelings involved?"

Alec stared into his empty port glass. "I can't answer that. Certainly, she has been all that is pleasant during our conversations together."

"Lord above, Alec. One is pleasant to the barest acquaintance, until given a reason not to be so. That tells me nothing."

"I think she believes a marriage between us would be mutually beneficial."

"She's a starry-eyed romantic, then. I'm shocked."

"It is the way of most marriages, as you very well know," Alec said.

"True, but it doesn't have to be that way. You deserve the chance to find out."

"This isn't a time to be thinking about myself."

"You do know that it's acceptable to consider your own wants and needs on occasion?"

"You are not helping, Benjamin."

"If it were me, I'd wait until the bill was passed before announcing my intention to court another woman."

"But that is disingenuous."

"I prefer to think of it as hedging one's bets. And we all know that Lord Fitzsimmons is a gambling man. He'll understand."

"I can't do that," Alec sighed. "I'm meeting with my steward this afternoon, and the Hertford ball is being held this evening. It will have to be done tomorrow, but only God knows what I will say."

"For once, leave your head, with all of its notions and responsibilities, out of it," Marworth said. "Just speak from your heart."

Alec gave a grim laugh. "Who's the starry-eyed romantic now?"

• • •

"I did not think I would live to see it," Aunt Sophia said as Annabelle entered the breakfast room at Marchmain House. "You have slept past noon—and since I am not given to fits of paranoia, which would have me wondering if you are alarmingly ill—I see this as a very encouraging development. I'm having a positive influence on you."

"Of course you are. That and the fact that I am overtired," Annabelle replied as she took a seat at the Georgian satinwood morning table. Canby appeared with a small pot of tea and a plate of sweet rolls with creamed butter. She poured herself a cup of the freshly steeped blend, swirling in a small spoonful of sugar, and glanced with contentment at her surroundings. She wasn't used to seeing the sun shining so brightly in this room. Normally, she slipped in here after dawn, when the light was more muted and tinged with pink. At this hour, though, it made the room sparkle, its rays bouncing off of the silver tea service on the sideboard.

Everything seemed to sparkle this morning.

"I hope I'm not interrupting your meal, Aunt Sophia."

"Don't be silly, my dear. This is when the civilized world breaks its fast. So you did not sleep well?"

"No, I found myself wandering the halls just before dawn."

"Did that wandering have anything to do with the Earl of Dorset?" her aunt asked between bites of a buttered crumpet.

Annabelle nearly dropped her teacup. Did Aunt Sophia know that Alec had slept in the library last night? Could she possibly know what happened between them? "Why would you say that?" she asked, trying for nonchalance.

"I know you were upset by his presence here last evening. Did the two of you argue when I left the library?"

She felt a rush of relief. "No, we did not argue. Well, at first we did, because I wouldn't believe him." She proceeded to tell

Aunt Sophia what had happened. Well, not all of it, of course, but rather the pertinent details about Mother, and Alec's vow, and her own disillusionment.

"Oh, Annabelle, I wish I'd known. I've said before that it is pointless to regret past actions, but I do. Most sincerely in this instance. I should have made inquiries from abroad once I received that last, nonsensical letter from Charlotte."

"You would only have learned what Mother wanted you to know, Aunt Sophia, and you have nothing to be sorry for. In these past few months, you've taught me to live my life again. Father, too. His letters continue to improve, don't you think? He will be here soon, which is a miracle all by itself. And I'm just so happy to know that Alec did not abandon me. We can be friends again." She couldn't seem to stop babbling.

"Is that what you want?" her aunt asked, with not a little suspicion. "To be friends with Lord Dorset ... and nothing more?"

She was saved from answering by Canby's return. He was carrying the most beautiful arrangement—a mix of pink hydrangeas, French lilacs, and glossy white peonies with starburst centers—and her heart leapt in her chest.

One early summer day when Annabelle was twelve years old, she, Alec, and Gareth had been racing horses through the forests at the edge of Arbury Hall. She was winning the race, although there was every chance that the boys—really, they were men by then—were allowing her an unfair advantage.

Near the end of the course, she'd found herself in a sunlit field full of flowers. They were everywhere, an untamed riot spreading all the way to the horizon in bold slashes of color. She'd been by them any number of times, but on that day, she drew her horse up short, and watched as they swayed in the morning breeze. Alec noticed her unusual behavior, and teased her that admiring flowers was the start of bad things indeed. "Next, you will be oohing and ahhing over silks and satins and darling little hats, and you will expect men to spout poetry to you. There will be no more horse racing then."

She'd stuck her tongue out at him in response. "I don't have the slightest idea what you mean." But she'd wondered if he were right, if it marked the beginning of something strange and wonderful.

He'd smiled down at her, because his horse was easily a hand higher than her own. "It means that you are growing up, bit by bit. Someday, you will be a beautiful woman, and lovesick men will want to give you flowers."

He'd leapt off of his horse to wander in the fields, snapping off an assortment of blossoms at their stems, before returning to give her an elaborate bow. "Let me be the first to offer a tribute to your beauty, my lady."

She could still remember the rush of pleasure as she looked first into his smiling, handsome face, and then down at his makeshift bouquet—a mix of pink hydrangeas, French lilacs, and glossy white peonies with starburst centers.

"Annabelle … Annabelle! Come out of the clouds and back to the breakfast room, if you please. Who are the flowers from?"

"I'm sorry," she replied, embarrassed again. "I was caught up in a memory."

Canby set the arrangement on the breakfast table and turned to offer Annabelle the accompanying card, which was engraved with the Carstairs family crest. Heart fluttering, she turned it over. There was a short note, written in Alec's familiar hand, saying that he would think of her all day before he saw her this evening at the Hertford ball. He had signed it simply, just his first name. Like an infatuated schoolgirl, she clutched the note close to her heart before she could stop herself. "Alec Carstairs sent the flowers." She felt exhilarated, as if the world was full of promise, and no dream was too foolish.

"Well, that answers my question," Aunt Sophia said. "Not just friends, then."

Chapter 17

Hertford House dominated Manchester Square with an enormous stone facade five bays wide and three stories high. Its front entrance, centered beneath a large Venetian window and balcony, was flanked by high Romanesque marble columns, and the entire property was set in an elaborate garden, protected from the street by tall iron gates. So many carriages clogged the road leading to the mansion that it took more than an hour just to move around Manchester Square.

The annual Hertford ball was the biggest fete of the Season, and Isabella Seymour-Conway, the marchioness, was one of society's most influential hostesses. According to Aunt Sophia, she was also an especially close friend of the prince regent—the kissing kind—which explained why she'd just returned from an extended stay in rural Ireland. Supposedly, it was a common punishment for wives who courted scandal.

Annabelle could not judge her. She'd learned that passion could seduce you, hold you in its sway, and make you do shocking things. When she thought of the intimacies she'd shared with Alec and of her own uninhibited responses, her entire body flushed with warmth. Not that she regretted anything they had done. Something so wonderful could never be wrong. Unless, of course, her heart was crushed in the end.

When they reached the front door at last, she and Aunt Sophia were helped from their carriage and ushered into the home's front hallway by a phalanx of footmen, each dressed in the distinctive silver and blue Hertford livery. It was less a hall, though, than a cavernous, two-story room dominated by a broad double staircase. A long line of the ton's elite snaked up the steps, which led into the ballroom above, where an orchestra was at play. Annabelle recognized a few faces, smiling when she did. For the most part, though, she waited nervously for her turn at the top of the stairs, when she and Aunt Sophia would be announced to the assembled guests.

Was Alec already here? This ball might be a spectacle of sights and sounds, but he was the only person she wanted to see.

When the Hertford's butler announced their arrival, it seemed as if every set of eyes—lorgnettes and quizzing glasses, too— swerved toward them as the din in the room quieted to a murmur. She took a deep breath as she and Aunt Sophia stepped down into the elaborate ballroom, lit with hundreds of candles, and shining with satins and silks.

· · ·

"Miss Layton, will you honor me with the quadrille this evening?" Viscount Petersham called out, barely visible in the crowd that collected as she and Aunt Sophia finished their introductions in the receiving line. Annabelle felt as if she were being swallowed whole. Were balls always such a crush of people? "Make way," Petersham called out again, nudging aside a young gentleman whom she'd met on Rotten Row last week, as well as several matrons with their sons. When she saw what he was wearing, her mouth nearly dropped open in surprise.

Dressed in shades of gold, from his heavily embroidered cutaway coat right down to the bell-shaped buckles on his jeweled evening shoes, he simply glowed, like the mythical King Midas. The brown tones he wore exclusively were nowhere in sight.

"Lord Petersham," marveled Aunt Sophia, clearly impressed. "If we were not at war with the French, I would compare you favorably with the brilliance of Versailles."

"You're too kind, Lady Marchmain," he said as he stopped in front of them. "These sartorial flourishes come easily when the exquisite Miss Layton is your inspiration."

Had she missed something? So many people were around her that Annabelle found it difficult to concentrate. "I wanted to pay tribute to your spectacular eyes, Miss Layton," he continued, "but I couldn't decide between the purest cerulean and the sparkling hues of a sapphire. How lucky that your golden tresses, in all of their glory, offered me the perfect palette. I hope you are pleased."

For a moment, Annabelle was speechless.

"I am ... touched, Lord Petersham. Indeed, I don't quite know what to say. You've gone to a great deal of trouble."

"I do nothing by half measure, my dear. If I may pencil my name onto your dance card, I shall look forward to telling you all about my new barouche, which is also gold. Its lovely sky-blue trimmings are particularly dashing. There's nothing else like it in all of London."

"I don't doubt it, Petersham," Lord Marworth said as he pushed forward and offered an elegant bow. "Lady Marchmain, how lovely you are this evening. Miss Layton, may I also ask you to honor me with a dance?"

"I'm flattered," Annabelle said, smiling as she extended her card, which dangled from her gloved wrist by a silken ribbon. Before either gentleman could sign it, however, a gruff, much older man maneuvered a path through the crowd. "Don't let them waste your time, Miss Layton," he called out. "Neither of these dandies knows how to please a woman."

Lord Petersham drew back in affront.

Annabelle was certain that she'd never met the man. He was slight of stature, with a bald head and a nose that was hooked like a talon. Surprised as she was by his indelicate comment, however, she was even more shocked when he turned to Aunt Sophia with a lascivious grin. "Too bad you are past the age for childbearing, missy. I would snap you up instead of going after the young one. I'd wager you know what to do with a man behind closed doors."

Several in the crowd stiffened with indignation, but Aunt Sophia merely smiled. "Lord Higgins, you made a similar proposal thirty years ago. If I recall, I said I would snap something off."

The old lord raised his nose a notch and turned toward Annabelle. "Miss Layton, we have not been introduced, but if you'd do me the great honor of becoming my wife, you'd save me a lot of trouble, and we could get on to the baby making."

Were she not so horrified by the prospect, she would have laughed out loud at his audacity. Had she stumbled into the center of a circus? "My lord, you don't even know me!"

"I don't need to, my dear," he replied with a leering smile. "You are beautiful and well placed, and that's all you need to be."

"You, sir, are an outrage!" Petersham gasped, as several gentlemen closed around Lord Higgins, bent on removing him from the ballroom. Luckily, the first strains of a Scottish reel started up, and Lord Marworth seized the opportunity to lead Annabelle onto the dance floor with an amused grin.

· · ·

Alec was trying to concentrate on what Lord Fitzsimmons was saying. He was. But when Annabelle had arrived, descending into the ballroom like a princess, her eyes sparkling, every sensible thought raced from his head. She was dressed in a white silk gown overlaid with embroidered tulle, the pattern a delicate tracery of flowers on trailing vines. Its short, puffed sleeves and sloping neckline highlighted the sweep of her shoulders, while the fitted bodice drew his eyes toward her breasts, then down to her waist and the sensuous curve of her hips. A flurry of excited whispers had followed her into the ballroom, and the men who'd tracked her so relentlessly these past weeks watched her too, eyes covetous as they swept her from head to toe.

He wondered how long it would take him to poke their eyes out.

Lord Fitzsimmons was still talking—as he had since their arrival—but his words droned meaninglessly, because Annabelle was dancing with Benjamin, smiling at him when Alec wanted all of her smiles for himself. As she spun about the room, he remembered how she'd looked this morning, her silk nightgown falling from her body, her lips swollen and wet. Desire flooded through him, but that wasn't the whole of it. There was something else too, something far deeper.

The realization nearly knocked the breath from his lungs.

He wanted all of her, as much as she could give for the whole of his life and beyond. He wanted her sighs and her laughter. Even though he didn't deserve her. Even though there was every chance that she'd merely been satisfying her curiosity last night. He'd promised to show her around the ton, to introduce her to eligible men. It was the right thing to do. She should have the opportunity to find out what sort of man she wanted. But for the first time in a long while, he didn't care about what was right or wrong or expected.

At long last, the dance was done, and as Benjamin bowed to Annabelle, Alec found the opportunity he'd been waiting for. He excused himself from his conversation with Jane and her father, moving toward the couple as they left the dance floor. When Annabelle saw him, she grinned.

All the candles in the room could not match the incandescence of that smile.

• • •

Was he thinking about what had happened last night? Was that why his eyes seemed to shine so brightly, and his gaze felt like an embrace? Alec was walking straight toward her, as if she were the only person in the ballroom.

Had he guessed it, then? Was her heart in her eyes, laid bare to the whole world? She was nervous, excited, and awkward all at once. In a heartbeat, he was beside her, giving a quick nod to Lord Marworth before turning with a look that made her legs feel like buckling beneath her.

"Miss Layton," he said, his voice warm and rich, his eyes dancing. "I confess I've been thinking of you since the early morning hours."

"You're not the only one, Dorset." Lord Marworth chuckled beside her. "Have you seen Petersham's get-up? The color is an homage to our lovely Miss Layton."

"The man is an offense to good taste," Alec said. "Annabelle wouldn't be swayed by such a ridiculous gesture." He turned back to her. "How was your day?" he asked gently. "Did you like the flowers? I remembered they are your favorite. I gave very specific instructions."

"They are beautiful."

"I warned you that lovesick men would send you tributes when you grew up."

"Is that what you are?" she asked, lowering her eyes to the intricate folds of his cravat, wishing that they were back in the library, alone, so that she could remove it from his neck, and kiss the pulse point at the base of his throat.

Marworth cleared his throat, as if to recall her attention. "I sense that my presence here is redundant," he said with a wry smile. "Ah! There is Miss Fitzsimmons, watching us all rather carefully. Perhaps I'll ask her to dance, to see if I chase her frown away. It will be a difficult task, but that's the fun of any challenge."

He kissed her gloved hand, and then with a scandalous wink, he wandered away. When Alec's eyes flared, Annabelle was torn between jealousy and a question she couldn't help but ask. "Do you mind?"

"That he just winked at you? Of course I mind."

"No. Do you mind that he is asking Jane to dance?" She hated the insecurity she could hear in her voice. "I know you care for her."

He grew serious then. "I do care about Miss Fitzsimmons, because she is a good woman, but my feelings for her are nothing like my feelings for you. Surely you know that?"

Looking into his eyes, she couldn't miss the sincerity there, or mistake the emotion. Joy swept through her, the force of it so strong that she wouldn't have been surprised to find that her feet were no longer touching the ground. It was only briefly dimmed by the sight of Aunt Sophia approaching with a horde of gentlemen in tow.

"They're like locusts," Alec muttered. "Quickly. Hand me your card before they claim every dance. I want all three of the waltzes."

"You know we can't dance more than two of them," she said with an impish smile. "Even I know that. People will be scandalized. Think of your reputation."

"Let them have their scandal," he said with a wink of his own. "The waltzes are mine."

• • •

Damien Digby moved through the Hertford Ball, focused on his revenge so long in the making. He had less than a month here in London, and it had taken every bit of his guile to negotiate that much leave. His regiment, the 10th Hussars, would have a new commander in place by the time he returned, and by all accounts, the man was a sober sort, distressingly disinclined to gambling, whoring, and drink—all the things, in fact, that made the barracks in Brighton tolerable.

Which meant that he had very little time to orchestrate the downfall of Alec Carstairs, the Earl of Dorset.

His life had taken a decidedly nasty turn since his last encounter with Dorset. The man had interfered with that highly lucrative Layton deal, and the result had been Gareth Layton's inconvenient death, not to mention his delectable sister's maiming.

Damien had returned to London to find his memberships at Brooks and Boodles rescinded. His account had been closed at Tattersall's, and suddenly, up and down Bond Street at the best haberdashers, his patronage was no longer welcomed. The consequences, it seemed, of being blackballed by a peer of the realm.

A gambler needed easy access to the ton, and without it, his creditors had been increasingly insistent. Painfully insistent. After a particularly frightening encounter on Fleet Street—one that left him with an ugly scar that ran from his left cheek to his chin— Damien had decided his country was calling. Surely the Peninsula was preferable to back-alley beatings.

As it happened, neither was pleasant. But he'd bribed his way back to England, preying on the vices of his commanding officers until he was posted to Brighton, a plum assignment if ever there was one. His uniform with its gold braided coat never failed to attract women, who one and all were drawn to gaudy, shiny things, just like magpies. If this evening went as planned, he would celebrate by pumping between a long pair of shapely thighs.

But first things first.

He scanned the crowded room. Long rows of chairs were set up on either side of the ballroom, with clusters of potted palms arranged in various alcoves, ideal for those who wanted to indulge in a flirtation away from prying eyes. However, he was headed toward the gaming tables in the ballroom's antechamber.

If he were careful in a place like this, the winnings could be grand indeed, but he had only one target tonight: Lord Reginald Fitzsimmons, whose daughter Dorset was courting.

He'd tracked Fitzsimmons to Sharpe's last week, a notorious hell for hardened fans of cards and dice, where Damien studied his every move. What his eyes betrayed when the cards were dealt. If he flinched when a stronger hand was laid down. If he perspired when a hand turned against him. If he cheated. In the end, Fitzsimmons had been guilty of all save the last. The fool. Making a habit of the last was the only way to mitigate the first three.

How convenient that Dorset's future father-in-law was a gambling man.

He spied the older gentleman in a corner, deep into a game of Pontoon with four other men, an empty seat beside him. Short and paunchy, with a receding chin and a hairline to match. His face was flushed, a tall snifter of whiskey by his side, another empty glass beside it. And Damien knew what that meant. The man was losing, and badly.

He made his way across the room, smiling at strangers to create the illusion of being widely known, before sitting down at the table. The play was deep enough that the others merely nodded their greeting, but Fitzsimmons took note of his uniform and smiled.

Before long, his smile vanished. One by one, the other players took their leave as Damien took control of the game and its winnings. Not Fitzsimmons, though. He played on as the stakes moved higher. Perspiring heavily, he downed another whiskey, and then another. His eyes took on that fevered look, the one that appeared when a man was gambling with money he did not have.

"My lord," Damien said after the final hand was played. "I believe the total owed is 3,000 pounds."

Fitzsimmons took another swig of whiskey. "Well, lad," he said, obviously trying not to panic. "I hope you will give me a few days to collect the funds. I do not, of course, carry that kind of money with me, but I'm good for it."

"I don't doubt it, Lord Fitzsimmons. I apologize for not introducing myself earlier. I am Corporal Damien Digby, of the 10th Royal Hussars, the prince's own."

"Have we met before?" Fitzsimmons asked, surprised to be called by name.

"I've not had that honor, my lord, but your reputation as a strong voice for our troops precedes you. May I speak for my fellow soldiers and offer our thanks?"

The old man brightened, puffed up by that bit of hyperbole. "I know the challenges you men face. I'm happy to make a difference in your lives."

Pompous ass. Weak men always touted their influence.

"I'm currently supporting the new soldiers' bill to make the return of lads like you more seamless. With the influence of its sponsor, Alec Carstairs, Earl of Dorset, we're certain to see it pass."

Damien pretended to rear back in surprise. "Carstairs, you say? Alec Carstairs, of Nuneaton?"

"I am glad you've heard of him, son. There's no better man in London."

"If he has your confidence, I shall say no more. No doubt he is much changed from the gentleman I knew years ago."

"What do you mean?"

"I hesitate to say it … but he was involved in a very unsavory incident the last time we met."

Fitzsimmons bristled visibly. "Are you doubting the honor of my future son-in-law?"

"Your future son-in-law? I didn't know of his relationship to your family, my lord!"

"It's all but settled. Dorset has been quite pronounced in his attentions to my Jane."

Damien couldn't have asked for a better gambit. "Your daughter must be that stunning blonde. When I saw Dorset earlier, he couldn't take his eyes off her."

Annabelle Layton. God, she stirred his blood, just as she had when she was eighteen, ripe for the plucking. How had she recovered from those gruesome wounds? He'd figured her for a cripple long ago. All this time, Damien had thought Dorset swooped in to spoil the Layton wager because of some outraged sense of duty, some notion of protecting the innocent. What a bounder. They'd had the same game all along. They'd both wanted the girl.

Fitzsimmons shook his head, befuddled. "My daughter, lovely thing that she is, is a brunette. You must be mistaken."

"You have my sincere apologies, then. May I have the honor of being introduced to her? I should like to offer my felicitations."

"Come with me. You'll see firsthand how things are between Dorset and my Jane. Everyone knows him as the hero of Badajoz."

They walked into the ballroom, and while it took the bleary-eyed Fitzsimmons a moment to track his daughter, Damien found her immediately. She was standing in a far corner, looking like her heart was breaking as she watched a couple on the dance floor.

Annabelle Layton and Alec Carstairs. They were spinning to a waltz, their bodies touching, their eyes locked on each other. And there was something in the way they moved that hinted at forbidden intimacies and barely suppressed passions.

Fitzsimmons gasped with outrage. It was all Damien could do not to smile. "I am sorry, my lord," he said, the picture of contrition. "That is obviously not your daughter."

"But he told me they were childhood friends."

"Could it be?" Damien was all sympathy and surprise. "How did I not recognize her? She is Annabelle Layton, the sister of my close friend, Gareth, God rest his soul."

"He shouldn't be looking at her like that!"

"Dorset has wanted her for a very long time. There's no doubt he has been leading your daughter on. There was never any chance he would marry her, not with Miss Layton in his sights."

If it was possible for a man to turn purple, Fitzsimmons nearly accomplished it. "He has been using Jane to get to me, to secure my support for that bill. How did I not guess, especially when Badajoz was such a nasty business? I'll call the blackguard out!" He made a drunken move toward the couple, but Damien quickly reached out his hand to restrain the man.

"My lord, think of the scandal that would cause, the damage to your own reputation."

"But he must be made to pay, and pay dearly," Fitzsimmons spat. "I'm speaking for the man before the House of Lords in just a few days' time."

"Let me help you, then. Together, we can do more than simply discredit the earl. We can avenge your daughter."

Even though his rage and the whiskey had dulled him, Fitzsimmons's eyes were suspicious. "What do you have against Dorset? What is it that you're about?"

"Come back into the gaming room and join me for a drink," Damien said. "I'll tell you everything I know about Alec Carstairs."

Chapter 18

They'd done everything they could. Alec had made some difficult concessions, but the result, he felt certain, was a bill to attract both Tories and Whigs. Today, it would be introduced in the House of Lords. Debate would begin, and if they were lucky, a vote would take place tomorrow, moving the bill on to the House of Commons, where its passage was virtually assured.

He adjusted the formal robes he wore in Parliament and waited anxiously to make his way into the chamber. He could not help but think of his father, who had wanted Alec to make his mark here. The earl had wanted many things, but this would have to be enough. After tomorrow, he would leave his father's expectations behind and forge his own way. If she would have him, Annabelle would be by his side.

The bell rang, announcing the call to chambers. He crossed from the antechamber where he had been making his final preparations into the hall of the Lords. The other members were streaming through the tall oak doorways lining the imposing room, and he could see Lord Fitzsimmons already seated beside the podium at which they would speak. Alec smiled his greeting. It was not returned.

Fitzsimmons had been noticeably taciturn of late. Hostile, really. Since the night of the Hertford ball, just four days ago, they'd barely exchanged a handful of words. Alec had paid a call to Fitzsimmons House the day after the party, knowing he needed to speak about the change in his intentions. He'd been told the family was not at home to visitors. The same excuse had been given the next morning, and the morning after that.

He took his seat beside the podium, trying to quell a sudden fit of nerves. The members took their spots along the benches flanking either side, and a hush fell over the room. The clerk indicated that he should stand. Rising, Alec laid his notes down on the podium, looked about, and began.

He could hear the emotion in his own voice. He'd known hundreds of the men he spoke about personally, had watched their lives bleed out on the battlefields of Portugal and Spain. Outlining the most salient points of the bill, he called for increased wages to those who'd fought in more than one campaign, support at home for those who'd lost their ability to work, and pensions for the families left behind when soldiers lost their lives. When he finished, there was a chorus of huzzahs and several loud grunts of approval. There were also voices raised in dissent, but so far, they were polite. The House of Lords was not above a ruckus, and the fact that the members were still congenial was a positive sign. He took his seat. Lord Fitzsimmons rose and walked to the podium. At the last minute, the old lord turned toward him and smiled.

Alec knew then something was desperately wrong. The smile was gleeful in its malice. Fitzsimmons cleared his throat, and began. "Lord Dorset speaks eloquently about the soldiers' bill, and the legislation itself has my passionate support. It addresses concerns that deserve our attention." Alec breathed a sigh of relief. He was merely jittery, it seemed, and overly anxious.

"However," Lord Fitzsimmons continued, pausing to great effect, "I cannot vote in its favor so long as Lord Dorset remains as its sponsor. I've learned things in the past several days about his character that bring shame not only to this body, but also to the memory of his honorable father."

Alec had not misread that smile after all. What could Fitzsimmons be talking about?

"There are two issues in particular that need to be referenced. With the first, I shall remain vague, as it involves a lady, and I only mention this because it underscores the depths that Dorset seems willing to plumb."

Alec's head was spinning. He'd done nothing to shame Jane. They had never even held hands.

"I have it on good authority that when Lord Dorset's interest in a girl of a very tender age was denied by her older brother, Lord Dorset suggested a horse race. The race ended with the death of the brother, under suspicious circumstances not explained to this day."

There was a collective gasp in the chamber, but surely none sounded louder than Alec's own. Who could have so horribly misrepresented the truth?

Fitzsimmons was hardly done. "This next charge I do not make lightly. As most of you know, I'm privy to certain secrets about our defensive efforts abroad." Several of the lords nodded their assent. "Lord Carstairs has been called the hero of Badajoz, but I learned recently that nothing could be farther from reality."

Fitzsimmons was crucifying his character! Already, he could feel the censorious eyes of a number of men upon him.

"Following Badajoz, dispatches from the battlefield show that several wild, undisciplined men—soldiers of the lowest rank and morality—sneaked into the town itself, committing the worst sorts of depravity.

"You'll recall our efforts in that city defended the Spanish natives of Badajoz. But these vicious beasts raped helpless women and, in some cases, children. They killed defenseless men. Hundreds were slaughtered."

The lords shouted their outrage as bile rose in Alec's throat. There'd been a similar instance at the battle of Ciudad Rodrigo, when a few mongrels dishonored the whole of the army with their actions. Wellington had dealt with them summarily. They'd paid for their sins with their lives. But he had never heard any of this about Badajoz. "My lords, please," Fitzsimmons called out, waving his hands to calm the chamber. "Their behavior was appalling, but we must remember that brutish hordes always look to a man of authority to lead them. In this instance, they were led by none other than Alec Carstairs. Lord Dorset is not the hero of Badajoz. He is the butcher."

The room erupted with angry shouts as Alec leapt to his feet. "I deny these charges in the strongest possible terms, Lord Fitzsimmons. I demand to know the source of these lies!"

Fitzsimmons turned, his hand pointed accusingly. "You have been identified by a man who was there, an honorable soldier who watched in horror as you sneaked your band of men into Badajoz. Just back from the front lines, he has only now been able to come forward with his story. My lords, I present Corporal Damien Digby."

And out he came from a nearby doorway, a figure from the past with an elaborate mustache now, his left cheek neatly bisected by a long, thin scar. Dressed in the formal uniform of the 10th Royal Hussars, Digby gave every appearance of the loyal soldier, bowing to the lords at his left and his right as he approached the podium. "I know this man," Alec cried out. "He's a scoundrel."

Digby pretended he had not heard him. He merely raised his voice and said, "What Lord Fitzsimmons says is true. I was there to witness Lord Dorset's shocking misdeeds at Badajoz."

"If any of this happened," Alec insisted, "I was certainly no part of it. I learned of my father's death following that battle. I was sent home by Wellington to report on the victory at Whitehall."

"But not before the crimes took place," Digby scoffed. "Not before your grief turned to rage."

Alec lunged, knocking Digby from his feet, thrusting his forearm against the bastard's neck, pushing with all his might. Fury consumed him, and only from a distance could he hear the shouts of others as several members tried to pull him away. He struggled against them until he heard Marworth's voice above the fray. "Dorset, this is no way to fight slanderous charges."

God, he was brawling on the floor of the House of Lords! He stopped struggling, and the men slowly released their hold. Digby pulled away, loathing in his eyes. "You see the sort of violence he is capable of."

Alec turned to the assembled lords, breathing heavily. "I apologize for my behavior, but I swear not a thing he says is the truth."

Lord Fitzsimmons stepped forward then. "You are no gentleman, Dorset. I call for a vote of censure against you. You should be barred from this chamber. You do it no credit."

"Lord Dorset deserves the opportunity to clear his name," Marworth said. "He has the right to defend himself. Why should we believe a stranger when we all know that Dorset is an honorable man?"

"Because Corporal Digby was there," Fitzsimmons replied. "Because I am vouching for his honesty. I've served in this chamber for more than forty years, and I say to the lords who are gathered here, do not confuse Dorset with his father. On this day, the eighth Earl of Dorset would turn from his son in disgust."

How had everything spun so wildly out of control? How could Alec begin to defend his name, his honor? "I will voluntarily leave this chamber while I fight these accusations," Alec said, struggling to calm himself, to think clearly. "I will recuse myself from the soldiers' bill. But I beg you to consider it carefully, now that it stands with Lord Fitzsimmons as its sponsor." He straightened his clothing in a halfhearted effort to make himself more presentable, and strode out of the chamber.

• • •

Alec wandered aimlessly into the sunshine. When he'd taken off his House robes, he'd felt like he was divesting himself of the last shreds of his decency. He climbed into his carriage, his driver surprised to see him so soon. The debate had been expected to take hours. Instead, it had taken less than thirty minutes to destroy so much he'd worked for, and everything he'd tried to be. Before nightfall, the first whispers would be traded at ton dinner parties, and over cards and dice at London's clubs. It would be all over the papers tomorrow. What if he couldn't prove his innocence? After learning of his father's death in Badajoz, he'd gone alone to his tent. He'd written a letter to Annabelle, one of the many that had never been sent. But he'd spoken to no one. He'd not met with Wellington until the following day. He had no way to account for the hours in between.

What would happen to the legacy his father had so meticulously crafted? The Carstairs name had always commanded respect. Would it now be linked with savagery? Fitzsimmons was right about one thing. Today, his father would turn away from him in disgust. And, God, his mother! She would be devastated by the accusations against him. Only her unimpeachable reputation would shield her from the worst of the condemnation.

But not Annabelle. His father had insisted she was the sort to invite scandal. How ironic that his own son had proved to be the contagion. Alec felt as if his heart had cracked open, spilling out his hopes and dreams. All of his feelings for her ... they were suddenly irrelevant, because he could not bear it if an association with him harmed her in any way.

She couldn't be seen with him. Not now. And very likely not ever.

• • •

The letter came by way of a special messenger from Dorset House, and Annabelle smiled when she saw it was addressed to her in Alec's hand. His bill was being debated today, and surely the note carried good news.

Even though he'd spent the past several days caught up in last-minute negotiations, Alec had paid her a call each afternoon. The day after the Hertford ball, he'd stopped at Marchmain House, although he'd been annoyed to share her company with the half-dozen other gentlemen in attendance. As Aunt Sophia once said, there was something marvelously invigorating about jealousy.

Afterward, they had gone walking in Regent's Park, and as they'd strolled together, her arm nestled in his, Annabelle had felt a wave of longing for the years they had missed. When he'd kissed her surreptitiously in the corridors of Marchmain House, she'd felt a very different sort of longing.

Somehow, it was easy to speak with him about the loneliness she'd felt since Gareth's death, about her mother's tragic decline, and about her fears for her father. Alec shared the suffering that he'd seen during the war. He talked about his fears that he'd prove unworthy of his father's dreams, and about the burden they sometimes carried.

All the while, Annabelle wondered if he could tell that she'd fallen in love with him all over again.

She thanked the messenger, tucked the missive beneath her arm, and hurried through the house to her favorite garden. She ran to the marble bench beneath the ornamental tree in the corner, sat down in a puff of skirts, and separated the sealing wax from the letter. Opening it eagerly, she scanned its contents, only to be shocked and then horrified by what she read.

It was impossible anyone could believe Damien Digby, who was at best a coward. Alec was a gentleman. Not because of his title, but because of his character. Yet he'd asked her to stay away from him, as if he were a toxin or a disease that might be catching. He worried the ensuing scandal would engulf her.

If Alec thought she would stand idly by while a cretin from the past spread lies, he was mistaken. She'd dealt with ostracism before, and she knew how debilitating it could be to feel alone and unwanted. She would not let him suffer that alone. She would trumpet his innocence to anyone who'd listen.

Chapter 19

"You must have been shocked by the revelations, Miss Layton!" Lady Fairbanks exclaimed, fanning herself so vigorously that the plum-colored feathers adorning her turban threatened to dislodge themselves. "At that lovely picnic on the heath, he was so handsome and distinguished. To think we dined with a murderer in our midst!"

"Lady Fairbanks, surely you can't believe Lord Dorset is guilty of these charges," Annabelle said, defending Alec for what was surely the tenth time in as many minutes. From the moment they'd arrived at the Danforth musicale, she and Aunt Sophia had been surrounded. Everyone knew the Carstairs family was helping to sponsor her this season, which meant they were at the center of the greatest scandal in a generation.

"But Miss Layton, Lord Fitzsimmons himself stands as the accuser!" Miss Traemore cried. "And it is all over the papers. *The Times* is calling it 'The Great Unmasking.' To think he fooled us all."

"Lord Fitzsimmons is mistaken," she replied, trying to remain calm. If she gave into her frustration, she would start slapping people, and that wouldn't sway anyone.

"*The Times* says he's the most hated man in all of London, beating out even the prince regent," Miss Traemore continued.

"The regent, even," Percy Billingsly said, shaking his head. "Can you imagine?"

"I grew up near Lord Dorset in Nuneaton," Annabelle said forcefully. "I've known him all of my life. He could never have done the things that have been alleged."

That declaration, however, merely recalled the other crime Alec had been accused of. The one the ton seemed to consider the greater sin, because it had supposedly been perpetrated against one of their own. And rumors had been running wild.

"Did you know the brave young lord he killed?" Lady Fairbanks asked. "Or the girl he left for dead? I like to imagine that she walks among us even now, waiting for revenge. But of course, she was horribly maimed, and I can't think of anyone with nasty scars in full view. Perhaps she wears a veil?"

"Perhaps she wears seven veils, just like Salome," Aunt Sophia said. "No doubt she dances around, demanding the head of Lord Dorset on a platter."

Lady Fairbanks responded with a blank stare.

"Just a thought. Now if you'll excuse us," her aunt continued, "my niece and I are eager to find our seats for the performance."

Thankful for the intervention, which had saved Lady Fairbanks from a painful encounter with her fist, Annabelle followed Aunt Sophia past the crowd. "Digby is turning an accident into a crime," she said in a low voice as she took two glasses of lemonade from the tray of a passing footman. "Why can't I admit my role that day? People know I believe in Alec's innocence."

"Lord Dorset does not wish to link the two of you in any way, given the scandal. You must remember that."

Not since the darkest days of her recovery had Annabelle felt so helpless. What was the point of being accepted by society when so many of its members were buffoons?

Aunt Sophia paused to survey the crowded room. Gilded chairs with tufted cushions were set up at the front of the parlor, where a small stage was adorned with instruments and a pianoforte. Chairs had also been placed near the entrance to a side hall. "Let us move to a corner of the room that lies close to a convenient exit. I've not heard good things about the Danforth girl's abilities." She took a sip of her lemonade as they moved forward, and promptly grimaced. "If this is the only libation we are to enjoy this evening, I will argue for an early departure."

"I would be devastated if Miss Layton left before we had the opportunity to renew our acquaintance, Lady Marchmain."

The man who had spoken was directly behind her, but Annabelle didn't need to turn around to know who he was. He had surprised her before, behind the aviary in the formal gardens at Astley Castle.

"Will you not greet an old friend, Miss Layton?"

At that, she spun around, eyes flashing. "You were never my friend, Mr. Digby. And you were no friend to Gareth."

He'd changed. He was older, of course, and there was a long scar now that ran down one cheek. But he still had the same smirking grin he'd worn that night, the one that told her she would not be safe with him in the dark. He leaned in, his voice lowered. "Surely you do not want our shared past to be known? Wouldn't the ton be surprised to know that Dorset's victim blooms like a flower among them, the fairest lady in all the land?"

"You are the one with secrets to hide," Annabelle said. "You're the one whose lies have set the ton on its ear."

"My dear Miss Layton. I have no quarrel with you. I sincerely regretted your brother's untimely passing, which we all know was Dorset's fault. I am also thrilled beyond measure that you are healthy and well. You've exceeded even the promise of your youth."

"I do not believe a word you say."

His face darkened. "Perhaps when we know each other better, you'll learn to agree with me." He turned toward Aunt Sophia, who was silently assessing their exchange. "I hope, Lady Marchmain, that you will forgive the lack of an introduction between us. Your resemblance to the late Lady Layton is remarkable. It's not difficult to see where your niece gets her beauty."

"You are a charmer, aren't you, Mr. Digby?" Aunt Sophia drawled. "Just not a very good one. Come along, Annabelle. The company is such that I suddenly find myself eager for the music to begin."

• • •

"I'm relieved to find that my ears are not bleeding, as I'd first suspected," Aunt Sophia announced later that evening, as she looked into the ornately carved mirror hanging above the escritoire in her bedroom. "When Miss Danforth attempted that final note of Mozart's *Queen of the Night* aria ..." Cringing at the memory, she turned to Annabelle, seated directly behind her on a chaise lounge. "No, we must not relive it. It was horrible enough the first time."

"But not as dreadful as our encounter with Mr. Digby." Annabelle was still unsettled by the experience, her fingers picking restlessly at the folds of her evening gown. "His eyes were on us the entire evening."

"He looked like a peacock in that uniform," her aunt sniffed. "Puffed up with self-importance, reveling in the attention of fools who consider him some sort of hero."

"This is all part of a campaign to destroy Alec. Why does no one else see it?"

"Do you think that this stems from the circumstances surrounding Gareth's death?"

"I think it must," Annabelle replied. "When Gareth arrived in Nuneaton for his party, he was very interested in the outcome of a horse race in London. He'd placed a bet on it with Digby, one I've no doubt he could ill afford. Even the race that killed him was prompted by some sort of wager between them."

"It sounds as if Digby recognized Gareth's weakness for gambling and preyed upon it."

"Which must be why Alec became involved." For so long, she had wondered why he'd raced that day. "Lord Marworth told me that after the accident, Alec made sure Digby wouldn't be able to get his hooks into anyone else."

"That would explain Digby's quest for revenge," Aunt Sophia said, her brow furrowed in thought. "But it does not explain Lord Fitzsimmons's complicity in the plan. Unless ..."

"Do you think he could be under Digby's sway, as well?"

"The man lied in front of the entire House of Lords, risking the loss of his position and prestige. This is about more than money."

"But the change in Fitzsimmons's behavior can be directly tied to Digby's arrival. Before that, he was actively encouraging a match between Alec and Jane. That day at the picnic, he could not have been more obvious about his hopes in that regard."

Aunt Sophia came over to sit beside her, pressing Annabelle's hands into her own to still them. "I'm afraid this is very much about those hopes, my dear," she said gently. "Anyone who has seen you and Alec in the same room together understands that Alec will not be marrying Jane Fitzsimmons."

At any other time, the observation would have thrilled her. Now, she was heartsick that she might have played a role in Alec's downfall. If only she'd not been so obvious in her affections.

"There has to be something I can do to help," she said. "*The Times* has been reporting on the horrors at Badajoz. They are indisputable, but we both know that Alec was not involved. Digby is lying. The question is, how can we prove it?"

"As a young, unmarried woman, Annabelle, there is very little you can do while staying within the bounds of propriety. If society turns against you, its judgment will be swift and uncompromising."

"I don't care a fig about society."

"My dear girl," Aunt Sophia said, smiling broadly. "I couldn't be more proud of you if you were my own daughter. Not that I have ever wanted children."

There was a soft rapping at the bedroom door, surprising them both as Mary crept in and made a nervous curtsy.

"Good evening, Mary," Aunt Sophia said. "I would have thought you abed by now. You did a marvelous job with Annabelle's hair tonight, by the way. The sapphire clips tucked behind each ear were lovely."

"Thank you, my lady. I hope I am not being a bother. I had wanted to speak with you privately, if I might." She was blushing profusely. "Will you mind, Miss Annabelle?"

"Not at all." She certainly didn't wish to embarrass Mary further, whatever her concern might be. "I have a letter I must write. Can you believe that my father is visiting in just two days' time? What a pleasant surprise he'll have, Mary, finding you here."

But it was obvious that Mary felt otherwise. "Yes, indeed," she said quietly, her eyes fixed firmly to the floor. What could have so unsettled her?

"Well then," Annabelle replied. "Good night to you both." As she passed through the door, pulling it shut behind her, she heard Mary say something about a burdensome secret. Knowing her as she did, though, she couldn't imagine that it was anything too terrible.

• • •

It was almost midnight as Annabelle waited beneath a cluster of oak trees at the edge of the Serpentine. Although the evening was not a cold one, she was bundled up in a voluminous black cape, so long that it trailed behind her in the grass. She pushed the hood back to keep her vision from being obscured, careful to keep her hair hidden from view. She'd promised Aunt Sophia yesterday that she would take every precaution to avoid being seen.

This was an assignation, after all. Or it would be if Alec showed up.

She turned at the sound of a horse galloping toward her, its rider also cloaked in black, his face barely visible in the moonlight, but she would know him anywhere. It had been days since she'd seen him, although it felt like a lifetime.

Alec brought Mars to a standstill beside her and slid from the horse. However, the arms she lifted to embrace him fell back when she saw his expression, rigid with anger.

"What in the world were you thinking, Annabelle? To come here as a young woman alone? Do you have any idea of the dangers that lurk in Hyde Park at night?" He pulled off his gloves, raking his hands through his hair. "All the way here, I've been imagining every kind of horror …"

"I'm not precisely alone, Alec. Thomas, our footman, is waiting with my horse on the other side of the bridle path."

"But are you in his line of sight?" he asked. "If someone had accosted you, how quickly would he have known it? Do you never think things through?" He seemed to be struggling to rein in his temper. He took several deep breaths, long and slow. "Don't you know that you are precious to me?" he said, his voice barely a whisper now.

She reached up to caress his cheek, but he stepped back, putting more distance between them.

"Why are we here, Annabelle?" he asked, his jaw tight once more. "In my last note, I thought I'd made it clear that we can't be seen together. I refuse to have my shame become yours as well."

"But you've done nothing wrong," she exclaimed. "Digby is lying."

"It hardly matters. I've already been tried and convicted by public opinion. In society, that's more than enough to find me guilty."

"Then society is governed by people who can't think for themselves."

"Perhaps," he said with a humorless laugh. "It has been a rather spectacular fall from grace all the same. There are no more invitations to ton functions, or calling cards left on the silver tray in the hall. Instead, I receive threatening letters from people who don't sign their names, and notices from my clubs announcing that I'm no longer welcome."

"Alec, there has to be a way to prove your innocence," she said, alarmed by his air of resignation.

"I don't know how I can," he replied. "I've written to Wellington, requesting an affirmation of my character, but even he can't say where I was that night. I was alone in my tent, grieving for my father. And it's not as if the real criminals will come forward to claim responsibility."

"Digby must have played a part!" She was thrilled by her deduction. "How else would he have known about the atrocities that took place?"

"I'm afraid there's no way to account even for Digby's whereabouts. Tens of thousands of men fought that day. Thousands died," he said, his eyes bleak. "Besides, Fitzsimmons serves on a committee in the Lords that is privy to war secrets. He could have leaked Digby the reports from Badajoz."

"Wouldn't that be a crime if it could be proven? Perhaps there is a way to track Fitzsimmons's involvement in this." It seemed impossible that dishonorable, vindictive men could so easily destroy the most honorable man Annabelle had ever known.

"Even if there were, the damage is done. In the last few days, I've gone from being a respected peer of the realm to being a rapist, a murderer. It would almost be funny were it not so devastating."

"There is nothing funny about this," she insisted, indignant. "And I don't care what people think. I only care about you."

"Annabelle," he said gently. "So many men admire you. You don't need a castoff from your childhood, especially one who can no longer give you the position and respect that you deserve."

"Don't you know that you are the only man I've ever wanted, Alec?" she said, desperate to make him understand the depth of her feelings, to make him realize that they could conquer anything together.

Still, he held himself back, hands pinned to his sides. And she knew with a sudden wash of grief that he would not touch her again, because he'd decided that there could be no future between them. Honorable to the end.

"Come now," he said. "Let me escort you back to your horse. I remember that your father is arriving tomorrow for your come-out ball. You'll wish to be well rested when he arrives."

They walked together in silence, Alec scanning the horizon all the while, as Annabelle fought to maintain her dignity. She wouldn't shame herself by giving into her heartache and bursting into tears. When they came upon Thomas, though, he must have sensed she needed one last moment with Alec, because he crossed to the other side of her horse, busying himself with her saddle.

"Alec," she whispered, pressing herself into him so that she could feel every long, lean line. "Won't you please kiss me?"

At first, she thought he would deny her, even as his eyes flared with longing. But then with a sigh that sounded like surrender, he slowly bent his head toward hers, and her lips softened with bittersweet anticipation, her pulse speeding with desire.

His embrace never came. Instead, he touched his mouth to her cheek in a chaste, almost brotherly kiss. He lifted her onto her horse, thanked Thomas for his care, and turned into the night, his cloak swinging behind him. She wanted to call out, to ask him not to go, because with every step, he was breaking her heart. But she stayed silent, even though she could no longer stop her tears from falling.

• • •

As Father stepped from the Chessher's carriage onto the sidewalk outside Marchmain House, Annabelle pasted a bright smile on her face to disguise her fatigue. Despite Alec's admonition, she'd barely slept the previous night. She'd been too caught up in her despair. "How was the trip from Nuneaton?" she asked. "How well you look." And it was true. Everything about her father—from his gaze to his attire—seemed less confused.

"It was liberating, my girl. There is no other word for it. On some stretches of road, we went so fast, I imagined I was flying, soaring up from the earth, untethered and free." He rushed forward, folding her into his arms. "All around us, there were signs of rebirth and renewal," he continued, stepping back to smile down at her. "And I've discovered that the unfamiliar can hold unexpected surprises."

She could feel her eyes widen with shock. "I am so glad to hear it. Has Mrs. Chessher been keeping you very busy, then?"

"Well, she has no patience for cataloging specimens, which was quite upsetting at the start. She made me take several walks into town, and I even went to services at St. Mary the Virgin. I was certain that no one could hear the vicar over the pounding of my heart. In the churchyard afterward, I saw the most beautiful butterfly perched on the stone wall there. I've never seen its like. I can't wait to show it to you."

"You must slow down," she said, laughing now. "I can't keep up with everything you say." As the doctor and his wife descended from the carriage behind them, she called out. "What have you done to my father? I can't remember the last time he was so talkative."

"He has been a dear," Mrs. Chessher said, stepping forward. "He is doing right well, too. I'm proud of him."

"I can't thank you enough for seeing him here safely. Are you certain you cannot stay? Lady Marchmain and I had hoped you would rest here before continuing on to Dover."

"I wish we could, Miss Layton," Dr. Chessher said with a quick bow. "I don't often get the chance to take time from my duties in Hinckley. We need to be under way as soon as possible." He glanced down at her. "Has your leg been giving you trouble?"

"It rarely pains me, Dr. Chessher, and for that, I have you to thank."

"I may have bandaged your leg," he said approvingly, "but your determination kept it. You were my bravest patient."

"I hardly felt so at the time," she replied. In truth, she'd had no choice but to be brave. The only alternative had been the darkest despair. But she would not think of such things today, not when Father was doing so well. After the coachman removed his bags and the Chesshers departed for Dover, she moved with him up the steps to the house. "Are you excited to see London, Father?"

"I am, my dear, but I'm happiest to see my glorious girl again. Come show me where you have lived these many long weeks."

They passed through the doorway into the impressive entrance hall, with its dizzying expanse of marble and gilt. "Aunt Sophia wishes to give us a few minutes," she said with a warm squeeze of his hand. "Let me show you to the drawing room. We will wait for her there."

"Were all of these sent to you, Annabelle?" he asked as they crossed into the room, still filled with flowers, arrangements of every size and color.

"It seems the thing to do. If a gentleman speaks with you, he must send you flowers."

"I am not so old that I don't remember the rituals of courtship," he said. "Before your mother and I were married, her drawing room was always filled with flowers. She was the toast of London, just like her daughter."

"I have received a flattering amount of attention," she said quietly, "but I'm hardly the toast of London. I'm not even sure I would want to be."

"Haven't you been enjoying your time here? Is it wrong to hope that you might wish to return home?"

"Society is capricious. People admire you in one moment, only to turn away in the next. The lies of one person can shake the foundations of everything you've tried to be."

"My dear, whatever is the matter?"

"People have told the most outrageous lies about Alec," she said as a now-familiar anguish settled upon her. "Everything that he is and has worked for is being threatened."

"Alec?

"Alec Carstairs. The Earl of Dorset. Did you know, Father, he did not abandon me? I'd thought he wanted nothing to do with me because of the accident, but Mother banished him from Astley Castle. She destroyed my letters to him, so he didn't know I had asked for his help. He needs my help now."

Father had gone decidedly pale. "Mrs. Chessher has told me it is a very bad thing to hide from yourself," he said slowly, his eyes wary. "And even worse to hide from the things you have done."

"But Alec did nothing wrong. Don't you see? It is Digby's fault, that horrible man who raced with Gareth. He is here in London, and he's made up vicious lies about Alec, not only about his service during the war, but also about the accident. He has hinted that Alec caused Gareth's death."

"That man ... he is here?" he said haltingly, as if speaking was suddenly difficult. "In London?" A faint sheen of perspiration had appeared on his brow, and he looked as if he might faint. She should have known better than to burden him with such things. He'd seemed so much better, so like the father she'd known as a child that she'd run to him, like a little girl, eager to confide her worries. He was not the same man. She'd been foolish to forget it.

Moving quickly, she guided him to the striped settee, sitting down beside him. She loosened his cravat, fanning her hand in front of his face to stir the air. "Can I get you something to drink? Shall I call for a doctor?"

Slowly, though, his color returned. He took a shuddering breath, hanging his head between his shoulders. "I am sorry, Annabelle," he said, nearly overcome. "I did not mean to worry you. The journey was more than I'm accustomed to. I will be all right." Something in his voice, however, gave lie to that statement.

Before she could ponder it further, Aunt Sophia swept into the room, her face wreathed in a welcoming smile. It was quickly extinguished when she saw him on the settee. "Frederick, you are shockingly pale."

"He was overtaxed by the journey, but I was too careless to notice," Annabelle said. "I was telling him about Alec and the letters and Corporal Digby. It was too much for him."

Father looked up then, hollow-eyed and sad. "Please, my dear. You mustn't blame yourself for my weakness. She is always trying to protect me from myself," he added to Aunt Sophia.

"I've noticed that." Her aunt's voice was oddly sharp as she watched him carefully. "Grown men should not be coddled, Annabelle. Let us get him settled into his rooms."

She helped Father stand, alarmed by the sudden and debilitating change in his behavior. He'd walked into Marchmain House with such confidence, but he shuffled now. His nervousness became even more pronounced when Aunt Sophia turned and said, "You should rest, Frederick. I need to speak with you privately before dinner is served."

• • •

As he sat in the study of his bachelor lodgings on St. James Street, Alec couldn't set aside a nagging thought. Two days ago in Hyde Park, Annabelle had asked him about Digby's whereabouts in Badajoz, about whether or not they could be ascertained with any degree of certainty. He'd replied that was impossible to track a single solider in a battle involving thousands. And that was true. Tracking a soldier's regiment, however, was another matter.

Fitzsimmons and Digby could not have had much time to work out their scheme. After all, little more than a week ago, Alec had been dancing with Jane at the Hertford Ball while her father looked on in delight.

Might the two men have overlooked crucial details in their story?

On the floor of the Lords, Fitzsimmons had claimed that Digby was just back from the Peninsula, which assumed that his regiment had been engaged in the battles there. But given what he knew of the 10th Hussars, a horse-mounted unit more frequently assigned to gaudy displays at the prince's Royal Pavilion in Brighton, it seemed unlikely.

Had Digby served with other regiments on the Continent, and if so, when? Where had he been stationed on the evening of April 10, 1812? If Alec could find that out, and thus prove his suspicions, all of their lies would unravel.

Of course, in the midst of this scandal, he was in no position to ask the War Office for service records. They would probably toss him out on the street if he tried. But fortunately, he knew someone who'd be met with a more favorable reception.

He'd just dipped his quill into an inkwell, ready to pen a letter, when a knock sounded at the door. "No, thank you, Potter," he called out. "I have no appetite."

"I'm not bringing the lunch tray, my lord. You have a visitor."

"Send the man away. I'm in no mood for another journalist hoping to interview the butcher of Badajoz."

"My lord, it is an older man, and a nervous one at that, if you'll permit me to say so. I have brought you his card." Potter walked forward to hand it to him. "He claims to know you from Nuneaton."

Alec felt a frisson of alarm as he read the name on it. Sir Frederick Layton was hardly the sort to pay a social call. "Please send him in immediately." Moments later, Annabelle's father walked hesitantly through the doorway. He was hardly more than fifty, but there was an unsettled grief that hung over him, making him appear older. He also seemed remarkably anxious. Alec stood, indicating that the older gentleman should take the leather armchair opposite his desk. "Sir Layton, it has been a very long time. I know your daughter has been looking forward to your visit. I hope nothing is wrong?"

"Annabelle has told me about the accusations against you, Lord Dorset," Layton said quietly as he took his seat. "She is very worried for you."

"Please tell her that I am fine," he lied. "Things will right themselves. Your daughter has grown into a remarkable woman."

"She has become so without my help, I can assure you." Layton was looking down at his lap, as if unwilling to meet his gaze. "I didn't want to come here today, but Lady Marchmain told me I must. There are things ... that must be said."

Alec stiffened. He knew what was coming. "I have already resolved to keep my distance from your daughter. I'll not let this scandal touch her."

At that, the older man looked up in surprise. "No, Lord Dorset. I'm not asking you to stay away from my daughter. That would hurt her, and I have hurt her enough already."

Layton stood then and began to pace. "I am referring to the day that changed everything. I should have known, you see. I had just returned from the fields with a singularly large Death's-head hawk moth, when he came up the drive with Gareth."

"Who was with Gareth?" He was confused by the abrupt change in topic. Was the man talking about the accident?

"Most collectors want nothing to do with them," Layton continued, as if Alec had not spoken. "They are a portent of grave danger. I should have remembered that. Perhaps then my son would not have died. My dearest girl wouldn't have suffered."

"Sir Layton, who came to see you with Gareth?"

"Digby has blamed you for my son's death, but it was his fault. He brought death with him that day."

Was Layton mixing the past with the present? He wasn't making any sense. "Digby can be blamed for many things, but not Gareth's death." He knew that better than anyone. "It was a terrible accident."

Layton stopped his pacing and dropped his head, his shoulders bowed with grief. "It was no accident. That is what I've been trying to say. I have the linchpin from your carriage to prove it."

The room tilted wildly then. To steady himself, Alec gripped the corners of his desk, his knuckles white with the strain.

"He sawed through it partially, so it would snap during the race," Layton said, his anguish evident. "I found it that night, when I returned to Two Boulders Road. I'd seen Digby combing the wreckage, and I knew he was looking for something."

"Why didn't you confront him?" Alec cried. "Why did you never report this?"

"Gareth was dead. Annabelle was horribly injured. I worried Digby would come back for the money that was owed. I needed leverage against him. How else could I protect what was left of my family?"

If Layton had known about his son's debts, why hadn't he done more to stop his destructive behaviors? Why hadn't he gotten justice for Gareth? For Annabelle? "Hiding away the linchpin accomplished nothing. Why did you not at least tell me? Damn it! My father was the magistrate of Nuneaton. You could have gone to him."

"I did not want you to know. Can you imagine the shame of it? Astley Castle was on the verge of insolvency. Annabelle is the only reason it still stands today."

Alec leapt up from his chair in disbelief. "Do you mean to tell me you kept her there, hidden away from the rest of the world, to cover up your shame?"

"No, I kept her there so that she would be safe." Sir Layton's eyes filled with tears. "And yet I don't know what I would have done without her. My wife was no longer herself. Annabelle was all that I had left."

It was then that Alec knew, and the realization stunned him. "Did you also destroy her letters?" he said. "The letters she sent to me?"

Layton covered his face with his hands, openly weeping now. "God forgive me. I never sent them. Mary, her maid, brought them to me, but I hid them away. When she found out what I'd done, I dismissed her, so that Annabelle would never know."

Were he any other man, Alec would have struck him. It would have been a small price to pay for the damage he'd done. As it was, it took all his determination not to turn away from the man in disgust. Perhaps Sir Layton hadn't been able to bear the thought of Annabelle leaving him. Alec could understand that. But he couldn't forgive him. "What did you do with the letters and the linchpin, Sir Layton?" His voice was bitter with anger.

"I have sent a note to Astley Castle," he cried, looking away once more. "They are in a case I have hidden there. It will be here by week's end."

"I have reason not to trust the mail where you are concerned. I will go to the castle myself. God forgive you when Annabelle discovers the truth. It will break her heart."

Chapter 20

Annabelle felt like a puppet at one of the Punch and Judy shows in Covent Garden. All evening, she'd smiled until her face was surely cracking. She danced every dance and thanked a parade of people for their compliments, but even the elaborate gown she wore couldn't disguise her hollowness inside. The whole of the ton was here, not only to enjoy the ball Aunt Sophia and Lady Dorset had so meticulously planned, but also to make a final judgment about her suitability. Was she graceful and gracious? Was she witty? Would she be an asset to their exclusive ranks?

They didn't realize Annabelle had already judged them and found them wanting, because they believed the lies of a charlatan over Alec, and she was powerless to change their minds. Her declarations of his innocence were ignored. She was too pretty, they'd decided, to worry her head about such things. It hardly mattered that she'd known Alec for a lifetime, because war could change a man. Just look what it had done to him! And his poor mother! How courageous she was to show her face this evening, smiling valiantly beside Annabelle in the ball's receiving line, when the world knew her son was a monster.

Lady Dorset was indeed brave. She didn't shy away from the many veiled accusations and innuendoes. Annabelle had wanted to cancel tonight's ball, but Alec's mother had declared it should be even bigger and more elaborate than originally planned. Anything less would be seen as a capitulation—or worse, an acknowledgment of Alec's guilt. So Lady Dorset smiled her way through the dancing and the multitudinous array of courses served during dinner. She offered a toast to Annabelle as warm and heartfelt as one would give a daughter, and when at long last, there was an appropriate time to depart, she did so with grace. Not once did she give in to her heartbreak.

Father was also putting on a brave face, considering the fact he'd been distracted and on edge since his arrival in London. Save for a mysterious morning call, he'd hardly left the confines of Marchmain House. Tonight, though, he was cornered by some of the ton's biggest gossips, drawn no doubt by his eccentricity, and he looked profoundly uncomfortable in his evening wear. His eyes darted over the crowd, as if searching for a means of escape. Annabelle saw him notice the door that led to the servants' back stair, and watched as he edged toward it.

Perhaps they could escape the ball together. She excused herself from a circle of young ladies she'd met at the picnic, and followed him. She'd gotten no more than a few steps when her cousin Estrella came up, clasping a hand to her shoulder.

"What a squeeze this is," Estrella said with the languid drawl she'd adopted since her arrival in London this past week. "Surely the whole of the city is here. To think that our own little girl from Nuneaton is the name on everyone's lips! Augustus is quite put out, I must tell you. He doesn't like to share."

In the months since she'd last seen him, Augustus had not improved either his appearance or his character. And surely the greater squeeze had occurred when Estrella was buttoned into her gown, a fussy crimson affair several sizes too small. Still, Estrella's attempts at matchmaking were increasingly halfhearted, and that had been the only positive in an otherwise dreadful week. Her heart ached for Alec. Even now, he was in Nuneaton, chasing down something to do with Digby. He might as well be on the other side of the world.

"Annabelle, I need your help, my dear," Estrella said, recalling her attention. "I've misplaced my fan, and it's so beautiful with my new ball gown. I will simply be devastated if someone crushes it. I drank champagne in the library earlier to calm my nerves, and

I may have left it there, but Marchmain House is so large I will never find it on my own. I should hate to become lost and miss the rest of your ball."

It would be difficult to lose sight of Estrella, but Annabelle welcomed the opportunity to escape. "I'll be happy to show you the way." It took a few minutes to slip through the crowd, but once they cleared the room, it was easier to move quickly through the house, down the stairs, and past the main hall. The library overlooked the square.

The door to the library was closed, but Annabelle opened it and stepped inside. A low fire burned in the grate, but the candle sconces had not been relit, making it difficult to see clearly. She could just make out one of the floor-length casement curtains fluttering in a soft breeze. A window was open, no doubt to catch the cool evening air.

"Estrella, will you show me where you were sitting? Perhaps on the sofa?" she asked, moving with slow steps in the darkened room.

The sound of a door slamming was her only answer.

She spun around, almost knocking over a large vase on one of the side tables. What could Estrella be thinking, to shut her up in the library alone? She wasn't going to wait here to find out. She felt her way back across the room, only to discover that she wasn't alone after all. A man stepped out from the shadows to block her path, and as he turned to face her, Annabelle bit back a scream.

God help her. She was alone in the dark with Damien Digby. She needed her wits about her. Obviously, Estrella had led her here for just this purpose. But why? Annabelle had told her how dangerous the man was.

"Miss Layton, may I offer you my compliments? You are perfection itself tonight."

"What are you doing here, Corporal Digby? This is a private gathering, and you were not invited." She struggled to keep her voice calm. She couldn't let him see how frightened she was. In the dim light, he looked like a specter, half of his face and body hidden in shadow, the other half lit by the dying embers of the fire.

"I felt sure that was an oversight, Miss Layton. After all, I am invited everywhere now. I'm not quite Wellington, of course, but I've been told I am a hero all the same."

"You are no hero," she spat, though she was quaking inside. "All you've done is spread contemptible lies about an honest man."

He merely chuckled. "My revenge was long in coming, but that makes it no less sweet. Dorset tried to destroy me, and I've repaid the favor in spades."

"What do you mean, destroy you?" He was creeping toward her, and she stepped back, to the left of the fireplace, where the tools were kept to stoke the fire. With any luck, he hadn't noticed them.

"Come now, my dear. Don't pretend you do not know. Your brother owed me a great deal of money, but we were to settle things with our race that morning. The Laytons would keep Astley Castle, and I would get what I wanted. But then Dorset had to involve himself. I was forced to take matters in hand. And what in God's name were you doing in Gareth's carriage?"

"I have no memory of the race," she said defiantly. "I certainly know nothing about debts owed to you."

Her answer seemed to surprise him. "No memory? By God, that's rich. Is that what Dorset has played off of all these years?"

"You had some sort of hold over my brother," she acknowledged, keeping her focus on the fire tools. "She needed to keep him distracted. "Alec raced that day to better Gareth's odds against you." Just a few more steps now.

"I think, instead, that Dorset wanted the prize as badly as I did."

"Gareth had nothing of value to wager. Any winnings would have been meager." The tools were almost in reach. She would grab the poker, and take great satisfaction in skewering Digby between his shoulder blades.

"My dear Miss Layton, that's where you are wrong." Digby smirked, his eyes lingering on her lips. "Your brother wagered you. You were the prize."

"You are lying!" she cried, the poker forgotten. "I will never believe it." The very idea was preposterous. Gareth would never have offered her in exchange for his debts.

"Members of the aristocracy regularly trade their women for money, my dear. It's what the marriage mart is all about."

She was trapped in a nightmare. This couldn't be happening. Nor could it be true. "You'd only just met me," she said.

"You don't seem to understand your worth, Miss Layton. And I don't merely speak of your beauty, which is motivation enough. You have a most generous dowry from your mother's estate, something on the order of 7,000 pounds per year. An income like that is the dream of any gambling man." He was edging around the sofa now, inching closer.

She wrapped her arms tightly around her stomach and leaned over, suddenly worried that she would be sick. She needed to get out of this room, needed air. "Why did Estrella bring me here?"

Digby smiled, his lips thinning to slits. "You are an innocent, aren't you, not to have guessed. Your cousin doesn't want to lose Astley Castle any more than your brother did, and of course, the Laytons' debts to me still stand."

She felt faint, but she couldn't show him any weakness. She fought to steady her breathing. "I will never marry you."

"In a few moments, Lord Fitzsimmons will come through that door with some of the biggest gossips in the ton. He'll catch the two of us in an indelicate embrace, and I will announce that you've made me the happiest of men. Deny it, and your reputation will be destroyed. I'll claim my right to Astley Castle, and throw your father out onto the street."

"I will not let you hurt my father. I'll fight you with everything I have." But she was terrified. The smile was gone from his face, and he was so close now, his hands lifting from his sides, his fingers flexing.

"Fight all you want. Just know that when I come into you, you'll scream with the pleasure of it." He attacked then, forcing her back against the wall, trapping her hands with one of his own before she could grab at the poker, pinning her hips with his body. She struggled, twisting her face away when he tried to possess her mouth, battling to break free. But her efforts only inflamed him. He was deceptively strong, and she'd never felt so helpless. His free hand forced its way into her bodice, pawing painfully at one breast before grabbing onto the gown itself. In a rush of horror, she felt the fabric start to give way.

Suddenly, though, a crash sounded, and Digby grunted, going slack against her. Heavy pieces of porcelain fell all around them as he collapsed unconscious onto the floor. Standing behind his body was Jane Fitzsimmons, holding the remnants of an antique vase in her hands, her eyes round with shock.

"Jane!" Annabelle cried, kicking past Digby to wrap the woman in a desperate hug. "Thank God you came when you did!" How had she found them?

"Annabelle, I am so sorry. I overheard Father and Digby plotting this after the Hertford Ball. And they recruited your cousin this week to lure you here. I thought if I hid in the room, Digby could not claim to have compromised you. I didn't know what else to do. I couldn't let him do such vile, terrible things."

"You knocked him senseless!" It seemed impossible that she'd been rescued. "I will never be able thank you sufficiently."

"There's more to this. It concerns Lord Dorset as well," Jane said between short, panicked breaths. "I should not have waited so long to act. I've sent a note to him. I expect him at any moment."

But it was not Alec who next opened the door to the library. It was Lord Fitzsimmons, followed by Lady Jersey, the Princess Lieven, and Lady Hertford. "Ladies, explain yourselves," Lady Jersey huffed. "This is most unseemly!"

But Annabelle could not stay here, surrounded by the shadows of what had almost happened, Digby still prostrate on the floor, moaning now with pain. She grabbed Jane's arm and pushed past the others, blinking at the sudden rush of light in the hall.

Fighting to regain her composure, she clutched at her bodice—loosened around the edge of one breast, but thankfully still intact—as the others shuffled into the hall. Digby had not exaggerated when he'd said the biggest gossips in the ton would be on hand. If Alec had worried about being the scandalous one, here was a scandal of epic proportions.

"Corporal Digby trapped me and tried to force his attentions on me," she said as calmly as she could.

"It's true," Jane added. "I stumbled upon them. Miss Layton was struggling and—"

"Jane, my dear, you are mistaken," Lord Fitzsimmons interrupted. "They're lovebirds, those two, although Miss Layton is obviously trying to disguise it, having been caught out. In my pocket," he continued, "I have a special license from the archbishop. I procured it as a favor to the corporal, who wanted to surprise Miss Layton with a proposal tonight. There's even a minister waiting in a carriage outside. I hope you've not spoiled it."

"I was very nearly violated," Annabelle exclaimed, furious that the fiend could lie so brazenly.

Digby walked into the hall then, holding a handkerchief to the gash Jane had opened on the side of his head. His neck was covered with blood, his dress uniform spattered with long crimson streaks. He was palpably furious, and she felt a sharp spike of fear. "Fitzsimmons," he said as a crowd began to gather, drawn by the commotion. "Am I to understand that your daughter did this? I was wrapped in my love's embrace one moment, and coshed across the skull in the next."

"I am not your love, Digby!" Annabelle cried, wishing only that she'd picked up a stray shard of porcelain in the library, so she could carve a matching scar on the other side of his face.

"My dear, you know we have discussed marriage," he said, fixing her with a dark stare. "Your father, in particular, is eager for our union." There was no mistaking the threat behind his words.

"He is lying!" she continued. All around them, people were streaming down the stairs and into the hallway, as news spread of the unfolding drama.

"Never say you have been leading me along, Annabelle." Digby's eyes glittered. "That night, when you gave yourself to me, you swore you loved me."

The gathering crowd rippled with shock.

Contemptible man. But his words had their desired effect. Even now, all eyes were on her. "I did no such thing," she said, desperate to make everyone understand. "He planned the whole of this to force me into marriage."

"How dare you accuse my niece of impropriety!" Aunt Sophia all but hissed as she pushed her way toward them.

"Miss Layton," Lord Fitzsimmons said, ignoring her aunt. "I advise you to stop this foolishness, or society will have nothing to do with you."

"But Father," Jane exclaimed. "You know full well that Annabelle is innocent!"

The front door of Marchmain House suddenly flew open with such force that it slammed against its doorjamb. Several people shrank back in fear as Alec rushed into the hall. But Annabelle's heart swelled as she watched him fight through the crowd.

"Annabelle, are you all right?" he called out. She had never seen him so disheveled and anxious. His cravat was a tangled mess above a riding coat and breeches spattered with mud. He must have come on horseback, and he'd lost his hat along the way, his dark hair brushed into wavy streaks by the wind. He carried something wrapped with a cloth in his hand, and he looked as if he might use it to clear a path to her. He did not take his eyes from her face. Heavens, the expression in those eyes. As if the fate of the world was tied to her well-being. As if he would do anything, risk anything for her.

. . .

Had he arrived in time? He'd no sooner returned from Nuneaton than he'd found Jane's note, warning that Digby was plotting something infamous for Annabelle's come-out ball. He'd pushed Mars, his horse, to the edges of his endurance to get here, finding only a moment's irony in the fact that his father's gift to him might help save Annabelle.

"Dorset," Lord Fitzsimmons shouted, to make himself heard above the growing chorus of outrage at his sudden appearance. "You don't belong here among respectable people." But Alec was already at Annabelle's side, searching her face and form for any evidence of injury. When he saw her loosened bodice, a black fury nearly consumed him. If Digby had hurt her, he was a dead man.

"I'm all right," she whispered, gazing up at him with a quick smile, as if they were the only two people in the room. But of course, they were not. He pressed her tightly to his side all the same, onlookers and propriety be damned.

"You know Lord Dorset and Miss Layton are innocent of the charges against them, Father," Jane Fitzsimmons said in a voice loud enough for the throng to hear, although it trembled. "I overheard you in the study that night. I know what you've done."

Was Jane really calling her father out in front of the ton? If Fitzsimmons's duplicity was discovered here tonight, her reputation would be destroyed as well.

The old man blanched. "My dear girl," he said soothingly, but Alec could hear the desperation in his voice, the unspoken plea. "You're overset by this evening's events. Please, let me take you home."

She stood firm. "Father, tell the truth. Stop this while you still can."

And in that moment, Alec knew that he would never be able to repay her. She was risking everything she'd ever known for Annabelle's sake. But would anyone believe her? "Lord Dorset is a man without honor," Digby shouted, entering into the fray. "Yet your daughter defends him, Fitzsimmons. I can only guess at the reason." Several in the crowd cringed at the insult, because the man had all but called Jane his whore. Noticing the dried blood on Digby's collar, Alec had a sudden, pleasurable vision of the man's life blood draining out into a puddle on the floor.

With a squeeze of Annabelle's hand, he took a menacing step toward Digby, taking grim satisfaction in the bastard's sudden step backward. "Do you recognize this?" He slowly pulled back the folds of cloth covering the object he carried.

All around them, bystanders leaned in to look. "Of course not," Digby scoffed.

"Let me refresh your memory," Alec replied "It is the linchpin from my carriage those many years ago ... the linchpin that failed, causing my left wheel to career wildly into Gareth Layton's path, forcing the collision that led to his death. You'll notice one side is neatly sawed in half, ensuring that the pin would shatter during the race."

His words echoed in the hall, as several onlookers began to shift uncomfortably.

"Does this mean Miss Layton is the woman with the veils?" an overstuffed matron called out.

"Why would Dorset tamper with his own wheel?" someone else shouted from high above on the stair. Annabelle was looking at the linchpin with dawning horror, but Digby remained defiant.

"I don't know what you're talking about," he said dismissively. "I had nothing to do with that."

"You killed the wrong man, didn't you?" Alec seethed. "There was no justice that day, was there? Your mark died, while I walked away." The devil would have his time with Digby in the end. But not before he did.

"No one here believes your lies," Digby said, pretending outrage. "You can't distract us, Lord Dorset, from your crimes at Badajoz. I saw you there in the shadows. Leading men to despicable behavior. Violating women and small children. Committing acts of murder."

Alec cursed as the crowd recoiled. Several men demanded that he be tossed from the premises, as women frantically waved their fans and begged for smelling salts. Annabelle, on the other hand, looked as if she wanted to stab Digby through the heart. His brave, beautiful girl.

"May I interrupt this unpleasant exchange?" It was Benjamin Marworth, pushing toward them, dressed in a tiered riding coat and breeches, a sheaf of papers tucked under one arm. "Alec, I have those papers you requested."

A quick look passed between them, telling Alec all he needed to know. Thank God. He quickly scanned the sheaf and formulated his attack.

"I have a few questions for you, Corporal Digby."

But Digby was not done fighting. "Why should I answer your questions?" he said, trying for nonchalance.

"I only seek to clarify your military service," he replied. "An easy enough request, when you've spent so much time discussing mine."

Digby regarded him suspiciously, but he had not forgotten the crowd surrounding them. "By all means, then. Unlike you, Dorset, I've served my country with honor."

"You were posted in Spain under Wellington?"

"Of course. He has command of the entire Peninsular Campaign. Surely you know that."

"Which unit were you with, Corporal?"

"I first served as a foot soldier, but my skills were noticed by an officer with the 11th Light Dragoons."

"They're rather infamous, aren't they? Weren't they picking cherries in an orchard in Spain, frolicking among the fruit trees, when French forces caught them off guard and attacked?" Several men chuckled openly in the crowd. Good. The more derisive, the better. It would distract Digby. "Were you one of the Cherry Pickers, then?"

"I was transferred out long before that embarrassment," Digby insisted.

"Really? How convenient for you," Alec replied, dripping sarcasm. "Is that how you ended up with the 10th Royal Hussars, then? I couldn't help but notice your uniform."

"I was promoted to the Hussars in June of 1810, so I couldn't have been part of that orchard incident. I've served with them ever since. Really, though, these are pointless questions."

"The 10th Royal Hussars are stationed in Brighton?"

"Yes, we've been there since 1809," Digby said with an exaggerated sigh. "But what has any of this to do with your crimes, Lord Dorset, the ones that have shamed everyone here?"

"I confess to some confusion, Digby. If you've been stationed with the Hussars since 1810, how is it that you fought at Badajoz in 1812?"

A wave of shock rolled across the assembly as his words rang out, and Alec knew a moment of pure triumph. The bastard had been trapped by his own arrogance.

"You are mixing things up in my head," Digby insisted. "I was there at Badajoz! I know what I saw."

"You have marvelous eyesight, then," Alec observed, his voice dismissive. "There aren't many who can see Spain from the beaches of Brighton."

The room erupted in sound. Men were shouting words like "liar" and "cheat," as hundreds of eyes fixed on Digby, cold with condemnation.

"Everyone, please quiet down," Lord Fitzsimmons said, obviously shaken. "We'll sort this out tomorrow, when heads and minds are clearer. Let me escort Corporal Digby home. There's no need to rush to judgment." He glanced at Alec, eyes imploring, as if begging for forgiveness. But it was far too late for that.

"Didn't you rush to judgment, Lord Fitzsimmons?" someone called out.

"Wellington himself called Dorset a hero," another said. "Yet you believed the lies of a stranger."

"Did you never investigate this Digby's claims, Fitzsimmons? Or did you willingly set out to destroy an honorable man?"

"I'd say it was the latter," Alec said with deadly conviction. "In fact, I'd lay odds on it."

• • •

Alec was immediately caught up in a circle of well-wishers, men slapping him genially on the back to offer their congratulations, as Lord Fitzsimmons and Digby were escorted from Marchmain House. But Annabelle would not let Jane leave with them. "I do not want you to spend one more moment in that wretched man's presence," she said. "Your father can take him home." Jane, stiff and pale, merely nodded in agreement.

"Why did you do it?" she couldn't help but ask. "To risk so much for someone you hardly know?"

"I must admit," Jane said quietly, "that I did not particularly like you at our first meeting. I knew I would not be shown to advantage at the opera, with you there beside me. I had hopes, you see, for Lord Dorset."

What could she say in reply? "I know that he holds you in the highest esteem."

"Perhaps not the highest," Jane said with a wan smile. "He has certainly never looked at me the way he looks at you, when he thinks no one is watching." She started to protest, but Jane lifted a hand to quiet her. "It's alright. I could never shake the feeling that his courtship was half-hearted."

"Then why did you help us both?"

"Because I still hope that one day, a man will love me for who I am, and I want to be worthy of that devotion." Jane blushed, as if embarrassed by the admission. "And I could not allow my father to ruin Lord Dorset because of a perceived slight to me. I could not allow Digby to force himself upon you. Not if I wanted to live with myself."

"You will always have my thanks, Jane," she said, truly humbled. "My thanks and my devotion."

"Why not simply thank me for my shawl?" Jane said, pulling a cream satin wrap from her shoulders and tucking it around Annabelle's neck, to better hide her bodice. "If we don't cover you up, the men may never leave."

She'd almost forgotten that they were in the middle of a ball, which was buzzing as Aunt Sophia climbed to the top of the stairs, drawing everyone's attention.

"Lady Dorset and I thank you for joining us. Given this night's excitement, I think it best we conclude the evening." At that, the crowd scattered quickly, everyone obviously eager to spread the story of Alec's redemption. And it infuriated Annabelle that as people passed by Jane, many looked away, as if she were no longer worthy of their notice. When Jane had proved, against every expectation, to be a true and loyal friend.

She could not say the same for the Simpertons, who were herding toward the door with the other guests, hoping to be lost in the throng.

"Estrella and Cousin Augustus," she called out. "Could you stay for just a moment, please?" After hesitating, they turned, and she was perversely satisfied to see Estrella lose all semblance of color. Something bright and delicate hung from her wrist by a ribbon.

"I see you've found your fan," Annabelle said as the two came to a halt in front of her.

"Indeed! Imagine my relief."

"It was not in the library, then," she said, rather impressed that she hadn't already snatched the thing, and snapped it in two.

Estrella flushed an unbecoming shade. "No, it wasn't there after all. I'd forgotten my son was holding it for me. Weren't you, my dear?"

"It was a happy surprise," Augustus said, "to discover that it complemented my ensemble so well." He was wearing a glittering cutaway jacket embroidered with a profusion of colored crystal beads, over tight gold trousers.

"Rather like sparks complement an explosion, I should think," Aunt Sophia said as she came up behind them, having sent Jane up to her rooms. "You look like the fireworks display at Vauxhall Gardens."

Augustus seemed absurdly pleased by the comparison, but his mother was more wary. Rightly so. "We should return to the hotel."

"No, please stay just a moment more, Estrella," Annabelle said. "I want to know why you locked me in the library with Corporal Digby."

"Would you repeat that, my dear?" Alec's voice was deceptively calm behind her as he placed a protective arm at her waist, suffusing her body with tingling awareness.

"Happily," she said, leaning back into the solid wall of him. "You did not know, perhaps, that this evening's drama began when Estrella lured me into the library and trapped me there. I've just been asking for an explanation."

"I am eager to hear it," Aunt Sophia added. "Especially since the Simpertons are my guests at their hotel here in London, wearing clothes they've charged to my accounts, along with any number of additional fripperies."

Being too large to move with any speed, Estrella seemed to realize that a hasty escape was not an option. Instead, she opened and closed her mouth for several moments, reminding Annabelle of a round fish caught on a lure. "Corporal Digby told me they were in love," she said at last. "I have ever been one to further the cause of romance. I thought they'd make a fine match."

"In the same way Augustus would be a fine match for Princess Charlotte," Aunt Sophia offered.

"Precisely! I'm so glad that you see it, too."

"And because in handing Annabelle over to Digby, you'd have Astley Castle all to yourselves."

"Yes, indeed," Estrella replied. "I mean, no. No, not at all! That was never our intent."

But Annabelle knew better. It had been their plan all along.

Alec stepped around her. "I think you and your son should leave before I fully comprehend the depths of your deception."

"Right, then," Estrella agreed. "We'll be off straight away."

"I will give you until the morning to collect your things from the hotel," he continued, "and then I want you gone from London."

"And from Nuneaton, as well," Annabelle added. How satisfying it was to say it.

"You can't banish us from Astley Castle," Estrella huffed, stiff with outrage. "It is Augustus's birthright!"

"It was my brother's birthright before he was killed by Digby, the very man with whom you plotted to entrap me. I may not be able to keep your son from inheriting, but that doesn't mean I will suffer your presence in my childhood home until then."

"We have no money," Estrella cried, her hands shaking. "No place to go!"

"The sale of your new clothes should net you something," Aunt Sophia said. "And you hail from Manchester, do you not? Perhaps Augustus can find a position with a haberdasher there. He has that impressive flair for fashion."

• • •

Once the Simpertons had been dispatched, Alec pulled Annabelle into a quiet corner, away from the last remaining guests. "Are you certain that you are all right?" he asked, his face grave with concern.

"I am fine," she said, even as a shiver ran through her, recalling Digby's lies about Gareth and the race that day. The charges were so preposterous she would not repeat them. "To think that Digby meant to hurt you, or worse. And poor Gareth!" She wrapped her arms around him, hardly caring who saw, wanting only to revel in his warmth, to set aside her foolish fears, and pour out her feelings. For a glorious moment, he hugged her tightly against him, brushing the whisper of a kiss behind her ear. But then he pulled away.

"You have been so brave, Annabelle," Alec said with a gentle caress of his fingers along her cheek. "Can you be brave just a little while longer? I can't shake the feeling that there is still unfinished business tonight." He looked up and motioned to Lord Marworth, who was beside them in several long strides.

"I'll be shocked if Digby doesn't try to make a run for it tonight," Alec said. "Can you station a few men outside of his lodgings in Marylebone? I have some favors I need to call in at the War Office. Afterward, I will meet you there."

Here was the man so many soldiers had followed in battle, all brisk, military efficiency.

After Marworth departed, he turned again toward her. "I know you have questions about all that has transpired, but will you wait for me? I have things I must say, and I want to say them without distractions."

The inflection in his tone felt like silk rubbing along her skin. "I'll always wait for you, Alec."

His eyes flared as he treated her with one of his beautiful smiles, and then he bent down, kissing her firmly on the lips, in full view of the last remaining guests. "There goes my reputation for restraint," he whispered in her ear. Then he turned toward the door, walking out into the night.

• • •

After checking on Jane, Annabelle made her way to her father's chambers. She was surprised to find the door slightly ajar. When she knocked quietly and pushed it open, he was not inside. She'd been certain he would be sleeping, exhausted by the demands of the evening.

She wandered back downstairs, looking into the drawing room, the library, each of the front parlors, even the kitchen below, where the staff was enjoying the remnants of the evening's grand feast.

She was happy to see Mary among them, and with a heartfelt smile, Annabelle thanked everyone for their efforts before returning to the second floor to peek into the ballroom. Several housemaids were extinguishing the chandeliers, while footmen removed the dozens of tables set out for the dinner. So much effort had gone into her come-out ball, and it had come so close to disaster. Even now, she might have been at the mercy of Damien Digby.

Annabelle continued her search of the public rooms, increasingly worried. It wasn't like her father to venture out at night alone. Perhaps he'd spotted an unusual moth from the window of his suite? Determined to find him, she rushed back to her own rooms to change. A ball gown was ill-suited to searching the grounds. With the door to her chambers wide open, she hurried past her sitting area to the bedroom beyond.

What she saw paralyzed her with shock. Her father was sitting on the edge of her bed, his eyes lit with a wildness she'd never before seen. In one hand, he held a mounted butterfly encased in glass. There was a cocked pistol in the other. After glancing at her, he returned his dazed focus to the doorway. "Father," she whispered. "You must put the gun away. You are going to hurt yourself."

"But he's come back. And the gun will keep us safe."

"Who has come back? All the guests have left."

"His voice ... I heard it rising up from the hallway. It's been beating about my head."

"Whose voice, Father?"

"I imagined you were already here," he said, gesturing with the hand that held the encased butterfly. "See how much you look alike? The gold and the blue? So pretty and perfect."

She could feel tears welling up inside of her. Had he finally given into madness?

"But I have mixed up things in my head again," he said. "Come stand behind me. He will walk in at any moment."

"Father, please," she begged. "Who will walk in?"

"Digby, of course!" His eyes never wavered from the door. "The Death's-head hawk moth. He steals from the hive of the honeybee. Even the guardian bees cannot harm him. He's immune to their poison ... but not this pistol."

"Father, you are not making any sense, but I know you sometimes have problems forming your words and making yourself understood. Digby was here, but he has gone. He's going to be brought up on charges of slander, and perhaps murder." She paused, not sure if what she'd learned tonight would unsettle him all the more. "Please put the gun away. We are both safe. I have so much to tell you."

His eyes were still haunted, but some of the tension seemed to leave his body. "I tried to keep you safe, Annabelle. Even when I did wrong, I tried to keep you whole."

She watched as he lowered the hand holding the gun, settling it upon his thigh, pointing it at no direction in particular. "Will you hand the pistol to me, Father?" she asked carefully, terrified he would set it off inadvertently and harm himself. "Can I secure it for you, so that I can keep you safe?" The tone of her voice seemed to settle him. He slowly uncocked the pistol and shifted it toward her. Annabelle lifted it from his lap, and moved purposefully to the fireplace mantel. Placing it there put it clearly out of his reach.

"Digby is the Devil's own," he said. "I knew it when he came to Astley Castle once upon a time, with a wager to offer."

"Do you mean the night of Gareth's party?"

"He'd been to Astley before," he replied, increasingly cogent now. "He offered your brother a quick profit on a bet, and we needed money. Gareth vouched for him."

Father had known Digby before that night? "Did you bet with him, as well?"

He hunched his shoulders. "At first, we made money, and I was happy. I've never had a head for figures, as you know. But then we started to lose, and rapidly. The worst of it was the Sherford-Chetwiggin race. We couldn't recover from the debt."

Sherford-Chetwiggin.

The name stirred a memory, but Annabelle couldn't assign it to a time or place. "How much did you lose, Father?"

"Together, we lost 8,000 pounds."

Eight thousand pounds!

A disquieting numbness came over her. The number was strangely, horribly familiar. "Surely Gareth didn't risk so much on a carriage race in the country," she said. "Alec would have argued against such lunacy."

Father looked up at her from his vantage point on the bed, eyes wide and sad, his voice cracking with emotion. "Digby had seen you. He wanted you. He told Gareth he was willing to forget all of our debts for you."

Rather than the crushing grief she should have felt, Annabelle felt the strongest rush of anger she had ever known. "You and Gareth were going to barter me for Astley Castle?" Digby had said as much, but she'd refused to believe him.

"No! I would never have let him have you. Gareth was drunk when Digby suggested the wager. He wasn't thinking clearly."

"That is not an excuse!" To think the brother she'd mourned had planned to trade her for the price of his debts.

I am the worst of brothers. I am so sorry.

"Dear God," she whispered, wrapping her arms around her waist. Why was she suddenly seeing bits and pieces of a day she no longer wanted to remember?

"Gareth came to me before dawn and told me about the race. I insisted it be canceled, but he believed Digby would do anything to have you. I told him to take you and steal away. He was going to go first to Arbury Hall, and then vanish from there."

"I've brought you a quick change of clothes, an old set of mine."

"After you were safe, I was going to give Digby the note to Astley Castle, and sell my collection to cover the rest. But the race began before it was meant to." His voice was tortured. "Digby must have suspected something."

"Such a surprise, to see you out and about so early, Gareth. Are you making an escape?"

"I was too late to save your brother," he moaned. "And you were like a beautiful doll that had been ripped in two."

She did not want to ask it. She was terrified of the answer. "Did Mother know?"

He looked up, his face contorted with grief. "That night, I told her about the debts we'd incurred. About the race and Gareth's wager. I think she went mad with the knowledge."

The pressure building in her head was nearly unbearable. All this time, so much had been kept from her. "Why have you never told me any of this? Didn't I have a right to know?"

"I wanted to keep you safe with me. Nobody knew how well you'd recovered. Digby had forgotten your existence."

"But you still owed him money. There was every chance he would return."

"If he came back, I had proof of his perfidy! I'd found the linchpin. I could protect you."

"But Alec found the linchpin. He confronted Digby with it this evening."

"I told him where it could be found," he said, tears gathering in his eyes. "I kept it in the locked case on my desk, along with all the things I hide from myself. I am a coward, you see."

She tensed, as if preparing to absorb a body blow. There had been something in the sound of his voice. "What other things have you been hiding, Father?"

"My Aporia Crataegi specimen. It was so like your mother, you see. And a lock of your brother's hair. I clipped it before he was buried. It was dry and lifeless in my hands, just like my poor boy."

He shuddered, tears slipping down his cheeks. "And your letters. I kept those hidden too."

Her heart was pounding, ringing in her ears. "Which letters?"

"The ones you sent to Alec Carstairs," he whispered.

A white hot flash of loss almost drove her to her knees. She nearly groaned with the pain of it, certain she would crumple under the weight of her anguish. All those years, she'd felt so unwanted and alone. Did he understand what he'd done? His mind had a strange way of viewing reality, and of responding to it. But at this moment, she could only feel a deep sense of betrayal.

"You say you wanted to protect me. In truth, you were only protecting yourself."

"No, Annabelle!" he sobbed. "I know now that I was wrong, but I only wanted to keep you close. I wanted to keep you safe."

She didn't reply. Instead, she went over to the mantel and removed the bullets from her father's gun. Then she walked out of the room, shutting the door behind her. Canby, having closed up the house for the night, was making the last of his rounds in the hall. It took every bit of her composure to speak calmly. "Would you please have a carriage brought around for me? I need to speak with Lord Dorset."

He couldn't mask his surprise. "It is rather late, my lady. Are you sure that's wise?"

"Probably not. But with or without a carriage, I am going to find him."

"Shall I send a maid for Lady Marchmain?" he asked, his distress obvious. "I feel certain she would not wish you to travel about unescorted."

"Please, Canby. This is something I prefer to do by myself." She needed to leave now, before she shattered into pieces.

He seemed to sense that, because after a searching glance, he offered her a respectful bow. "I will see to it right away."

• • •

It was almost dawn when Alec turned Mars onto Welbeck Street in Marylebone. It was a respectable address, home to well-heeled tradesmen, writers, and professional men. Yet a murderer lived in their midst.

Several uniformed men were clustered outside of the Digby's rented lodgings, Marworth waiting nearby. Alec pulled up alongside him. "Any movement yet?"

"Not yet, but I have a feeling you're just in time for the fun. If he waits much longer, he'll lose the cover of darkness."

"I say we don't bother waiting." He slipped from his horse and threw the reins to one of the other men. "I say we go in after him." The two approached the door of Digby's modest building. "Let's smash it open … " Alec said, no longer interested in leashing his anger.

"That won't be necessary," Marworth said with a brief smile, as he pulled a ring with several brass keys from his pocket. "His landlady was more than accommodating."

After a nearly noiseless entry, they passed into a narrow hallway, two doors opposite each other at the bottom of the stairs, two more at the top. Digby's was the second to the left, bathed in a slant of moonlight from a small window.

Slipping up the stairs, they stopped outside his door, Marworth ready to reach for another key, when the door suddenly swung open, and a dark figure rushed out, barreling toward them He crashed into Alec with a satisfying thump before crumbling to the floor at his feet. Too bad Digby hadn't bothered to watch where he was going.

"May we assume that you're going out?" he asked as the bastard struggled to force air back into his lungs. He was dressed in undistinguished clothing, a bag and its contents splayed beside him. "What are you doing here?" Digby wheezed as he tried to regain his footing. "You have no right to accost me in my home."

"I'm not sure it's yours anymore," Marworth said. "It seems your rent is in arrears." Together, they pushed him back into a dingy parlor and closed the door behind them.

"I'm free to go if I please," Digby insisted. "I've not been charged with a crime."

"Please," Marworth drawled. "We all know several charges are forthcoming. Even as we speak, you've busied detectives from Bow Street to the Peninsula."

"What of it? You can't hold me here."

"Go ahead, then. Try to push past," Alec said. "I'd welcome the opportunity to wring your neck." In fact, nothing would give him greater pleasure. His hands fairly itched to encircle the man's throat, and squeeze just so.

"You have a habit of trying to separate my head from my body," Digby sneered.

Really, the man's bravado, given the circumstances, was offensive in every way. Alec rewarded it with a vicious jab to his gut, and Digby doubled over in agony, clutching his stomach. "I can stay away from the head then," he said, "if you like."

"Do you know what the punishment is for slandering a peer?" Marworth asked casually.

"I didn't plan on being here long enough to find out," Digby panted, slowly righting himself. "Miss Layton and I would have been far from London by now, if Jane Fitzsimmons—that dried-up spinster—hadn't interfered."

Yet another excuse to punish the man. Alec slammed his fist into Digby's jaw, and a resounding crack echoed in the room.. "Mention either woman again," he said, brushing spittle from his knuckles, "and you won't live to see the morning." Really, he hadn't expected this confrontation to be so rewarding.

"I am starting to believe that's inevitable," Digby slurred, wiping his sleeve across his mouth to sop up the blood streaming from it. "I think you broke my jaw."

"It looks like a few teeth have gone missing as well," Marworth pointed out, as Digby spit several onto the floor. "But back to your fate … "

"Why the hell are you here?"

"For justice, of course, but while I would like to see you hang for your crimes, Dorset here has another plan. I think you will prefer it."

"What did you have in mind?" Digby was swaying on his feet.

"There will be a public trial if you are formally charged with your crimes," Alec said. "Painful truths will come out. I don't want either Miss Layton or Miss Fitzsimmons to suffer through that."

"Say the word, then," Digby said, suddenly sounding hopeful. "I will vanish. You'll never hear from me again."

He gave a bark of laughter. "I'd rather see you drown in the Thames than go free."

"Then what are you suggesting?"

"Your regiment expected you back last week. Which makes you a deserter."

"That was an oversight on my part. I'll happily return to my regiment, if that's what you're proposing. I will leave for Brighton right now."

"You're not going back to Brighton. I've arranged to have you transferred to a new regiment, once the flogging is done with. Escorts are waiting for you downstairs."

"What do you mean … flogging?" Digby's eyes were wide with horror.

"The Royal Hussars want three hundred lashes."

"That will flay me to pieces!"

Would that Alec could be there to see it. He deserved far worse, because of what he'd done to Annabelle. "You'll be sent to the front lines with the 2nd Regiment of the Foot. The paperwork is already on its way to the Peninsula."

"But I am a Hussar," Digby said weakly, fresh blood pooling in his mouth.

"The army no longer has a horse to spare for you, and the 2nd needs men. It has been in more battles than any regiment should, and its numbers have been decimated. You'll be in the thick of the fighting.

"And there's something you should know," Alec continued. "The general in charge of the 2nd Foot has a fearsome reputation. Anyone caught gambling is dealt with severely, and soldiers fleeing from the battlefield are shot on sight."

"Why are you doing this?" Digby said, his voice panicked.

Alec pinned him with a cold stare. "We have lost too many good soldiers on the front lines. I'd rather see you die to save one of them than have to kill you myself."

Chapter 21

The morning was new, and as the sun rose over the horizon, Alec felt an unexpected lightness. Despite the fact that he had just, in all likelihood, consigned a man to his death, he couldn't muster any remorse. Perhaps Digby would find redemption in dying for his country, but little else would save him from damnation.

After passing Mars over to a footman, he walked up the front steps of his St. James Street residence. Before he'd even raised his hand to knock on the door, it swung open, revealing his wide-eyed manservant. "Goodness, Potter." He smiled. "That was unexpectedly prompt service. Is it time to review your wages again?"

"You have a visitor, my lord. She has been here for quite a few hours, in fact. She is unescorted, and of course, that is not at all the thing, but I could hardly turn her out. A lady like that is not safe on the streets alone." He'd never seen Potter, who was congenitally unflappable, in such a state.

"Such a lady, she is, my lord! She calls to mind that painting of an angel you have at Dorset House. May I say if Miss Layton was the inspiration behind it, it does not do her justice."

The rest of Potter's words were lost as Alec swept past him and headed for the small front parlor, where guests were usually seated. He pushed through the doorway, scanning the room for a glimpse of Annabelle. When he didn't see her, he moved toward a settee facing the fireplace and peered over its edge. She lay there sleeping, still dressed in her ball gown from the evening past. His eyes caressed the sweep of her brow, the generous swell of her lips. He resisted the urge to touch them with his own. What had happened to drive her here at this hour?

Her eyes fluttered open, their blue depths crystalline in their sparkle. She blushed, and hurriedly sat up, brushing her hands over the creases in her dress. She was adorably tousled, her hair a tumble of curls and dislodged pins. "Alec, you are finally home."

He liked the way that word sounded on her tongue.

"Potter told me you were here," he said, coming around to the front of the settee. "You must know you're risking your reputation again. You cannot visit a bachelor's lodgings." It was what a responsible person should say, but his voice lacked conviction. His heart had nearly burst at the site of her.

"Given the behavior of so many in society last evening, I'm no longer sure I wish to stay in its good graces," she said. "You have been treated abominably."

She'd always been loyal, his Annabelle. But there was an air of sadness about her. She'd braved the early morning and its dangers for a reason. "Something is the matter," he said. "Will you tell me what it is?"

"I learned any number of terrible things last night." Her voice was barely above a whisper. "Not only about my father and Gareth, but also about bets that were made, and letters that were never delivered."

It had happened, then. She'd learned the truth. "It's not always easy to understand the decisions people make," he replied carefully. "Everyone has done things they regret."

"Alec, I asked you this once before, but you would not reply. I need you to answer me." She was looking up at him, one hand gripping the edge of the settee. "Why did you participate in the race that day?"

He felt a flash of panic. She deserved his honesty, but there was every chance she would never forgive him. He had yet to forgive himself.

"You have been told what the stakes were. At least, as they were first presented."

She nodded imperceptibly.

"The truth is … I wanted you for myself. I've wanted you since I saw you dancing in the fountain."

She leapt up if she'd been burned by a cinder from the fire, and hurried past him to the opposite side of the room.

"But not as some sort of prize," he insisted, following her with his eyes. She was standing by the window a few feet from him. "I came upon Digby discussing the wager with Gareth. I'm not sure your brother even realized what the bastard was proposing, but I did, and I wanted to kill him for it. You stumbled upon us when I had my hands around his neck. You probably saved his life."

She watched him mutely.

"I couldn't let Digby get away with his vile proposal. So I proposed a new wager, one he couldn't resist."

"I was no longer to be traded for my brother's debts?" she asked quietly.

"God, no! I bet Digby 10,000 pounds that I would beat him in the race. It was everything I had on my own at the time." He heard her sharp intake of breath. "If I lost, he would win more than he was owed. But if either Gareth or I won, he would forfeit all claims on the Layton family."

"Father owed him money too. Gareth was not alone in this."

Since Sir Layton's visit, he'd suspected as much. "One of the terrible ironies is neither Marworth nor I can find any evidence that Digby placed bets on the Sherford-Chetwiggin race. He planned to cheat them from the start."

"So you decided to fight him for us," she said with a dawning smile.

He looked into the fire. "No, Annabelle. It was nothing as noble as that." He was swamped by a familiar wave of guilt. "I could have stopped the race from ever taking place. I could simply have given Digby the money. He'd have taken it. But I wanted to win for you. I wanted to play the hero for you one last time, like all those games from our childhood, so that I could finally put you in my past."

"What do you mean, put me in your past?"

God, this was hard to admit. "My father had plans for me. They didn't involve you or the Layton family. I went to Gareth's party to see you and say goodbye. I was going to return to London and take my place in Parliament. I was going to marry someone suitable, probably Jane Fitzsimmons, and make a name for myself."

He could see that he'd wounded her terribly. Her face was ashen. "I have never been suitable, have I?" she whispered.

"No, that's not it," he said gently. "You have never been ordinary, which is a very different thing. You were my childhood friend, but after that morning in the fountain, I could no longer pretend that was all I wanted you to be. That made you unsuitable, because desire and passion and love are very messy emotions. They are a distraction when you're supposed to spend all of your time accomplishing important things, as my father intended."

"But what about you?" she asked, her eyes inexpressibly sad. "Didn't you want a different sort of life for yourself?"

"I wanted my father's respect, not only for me but also for my mother. We were inextricably linked. Whenever I disappointed him, she, too, paid a price. For years, I was willing to sacrifice everything else—including my friendship and the chance at a future with you—in order to be worthy of his love. After the accident, though, it was no longer enough. I went away because it was the only way I could regain some semblance of control over my life. I'm not sure he ever forgave me for leaving, but at least he and my mother grew closer once I was gone."

"But why the war?" Her eyes were unwavering as she approached him.

"I raced that day for a pathetic reason, one that cost Gareth his life. And when I found you in the wreckage ..." He gave a helpless shrug of his shoulders. "I put myself in harm's way, because that was exactly what I'd done to you. There was nothing noble about it."

"No, Alec." She was beside him now. "Father and Gareth did that. They didn't intend to, of course. My brother tried to sneak me away. That's why I was dressed in boy's clothes when you found me." He looked up, astonished. "Gareth was going to take me to Arbury Hall, but Digby was at the stables when we arrived. I tried to hide in Father's carriage, but in a panic, I climbed into Gareth's by mistake."

"You remember what happened?"

"Only bits and pieces. Gareth and Digby were talking. When you arrived, Digby pushed for an earlier start. He must have been worried that you would inspect the carriages. I could hear the horses being harnessed. I was too afraid to move."

"What else do you remember?" he asked, unable to stop himself.

"The terrifying sway of the carriage. Flying through the air. A terrible, slashing pain."

He took her hands in his, kissing each one gently before releasing them. "I'd give my life to have saved you from that pain. I would do anything, risk anything for you."

She ran a finger down his cheek. "You say you are not noble. You are the most noble man I've ever known."

He cleared his throat and stepped away. "We have to find a way to get you home, Annabelle. I have a small carriage without my crest. I will ask Potter to have it called up, and hopefully, at this early hour, we'll pass without notice."

Was that disappointment in her eyes? God knew he wanted to crush her to him. He wanted to run out into the street and shout that she was here, that she'd been here for most of the night. He wanted to take her to Rotten Row and kiss her in front of everyone, so that the whole of society would know she was his.

But all he had left was his honor. And she'd been denied choices for too long.

He moved toward the door to call for Potter, but turned when she spoke. "Alec … did you see my letters in the box that held the linchpin?" She sounded embarrassed now.

"I did, but I haven't read them. I wanted to ask your permission."

"They're just ramblings," she said, looking away. "At turns heartsick and angry and terribly personal. Perhaps it would be best if they were forgotten."

"I will do that, if it's what you wish. But I would like to read them. They are a piece of you that I've missed. The whole time I was gone, I wondered how you were, and if you ever thought of me."

She flushed. "You don't need to say that, Alec. You hardly had time to think of a lovelorn girl back home."

Lovelorn. He seized on the word. "It would surprise you to know just how often I thought of you, how much I missed you." His voice cracked on the words. "If you will wait here for a moment, there are some things I'd like you to see."

He turned and headed out into the hall. After speaking with Potter, he ran up the stairs to his bedchamber, his heart pounding in his chest. He'd never planned to show her his letters. He had said and revealed too much in them, but it was the only way he could think of to show her the truth. That he'd carried a part of her with him ever since that day.

• • •

Annabelle stared at the letters Alec had left with her before heading sheepishly upstairs, claiming he needed to shave before returning to Marchmain House. There were dozens of them. Each and every one written to her.

I arrived in Spain today on a transport ship. God only knows what I've committed myself to, but it's little better than I deserve. I am so far away from home. I've done little else but think of you, and I wonder if you are well.

I killed my first man today. We fought each other at Sabugal, and I'll never forget the look in his eyes as my sword pierced his heart. I couldn't shake the feeling he cared less about dying than about those he was leaving behind. Perhaps a family, or a woman he loved. After the battle was won, and my duties were discharged, I hid in my tent, but I couldn't hide from myself.

I made love to a woman tonight because she had long blond hair and fair skin and blue eyes. In the dark, I pretended she was you. It is a just punishment, I suppose, for wanting you so desperately.

My father has died … You understand the shock of a sudden death all too well … I miss you.

She had never imagined the things he'd suffered. As a young woman, she'd made him into a kind of storybook hero. In reality, Alec was far more human. He was flawed and imperfect, and after reading the letters he had never expected her to see, she loved him all the more. If she were very lucky, perhaps he felt the same way. Taking a deep breath, she decided it was time to find out.

His lodgings were not overly large. Indeed, they were modest for a man of his position. He'd told her that following the war, he found it difficult to take up many of the trappings of his privileged life, and she could now understand why. Walking through the upstairs hall, she knocked tentatively on one door and then the next. When there was no answer, she moved to a third, rapping her hand against solid oak.

"Yes, Potter. Come in." Alec's voice was muffled through the door.

She didn't bother to correct him. Instead, she turned the handle until it clicked and slipped into the room. Alec was standing with his back to her, naked to the waist, running a sharp blade down a lathered cheek as he stood above a small wash basin. He was peering into a minuscule mirror, surely a remnant from his army days. She'd never seen him like this … in the bright morning light, shafts of sun touching his shoulders before slipping down to his narrow waist. He must have just bathed. His hair was still wet and inky black. Small droplets of water dripped from the curls at his neck, and ran over muscles and sinew.

"Does Miss Layton require anything?" he asked, still intent on his shaving. When she didn't answer because her voice had died in her throat, he peered at her in the mirror, dropping his blade with a clatter into the basin.

"Annabelle!" He grabbed a towel that lay beside him on the washstand and quickly wiped the remaining lather from his face. A fresh linen shirt was draped over a nearby chair, and he reached for it. "Please don't," she said, shocked at the sound of her voice, strangely thick and throaty.

He went completely still.

"Don't put your shirt back on. You are far too beautiful for that."

"Annabelle, you cannot say such things to a man. What has your aunt been teaching you?"

"She told me if I was ever lucky enough to fall in love, I should do everything in my power to hold onto it." Her heart was beating furiously. "She said I should never shy away from telling that man I found him beautiful."

His eyes glinted with emotion as she walked to him. She felt mesmerized, as if she were being pulled by an unseen force to run her hands along his face, and across his chest, to marvel at the feel of his warm flesh beneath her own.

His breathing went raspy at her touch. "Annabelle, despite your bold claims, I don't think you know what you are tempting me to."

She smiled then, because she couldn't be so close to him and not feel his body with her hands. "In all truth, I don't know. But I am eager to find out. I remember that night at Marchmain House, the way you made me feel. I want to make you feel that way."

With a low groan, he reached for her, pulling her tightly against him. He smelled of soap and shaving cream, but there was something else. Something thrilling, because it had to do with passion in a way she didn't yet understand. He captured her lips with his own, pulling at the bottom one, begging his way into the warmth of her mouth. As his tongue met hers, she curved her hands around his waist, teasing at the place where fabric met skin. He shuddered, and her body flooded with warmth, especially in that place where he had touched her before.

"Alec," she whispered. "I want you to forget that woman you held. I want to replace all of your thoughts of her with thoughts of me."

"God, Annabelle. It has always been you. You can't know how I have dreamed about feeling your body beneath mine, of feeling myself inside of you."

"Then show me."

Lifting his head, he stared into her eyes. "Do you know what you are asking? Because if I start, I will not stop. I won't let you go."

"That is all I've ever wanted."

He lifted her off her feet and carried her to a large, imposing bed in the corner of the room. Laying her down gently, he smoothed her hair across his pillow, running tentative hands down the length of her arms, molding them to the span of her waist, and down the curve of her legs.

"You cannot have any idea of how stunning you are, Annabelle," he said softly. "If this were not morning, I'd swear I was dreaming. So many times, I've imagined you here. These last weeks, I wondered if I'd spend the rest of my life watching you from a distance."

She pulled him down, angling his head in her hands as she brought his mouth back to hers. Moving her hands down his body, she instinctively cradled his hips against her, even as she felt a hard jutting at the apex of her thighs. The weight of it sparked a flame within her, and when he groaned, she fought to peel away the layers of clothing still between them. She fumbled with the buttons of his breeches until he gave a weak laugh, grasping her hands with his own.

"You're going to be the death of me, Annabelle. Let me savor you. Let me see you naked in my bed."

She sat up so he could loosen the innumerable buttons running down the length of her back. Her glorious dress was a crumpled disaster now. All the more reason to strip it off.

"I thought this so lovely earlier," he murmured. "I'm less fond of it now."

"I think women's fashions should make a better use of ties," she said. "One pull and they are open."

His arms encircled her, his hands working at the buttons. When his fingers trembled with the last of them, she reached behind her to tear the buttons apart. She felt hot now; her clothes couldn't come off fast enough. As he pulled the dress from her body, then her corset and her pantaloons, she nearly gasped with pleasure.

Then she remembered, and she grabbed at the sheet, swiftly pulling it over her legs. She didn't want to see him draw away in shock or, even worse, pity. He said she was beautiful, but he'd never seen her like this—mangled in places and grotesque.

"Let me see you, Annabelle."

It took every ounce of courage to loosen her grip. Heart slamming in her chest, she watched his eyes caress her body, lingering on her breasts as he pulled the sheet away. They followed the line of her stomach, past the curve of her hips to the top of her thighs. Lower still they traveled, nearly black with desire, past the sweep of her legs, down to the pink tips of her toes. Every movement was tense and tightly controlled, as if he were wound like a spring.

How could he not have seen them? But of course he had. With a shuddering breath, he ran his fingertips along the arch of her left foot, giving only the barest smile as she squirmed at the sensation. His fingers continued past her ankle, smoothing along her calf, dipping into the shadows behind her knee until he reached the angry ridge of her scars, purple and distended, even after all this time. As she held her breath, he brushed his hand gently across them, his touch soft and light as he traced them.

"They are horrible to look at, I know," she whispered.

"Annabelle, it would be so easy to pretend you are fragile, that you need me to protect you and keep you safe. But I know what you have survived. This is the proof of it. It is not your beauty that makes me love you. It's your strength."

She melted then, her breath easing from her on a sigh because his hands continued their slow perusal, moving along her inner thigh to settle at the folds between her legs. He tucked a finger between them and inside, and she nearly came apart. "Of course, this part of you has its merits, too," he breathed.

She could feel the moisture, slick on his fingers, as he withdrew them and eased upward, teasing the bud there until her hips began to rock uncontrollably. The pleasure was nearly unbearable. Helpless, she looked at Alec. His eyes were dark and intent, his jaw tightly clenched as he watched her writhe. And then, just as before, waves of sensation engulfed her. She moaned aloud, driving her hips against his hand, her body heightened to every nuance of pleasure.

"God, Annabelle." He was looking down at her, his breath coming in labored pants, his body still tense, his pulse throbbing at the base of his throat. She reached up, trailing her hand down his chest, pausing to brush a fingertip across one nipple before continuing downward to settle her hand on the hard ridge pushing against the fall of his britches. He moaned as she ran her fingers up and down its length. She couldn't help but marvel at its heat and hardness.

"You were supposed to show me all about this. Do you remember?"

He reached for her hand then, pushing it against him briefly before edging away, just out of reach. "You have always been a curious sort," he said with a pained laugh. "And I'll live for the day when I can indulge that curiosity, but this must wait. I want us to be married.

"You will marry me, won't you?" he asked, suddenly sounding unsure. "I love you with all my heart."

"I'll only marry you on one condition," she said, her face gravely serious.

"Anything. Name anything."

"I don't want to wait. I'm far too impatient." She sat up, and tore at the buttons that separated him from her, until a hot throbbing met her hands. He groaned, as if waging some final battle, and then he gave into her, urgently freeing himself from the britches he wore, kicking them away as he pushed her back against the bed. When he covered her body with his, she almost cried out, because that restlessness had begun to build inside of her again.

She'd never felt anything like his weight upon her, warm and pulsing. He kissed down the curve of her cheek, between the valley of her breasts and up to their tips, taking each into his mouth until she was certain she'd scream. All the while, she could feel the insistent throbbing, so close to her heat.

"Annabelle," he said, staring into her eyes, sweat beginning to bead at his temples. "Are you sure? There will be pain this first time."

She didn't care. "I've known my share of pain, Alec. I want you as close to me as I can have you."

He kissed her then, deeply, as he edged open her thighs. And as he entered her gently, even through the initial flash of pain, she felt something tugging deep at her heart. He raised himself above her, arms cradling her on either side as he slowly moved in and out, her body adjusting to the slick friction between them until there was more pleasure than pain. She watched his face as he gazed at her, both of them unblinking. With each stroke, his eyes softened, his breath hot against her body. Could he feel this thing she felt? The hot frisson, the building heat that crept up upon you, stealing your thoughts, until there was only sensation?

She loved the sound of their bodies moving together, the tangle of his sheets around her legs, the feel of him as his muscles tensed. She was straining toward that feeling. She only knew he was at the center of it, building in pressure, pressing upon her until suddenly the most exquisite sensation took hold, stunning her with its power, its pleasure magical. When she cried out, he buried his head into the curve of her neck, moaning her name as his hips bucked against hers.

Later, when their breathing settled, he pulled her against his chest, her breasts nestled against him, his arms enfolding her in a possessive embrace. "Do you know how long I have loved you?" he whispered.

She smiled into the crook of his shoulder. "This will be a competition between us, then. Because I have always loved you."

• • •

There was a hesitant knock upon the door. "Potter," Alec called out. "Whatever it is, it will have to wait."

"I am afraid that's impossible, my lord," came the stern reply. "Miss Layton's aunt has come to call, and she wishes to speak with you."

In truth, Alec was surprised she'd only just arrived. As Annabelle let out a squeak of dismay, he gave her a gentle, lingering kiss, easing from the bed to wrap himself in a dressing gown. Because he couldn't seem to stop himself, he stole a glance at her, his heart skittering wildly. She'd said she loved him—

"If you are trying to preserve my maidenly sensibilities," she said with a naughty grin, "you're too late."

"Your aunt will probably beat me to death for that very reason. But the pain will have been worth it."

He dressed quickly and slipped down the stairs, smoothing his hands over his hair before proceeding into the front room to greet the countess, who was a vision in a blood-red day gown. "My dear Lady Marchmain, may I compliment you on the color of your dress? It's stunning with your complexion."

She gave him a sly smile. "No wonder my niece is so enamored with you. You're the picture of vitality at this early hour of the morning. However, flattery and your impressive good looks will not distract me. I understand Annabelle has been here since before the daybreak."

"I am afraid so. But your niece behaved with the upmost propriety. She has done nothing but conduct herself with dignity, and I've tried ..." He cleared his throat awkwardly. "I tried to act the gentleman."

She considered him for a long while before answering. "If you have acted the gentleman this entire time, you're not the man I thought you were. If you've squandered these few hours alone in each other's company, you have no one to blame but yourself."

"I didn't precisely squander them," he admitted. "But you must know I love your niece desperately. I've asked her to marry me."

"And of course she accepted. I'm something of an expert on marriage, and I know love when I see it."

"I'll give her the world if I can," he declared, only faintly embarrassed by the excessive, extravagant promise.

"That won't be necessary. I rather think the only thing she wants is you."

Chapter 22

Nine months later

Sophia Marchmain took a brief sip of tea as she studied the two-day old news sheets from London. Lord, the stuff was ghastly. Civilized people took a bracing shot of brandy at this hour of the day, but she was in the country, and she needed her wits about her. Annabelle would give birth at any moment. At least Mrs. Chessher had finally allowed Alec into the bedchamber to stand by his wife's side. Sophia had almost been tempted to violence by his ceaseless pacing up and down the hall, like a restless animal.

He'd certainly gotten Annabelle pregnant in short order—not that she'd doubted he would, strapping specimen that he was—but surely Alec's decision to witness the birth was unwise. That called for an especially strong stomach. She'd be there the instant the child was cleaned up, and not a moment sooner.

There was a certain comfort in reviewing news of no import on this unsettling morning. Lady So-and-So's soiree had proven a success. Miss Ingenue had created quite a splash. Lord Down-on-His-Luck was making a move for Miss Money. And the season, thus far, had been accounted quite dull since the marriage of the luminous Annabelle Carstairs, Countess of Dorset.

The wedding, of course, had been lovely. Alec and Annabelle had invited only their closest friends to a morning ceremony at St. George's. Handsome Lord Marworth stood with Alec, while Jane Fitzsimmons acted as maid to Annabelle. That girl had been shamefully treated by society since "The Incident," as Sophia called it. Her father was an outcast, censured in the House of Lords, but Sophia had plans for Jane, a woman of rare courage and substance.

She and Lady Dorset had stood in the first pew behind the happy couple, and Frederick had also been in attendance. He and Annabelle were slowly finding their way back to the closeness they'd once shared, although the path was a difficult one. In a particularly moving moment, he'd released dozens of colorful butterflies into the air after Annabelle and Alec repeated their vows. How the creatures found their way out of St. George's, she couldn't say.

A number of "mourners" had gathered outside of the church during the ceremony. Lord Petersham, still garbed in fabulous shades of gold, wore a black armband to signal his loss, and Thomas Rowlandson, the famed print artist, had also commemorated the occasion. His etching of Annabelle as a bride had caused a near riot at Ackermann's Repository upon its release.

Sophia heard her niece cry out in pain, and she steeled herself against the weakness of tears. If anyone could triumph over the rigors of childbirth, it was Annabelle. And Alec would never leave her side.

When another cry rang out, Sophia returned her attention to the news, convinced now that a review of weightier matters was called for. There were reports that French forces had been defeated at the battle of Vitoria, dealing a death blow to Napoleon's hopes in Spain. Perhaps soon, she'd once again be enjoying brandy in the shade of her olive orchard there! Another article was devoted to Alec's bill, which was officially law now, but she already knew everything there was to know about that, so she moved on to the next page, only to find the death notices from the war.

Such a dreary topic. Hopefully, the fighting would be over soon, the lists vanishing all together. She gave them a cursory glance, and would have gone on to yet another page if one name hadn't caught her eye. Corporal Damien Digby. Lost at sea. Evidently, his transport ship had gone down off the coast of Spain. He was the only man who hadn't been rescued. No doubt his fellow soldiers left him to drown on purpose.

What a lovely start to the morning! The news would be one of her gifts to Annabelle. When she heard the cry of an infant, however, all thoughts of Digby vanished. She threw aside the paper, rushed out of the chamber, and ran down the hall to her niece. When she swept into the room, Alec was holding his wife as if the world would be lost without her, while Annabelle held their newborn son in her arms, smiling so brightly that she sparkled.

A Sneak Peek from Crimson Romance
(From *Mischief and Magnolias* by Marie Patrick)

Natchez, Mississippi
September 1863

Shaelyn Cavanaugh leaned against the railing of the second-floor gallery of her home and focused on the two men coming up the road, their blue uniforms unmistakable. They rode at a swift pace, a trail of dust behind them.

Since Natchez, Mississippi, surrendered to the Union forces, it wasn't unusual to see blue uniforms, especially since they'd made Rosalie, the home next door, their headquarters. But the two men didn't turn into Rosalie's drive as she expected.

Her breath caught in her throat when she glimpsed light auburn hair, much like her brother's, gleaming in the sunlight. "Ian!"

His companion had raven-black hair, though it too reflected the sun's light. Traveling with Ian, he could be only one man—the one she had promised to wait for. "James." Her hand gripped the wrought-iron railing, her knuckles white. Tears blurred her vision. Her heart beat a frantic rhythm in her chest as excitement surged through her veins.

"They're home!" she cried. "Mama!"

She lifted her skirts and ran for the outside staircase at the back of the house. "They're home!"

She jumped, missing the last few stairs, and hit the veranda at a run, her skirts held high as she ran into the house through the French doors in the small sun parlor.

"Mama!" Shaelyn darted into the central hallway, her footsteps clicking on the marble tiles as she ran to the front door, flung it open, and rushed headlong into a pair of strong arms. She rested her head against a firm, hard chest, and squeezed tight. A button pressed into her cheek, but she didn't care. They were home. "Thank God," she whispered into the uniform.

"Well, that's quite a greeting," a deep, rich voice as smooth as drizzling molasses responded. Laughter rumbled in his chest. "Not expected, but certainly welcomed."

"Hmm. Where's mine?" his companion asked in the clipped tones of New England.

Shaelyn recognized neither voice nor accent and turned her head to glance at the auburn-haired man. Ian Cavanaugh did not look back at her, which meant she did not have her arms around James Brooks.

Her face hot with embarrassment, Shaelyn pulled away from the man. She drew in a shaky breath and stared. The most beautiful pair of soft blue-gray eyes she'd ever seen stared back. "Forgive me. I thought you were someone else."

"Obviously," the man replied. "Perhaps introductions are in order, although after your greeting, it may be too late." Amusement gleamed from his eyes as a wide grin showed off his white teeth in a charming smile. She wanted to touch the dimple that appeared in his cheek. "Major Remington Harte." He gestured to the man beside him. "This is my second in command, Captain Vincent Davenport."

"Miss." Captain Davenport bowed from the waist.

Shaelyn nodded in his general direction, but her focus remained on the major. She'd never seen hair so black or so thick. An insane impulse overwhelmed her—she wanted to run her fingers through that mass of thick, shiny hair and feel its silkiness. Struck by her own inappropriate thoughts, she stilled. He wasn't James. She shouldn't want to run her fingers through his hair.

"Are you Brenna Cavanaugh?"

"What?" Startled, Shaelyn shook her head. "No, I'm her daughter, Shaelyn."

Footsteps rang out down the hallway. Shaelyn dragged her gaze away from the man in uniform for just a moment as her mother joined them at the door. "I am Brenna Cavanaugh." A sweet smile accompanied the hand she offered the major. "May I help you?"

Introductions were quickly made, and Shaelyn watched the exchange of pleasantries, but her gaze was drawn back to the major. He looked dashing in his uniform. The dark blue complimented his eyes quite nicely. The material molded to his body, emphasizing his broad shoulders, lean waist, and slim hips. He stood tall, well over six feet she guessed, as her gaze swept the length of his body with admiration. She noticed a silver-tipped cane in his hand, which he leaned on. He must have been injured in battle.

She had always loved seeing a man in uniform. They stood differently: straighter, taller. Proud. They acted differently, too, as if wearing a uniform had something to do with how the world perceived them.

Her gaze met his and she felt the warmth of a blush creep up from her chest. A smile parted his full lips and her face grew hotter. She'd been staring at him and he knew it.

"Is this about Ian, my son?" Hope colored her mother's tone, a hope she had tended carefully, like one tends a garden.

"Or James Brooks?" Shaelyn added.

"May we go inside?" Major Harte gestured toward the open door.

"Where are my manners?" Brenna smiled. "Of course." She turned to Shaelyn. "Please show our guests into the sun parlor, dear. I just finished making tea."

With effort, Shaelyn dragged her gaze away from the major and the pulse throbbing in his neck, above the collar of his uniform, which had mesmerized her. "Please follow me."

Major Harte's uneven footsteps echoed in the hallway and the tip of his cane tapped on the marble tiles as Shaelyn showed them into a small, comfortable, sun-filled room at the back of the house, while Brenna pushed through the swinging door to the kitchen. "Please, make yourselves comfortable."

"Thank you." The major moved to the fireplace and rested his arm on the mantle while Captain Davenport sat on a rattan love seat.

Shaelyn sank into a chair across from the captain, her fingers settling into one of the rattan grooves, and let out a slow breath— anything to still the anxiety plucking at her spine with its icy fingers and chilling her from the inside out. After a moment, the heat of the major's gaze rested on her, negating that chill. He didn't speak as she turned to face him, nor did he smile, but the warmth in his slate-colored eyes captured and held hers.

She opened her mouth, but no words issued forth. She didn't know what to say. Or do. She'd never had to entertain Union officers, although her brother had marched off to war wearing blue. In all truth, she hadn't entertained in a very long time, and the lessons her mother had taught her about proper decorum and genteel manners simply escaped her.

Captain Davenport didn't speak either, and a heavy stillness filled the room, the only sound the rhythmic ticking of the grandfather clock in the corner. An ominous sense of foreboding stole through Shaelyn with each passing minute. Her heart pounded, not with excitement now, but with dread. A lump rose to her throat. She knew, deep down, whatever the reason for these men to be here, no good would come of it.

Brenna entered the parlor and broke the silence. "Shaelyn, would you please pour?" Her mother placed a silver tea service on the table in front of the divan and took a seat in her favorite wicker chair.

Shaelyn rose from her seat, though her entire body trembled. With shaking hands, she lifted the teapot and started to pour. A few drops of the dark brew spilled onto a linen napkin on the tray and stained it brown.

She glanced up and caught the major's wince before he addressed his second in command. "Captain, would you be so kind?"

"Of course." Captain Davenport leaned forward and took the pot from her hands.

Shaelyn gave him a tremulous smile. Every muscle and sinew in her body tensed with apprehension as she moved behind the settee, her hand resting on her mother's shoulder.

Captain Davenport handed Brenna her teacup and attempted to give one to Shaelyn as well, but she declined without a word, afraid her voice wouldn't work over the lump constricting her throat.

Major Harte straightened and limped over to the chair opposite the divan, a grimace tightening his features. Shaelyn watched his painful progress and a surge of sympathy rippled through her.

"Now, Major, please tell us why you're here. If it's bad news, don't make us wait, I beg you." Brenna's voice shook as she said the words. She grabbed Shaelyn's hand and squeezed.

He hesitated. Shaelyn wanted to drag the words from his mouth. Whatever he needed to say, she just wished he'd do it. He took a deep breath. She prepared herself, swallowing hard against the bile burning the back of her throat.

"Mrs. Cavanaugh, are you the owner of Cavanaugh Shipping and the steamboats the *Brenna Rose*, the *Lady Shae*, and the *Sweet Sassy*?"

"Since my husband passed away," Brenna replied. "Yes, I am, but Shaelyn runs the business. She's quite good at it, despite this terrible war."

"And are you the owner of record for this home, Magnolia House, and the warehouse and shipping office located in Natchez-Under-the-Hill?"

"What is this all about, Major?" Shaelyn asked. She didn't like the expression on the major's face at all. He seemed sad almost, as if he didn't relish what he needed to do, and her dread intensified, those icy fingers no longer plucking at her spine, but squeezing her heart. She stiffened against the blow that was sure to come.

He removed a document from his uniform pocket, slowly unfolded it, and began to read. "By the order of the government of the United States, for the duration of this war or until they are no longer needed," he said softly, "you are hereby commanded to relinquish your home, steamboats, warehouse, and shipping office to the Union Army. Specifically, me." He glanced at Shaelyn, an apology in his eyes.

"What!" Shaelyn let go of her mother's hand and came around the sofa on legs that felt like wooden stumps instead of flesh and bone. "You can't do that. They belong to us."

She stopped in front of Major Harte and stared at him. The brief moment of sympathy she'd had for him vanished, and her face burned with anger. Indeed, her entire body felt as if fire consumed her. She grabbed the document from him, but her hands shook so badly, she couldn't read the paper in front of her.

"Indeed, I can, Miss Cavanaugh," he said, his voice no longer soft, but commanding and strong. "I have my orders." The expression in his eyes hadn't changed, though. They were still apologetic.

She knew the army, on both sides, frequently took homes and other possessions, but it didn't assuage her anger one bit. "Why my steamers? And my home?"

"The Union Army has need of your boats to transport men and supplies and your home, being in such close proximity to Rosalie, is perfect to quarter my men."

"What are we supposed to do? How will I support us if you take my steamboats? Where are we to live?" Incredulity made Shaelyn's voice sharper than normal. Although she was usually unflappable, even in the most dire of circumstances, this whole tableau had her feeling like she was someone else, someone she didn't even recognize. "What if I refuse, Major? What will you do then?"

A muscle jumped in the major's cheek as he stood to tower over her. "You have no choice in this matter, Miss Cavanaugh." His voice remained strong, but the warmth of his eyes conveyed another message. "It's nothing personal. Consider this your contribution to the war effort."

The lump constricting her throat threatened to suffocate her. She took a deep breath and swallowed hard.

"My my mother and I have already contributed far more to this blasted war than you could ever imagine." Her voice barely above a whisper, she almost choked on the words. "My father suffered a stroke when war was declared. I watched him struggle for life for two months before he succumbed." She blinked against the tears filling her eyes. "I have heard nothing from my brother or my intended in over a year. I can only hope they are still alive and were not at Gettysburg. I have lost two riverboats to shell fire. They lay at the bottom of the Mississippi, along with the people who were aboard."

She drew in her breath, tried to control her shaking body, and tried but failed to control her temper. "Now you will take my home and my business, and I am to give it to you graciously? I don't believe I can, Major."

A strong desire to do him bodily harm made her clench her fists as he stood before her, his expression impassive.

"I am sorry for your losses, Miss Cavanaugh, but we have all made sacrifices," he replied softly. His gaze held hers and he shifted his weight to his other leg, as if mentioning the word *sacrifices* made him remember his own. "Some more than others. It is the way of war."

"Your war, not mine!" The words exploded from her, despite the constriction in her throat. How much more would this blasted war take? How much more could she give? Had she brought this on herself by applying for a government contract? She'd been denied, of course, and immediately tried again and again. Had she drawn attention to Cavanaugh Shipping by her sheer persistence? Instead of getting the contract she so hoped for, she had her possessions taken.

A small sound drew her attention. Shaelyn tore her gaze away from the major and glanced at her mother. Brenna had not moved, had not uttered a sound except for a small whimper, but her face had lost all color. Her chin trembled and tears shimmered on her lashes. Pain and confusion flashed in her eyes. Shaelyn's heart came close to shattering.

She had promised her father she would always take care of her mother, a privilege she gladly accepted. She wouldn't break her promise now. She took a deep breath and managed to smile at her mother to let her know it would be all right.

"I'm certain you are a reasonable man, Major." She forced her gaze away from Brenna and faced the man who stood to take everything from her. "We have nowhere to go, sir. No family left, no friends able to take us in. The war has seen to that." She took a deep breath and tried to keep her anger under control. "Perhaps we can strike a bargain?"

• • •

Intrigued, Remy cocked a dark eyebrow. He hadn't missed the look she'd given her mother, nor could he mistake the devastation on the older woman's face and his part in putting the desolation there. He hadn't had this issue with the other homes where some of his men were now staying. "A bargain, Miss Cavanaugh? What did you have in mind?"

"Perhaps we can discuss this privately," Shaelyn suggested, and nodded toward Brenna.

"Of course," he conceded, and followed her from the parlor. They stepped across the hall, toward the front of the house, and into a well-appointed study. Remy limped to the desk and leaned against it, taking the pressure off his leg in an effort to alleviate the pain, which never seemed to abate.

Shaelyn shut the pocket doors then moved to the center of the room. A ray of sunlight fell on her, and Remy sucked in his breath. *Heaven help me, she is a beauty. Damn Jock MacPhee!*

Her light auburn hair, twisted haphazardly into a loose knot atop her head, left wispy tendrils to frame a lovely, heart-shaped, and at the moment, angry face. Bright patches of color stained her cheeks. Dark brows arched over smoldering eyes the color of cobalt. Her pert nose turned up slightly at the tip. He had no doubt her mouth, now compressed in annoyance, broke hearts when she smiled.

She had spirit. He'd give her that. Her rage was tangible; he felt the heat radiate from her from across the room. Her eyes never left him. They sparkled with dangerous intent.

"You have my undivided attention." He hid a smile as she stomped toward the desk, the lace at the hem of her dark plum skirt swishing like ocean foam. He wondered briefly if the skirt had had lace originally or if she had used it to hide a badly frayed hem like so many other young ladies did during these difficult times. She wore no hoops or crinolines beneath her skirt, but he did glimpse pristine white petticoats and the tips of her worn, scuffed shoes.

Shaelyn said nothing. The expression on her face spoke for her. Remy kept his gaze steady on hers, frankly admiring her blushing cheeks and flashing eyes.

"You're staring daggers at me, Miss Cavanaugh. Does the color of my uniform offend you?" he asked, unable to resist.

"The color of your uniform makes no difference to me, sir." Her eyes narrowed as she spoke, yet still glittered like rare dark sapphires. "What offends me is the color of the blood that runs so freely because of this war. What offends me is the way you all do whatever you all damn well please, without thought for the consequences of your actions. What offends me, at the moment, is you!"

"I'm sorry you feel that way, Miss Cavanaugh." He'd always admired a woman with strength and courage, with character, with what his mother called fortitude. Shaelyn Cavanaugh seemed to have all that and more, and he rather enjoyed this confrontation, despite the circumstances, despite how her attitude had changed. It made him feel alive in a way he hadn't felt in quite some time. "Regardless of your feelings, this is the way it is. You must accept it as fact."

He straightened and took a step toward her. Before they'd left the parlor, she'd been willing to swallow her anger and strike a bargain. Now, however, she didn't seem so willing. "I find it remarkable how much your manner has changed since we left the parlor."

She glared at him, her head tilting back on her slim neck, but she didn't move, didn't back down.

His attitude softened as she stood in front of him, defiant and bold. He expected her wrath, even her resentment. Almost welcomed it. He would have been in full fury if his home and business were taken away. "You wished to strike an agreement?" he reminded her.

"My mother is an excellent cook. She will prepare meals for you and your men and I will clean, do your laundry—" she paused and licked her lips "—and anything else you need to have done if you will allow us to stay in our home."

Her words finally penetrated his brain. No wonder she looked at him as if she would happily stab him through the heart. His blood ran cold as he realized she assumed by confiscating her home, he'd be asking—no, telling—them to leave, throwing them into the street. He'd seen it happen before. No doubt they had, too. Truthfully, he *had* planned to ask them to leave, though Jock had asked him to allow Shaelyn and her mother to stay. He hadn't quite made up his mind....not until he met her and then everything changed in a split second.

He should disabuse her of her misinterpretation at once but just...didn't want to. No one had dared to stand up to him such as she had in a very long time, and the longer they stood staring at each other, the more fascinated he became. She drew in her breath, the flesh above the décolletage of her white blouse turning red. A vein throbbed along the side of her neck, drawing his attention to the soft column of her throat. His gaze rose higher and he watched the subtle shading of her eyes darken to almost violet.

He hid the smile that threatened to turn up the corners of his mouth. "You and your mother may stay with conditions."

"And what would those conditions be?"

"You will treat my men with respect, regardless of the color of their uniform or the reasons they are here."

"I would have it no other way," she told him, her mouth set. "By the same token, I will have the same from you. My mother is a kind, gentle woman, Major, and naive in many ways. I will not have her abused or mistreated, by either you or your men. If we must treat you and yours with respect, then I demand you treat my mother that way as well."

"You aren't in any position to make demands, Miss Cavanaugh."

"I understand. I still ask you to honor my request."

Remy's heart skipped a beat as he gazed into her flashing eyes. They didn't merely sparkle; they danced in her lovely face. He detected no fear in those glimmering orbs of blue, just fury. What would she look like with her temper—or her passion—unleashed?

"It will be as you wish, Miss Cavanaugh," Remy conceded. "My men will show your mother the respect she deserves." He took another step forward and smelled the warm, inviting fragrance of her perfume. The alluring scent conjured images in his mind, images better left alone. He wanted to touch her, to kiss the spot on her neck where her pulse throbbed, to rub his thumb against her lips and feel them soften. "And what of you? Do you not deserve the respect of my men as well?"

"I expect nothing less."

Intoxicated. That's what he felt. As if he'd drunk all the whiskey his father distilled. Her scent wafted gently to his nose and a vivid vision filled his mind. He saw her in his arms, saw them making love until they were both breathless, moonlight glowing on her bare skin, passion flushing her lovely face—

She's taken, promised to another.

The reminder did little to stop the kaleidoscope of visions cascading through his mind. With a bit of disappointment, Remy mentally shook himself and moved away from her, more to save himself from her sensual, alluring fragrance and the images in his mind than anything else.

"I realize this is an inconvenience for you, Miss Cavanaugh, but I will try to make it as pleasant as possible." He gazed into her eyes. The most peculiar sensation settled in his chest, one he could not define, but which made his heart a little lighter. "I suggest we both make the best of a bad situation. I am willing to allow you and your mother to stay. Do we have an agreement?"

Slowly, she let out her pent-up breath and stuck out her hand. He grasped it firmly and a jolt of desire slammed into him. He wanted to pull her into his arms and kiss her tempting lips. Now. If she felt it too, she gave no sign.

He pulled his hand away quickly and cleared his throat. "Please show me the rest of the house."

"As you wish." She led him out of the study, her hands balled into fists at her side, and into the central hallway. Remy followed, admiring the subtle sway of her hips beneath the plum skirt, the long line of her back, the wispy tendrils curling at the back of her neck, begging for his touch.

From the study, they took the marble-tiled corridor toward the rear of the house. She poked her head into the sun parlor, where Brenna held Captain Davenport in subdued conversation. Her mother looked up. Shaelyn said not a word, but the expression of relief on the older woman's face could not be denied.

Shaelyn opened the swinging door to the kitchen a moment later and stood aside. She said nothing as he inspected the room, but her anger smoldered. The heat he'd felt earlier shimmered around her. He couldn't concentrate on the room's appointments. Instead, he felt the intensity of her stare and turned to face her.

A blush spread across her face, but her eyes never left his.

Is that a challenge I see?

He tore his gaze away from her and walked around the kitchen, opening all the cabinets and drawers, inspecting their contents, satisfied his stay at Magnolia House would be a comfortable one.

He finished looking into the cabinets and moved to a door to his left. His hand rested on the knob. "Where does this lead?"

"The cellar, backyard, and a small room where one can remove muddy boots." Her answer was clipped, bordering on rude. "Also the servants' stairway."

Remy ignored her tone as he nodded and limped to another set of doors. "And these?"

"Servants' quarters."

He opened the door to the first room, noticed it was clean, the small bed made, but vacant, as if no one had resided there in a long time. "Where are they now? Your servants, I mean."

"Gone. I couldn't afford to pay them anymore."

He closed the door and walked around the butcher-block counter in the middle of the room. A set of carving knives sat on the surface, and he wondered if he should remove them before they became an enticement for her.

Another swinging door led to the dining room. Shaelyn pushed through it a few steps before him and let it swing back. He drew in a deep breath and stopped the door from hitting him in the face with his hand.

This is going to be more difficult—and more entertaining—than I thought.

He didn't take more than a moment to glance around, but in that time he saw all he needed to see. The dining room table, covered in a lace cloth, seated twelve comfortably. Extra chairs lined one wall and a long sideboard sat across from it against another. The hutch stood empty—perhaps the fine china had been sold to put food on the table.

Shaelyn left and waited in the hall. Impatient, her foot tapped a beat on the marble floor. Remy grinned and slowed his pace to annoy her a bit more.

The ground floor of Magnolia House held a myriad of surprises, not the least of which was a billiard table in the game room and a fine piano in the music room. No artwork adorned the walls, but he noticed bright squares on the wallpaper where pictures had once hung. No carpets covered the floor, either, and the rhythmic tap of his cane seemed very loud, especially in the room he suspected was the formal parlor, which contained not a stick of furniture, not even a plant. Perhaps the furniture and paintings had been sold as well. Or bartered.

"This is a lovely home, Miss Cavanaugh."

"Yes, and I'd like to keep it that way, Major. I would appreciate it if you and your men leave it exactly as you find it." She led the way upstairs to the bedrooms at a quick step. Remy followed slowly, using his cane and the carved banister for support. After so many hours on horseback, his leg felt like a foreign appendage made of lead as he placed one foot in front of the other on the treads. Each time he put pressure on his leg, a fresh wave of pain shot through him. Sweat beaded on his forehead. Still, he endured, welcoming the burning rush. His circumstances, like so many others, could have been much worse and he could have died, several times, since the day he'd been shot.

Shaelyn waited at the top of the stairs, her fingers gripping the banister, knuckles white. He looked at her for a moment, saw how stiffly she stood, and forced himself to move faster. He had too much pride to show her his weakness.

When he reached the landing, he took a deep breath. He didn't apologize, nor did he acknowledge her as his gaze swept the upstairs hallway.

There were six bedrooms in all on the second floor, some with adjoining sitting rooms, some without. All led out to the gallery, which encircled Magnolia House. He inspected each bedroom, mentally naming who would occupy which.

The manse more than met his expectations. His officers, those who had elected to stay with him and not somewhere else in Natchez, including the apartments over the Cavanaugh warehouse, would be quite comfortable here for the duration of their stay. The proximity to Union headquarters at Rosalie was perfect.

Between the last two bedrooms stood a closed door. Thinking it held linens and such, Remy opened it. A smile curved his lips.

"The bathroom," Shaelyn said from behind him.

The small room contained a commode, a sink with brass spigots, and a large clawfoot bathtub. "Indoor plumbing," he remarked with pleasure. He entered the room and faced the sink, then turned the tap and waved his finger beneath the flowing water. Steam rose to coat the mirror and he wondered if there was, perhaps, a copper tank somewhere in the house that kept water heated. It didn't surprise him. Sean Cavanaugh owned steamboats. Surely he could devise something…or pay someone to devise something. Remy didn't ask though. Instead, he wiped the steam away and caught his grinning reflection. And something else—a tile-floored structure in the corner of the room. "What is this?"

"We call it a rain bath." Shaelyn moved into the room, opened the wooden door, and pulled the lever connected to the pipe leading up to a wide, round brass…thing. Water flowed onto the tile floor, like it sprinkled from the sky during a rainstorm, before she turned it off. "Instead of taking a bath, you can stand in here and let the water flow over you to get clean."

He'd heard about them, but had never seen one. And couldn't wait to try it. The structure gave a completely new way to keep clean, and after what he'd been through, cleanliness was something he valued. He said nothing more as she moved past him and stood by the door to the last room, her arms folded against her chest as she waited for him.

Remy poked his head through the doorway. He liked the stark simplicity of this room. The walls were papered in a soft white with sprigs of purple violets and green leaves. The draperies repeated the pattern. An intricately carved four-poster bed took up space between the French doors leading to the gallery. The bed looked inviting with its plump pillows slanting against the headboard.

"This will be my room."

"But…but this is mine," Shaelyn sputtered.

"No longer," he said as he made his way down the hallway. "Have your possessions removed before dinner. Your mother's also."

"And where am I supposed to sleep?"

He turned and grinned at her, couldn't help it. "You could stay with me."

Her eyes widened and color stained her cheeks. She drew in her breath sharply. "How dare you even…suggest…such a thing!"

Remy shrugged. "It's your choice." The idea of her warming his bed brought a vivid image to his mind.

"I am not that sort of woman!" Her eyes flashed with pride.

He took pity on her and relented. She didn't know him, didn't know his sense of humor. She couldn't have known he wasn't like most men, who would have taken advantage of this kind of situation. "You may move into the servants' quarters for the duration," he said over his shoulder as he continued down the hall.

"I thought we had an agreement, Major. You said you'd try to make your stay as pleasant as possible." She caught up with him and grabbed his arm, stopping his progress. Her eyes narrowed. "You said—"

"I know what I said, Miss Cavanaugh." He looked at her small white hand on his arm and felt an infusion of warmth seep through his sleeve. Her touch ignited a fierce yearning in him. In another time and place—he didn't allow himself to finish the thought. "I am allowing you and your mother to remain here, but make no mistake. I am in command. My orders will not be questioned. I don't accept it from my men and I won't accept it from you. Do I make myself clear?"

Shaelyn nodded and stepped back, releasing her grip on his arm.

"I'm glad we understand each other. We are in the middle of a war. We all must make sacrifices."

"Yes, Major, we are in the middle of a war," Shaelyn said, her voice strong with defiance, her body stiff and unyielding. "But your battle has just begun."

She spun on her heel and sashayed down the stairs. Remy watched her, fascinated. "If it's a battle you want, Miss Cavanaugh, it's a battle you shall have."

In the mood for more Crimson Romance?

Check out *Blinded by Grace*
by Becky Lower at *CrimsonRomance.com*.